Shark

Wes Brown

Ink Lines

SHARK
was first published in 2010 by Dog Horn Publishing

This edition published 2013 by Ink Lines
an imprint of Valley Press
Woodend, The Crescent, Scarborough, YO11 2PW
www.valleypressuk.com/inklines

ISBN: 978-1-908853-23-3

A CIP record for this book is
available from the British Library

Printed and bound in Great Britain by
Imprint Digital, Upton Pyne, Exeter

Acknowledgements

I would like to thank my editor, Alexa Radcliffe, Kester Aspden, and Danny Broderick for his suggestions on earlier drafts and his mentorship. Steve Dearden, Robb Barham, David Peace, Mick McCann, Gary Wigglesworth and Anthony Clavane. Mike Rossiter's brilliant *Target Basra* was key to many of the war flashbacks.

I'd also like to thank Nicholas Hogg, Jo Brandon, James Looseley, Dan Grant, Frank Earl, Matthew Noble, Jess Burrows, David Tait, Ian McArdle, Andy Hollis, Daniel Connelly and Jamie McGarry for help along the way.

'By "guts" I mean, grace under pressure.'
ERNEST HEMINGWAY

'The inner freedom from the practical desire,
The release from action and suffering, release from the inner
And the outer compulsion, yet surrounded
By a grace of sense, a white light and moving...'
TS ELIOT, *FOUR QUARTETS*

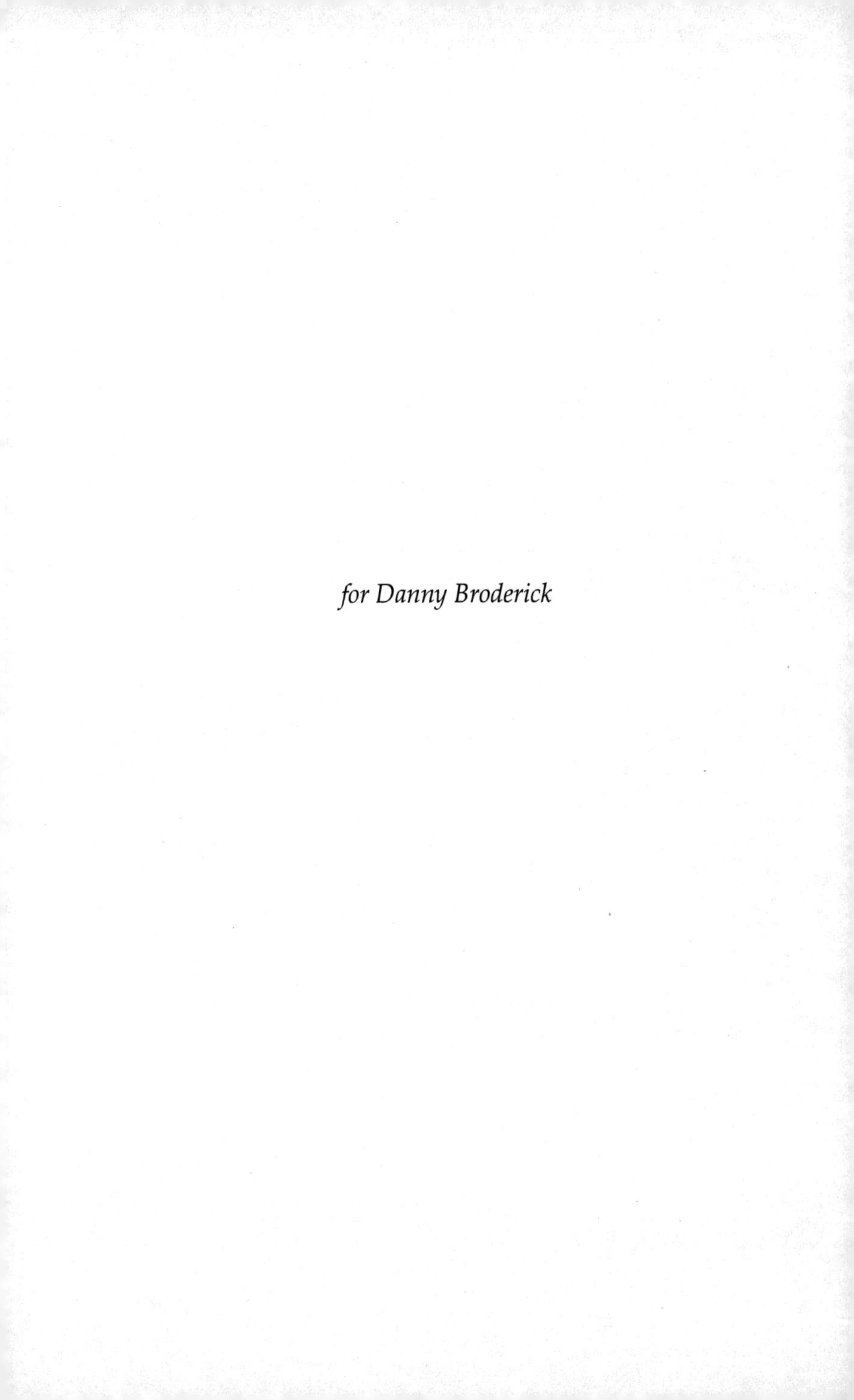

for Danny Broderick

I

JOHN USHER, with his six feet of height and his rigid hands, pedantically sets the table: triangle over the balls. Even though he's playing himself, there's somehow more to lose. He plays pool every Wednesday; today alone, playing before daybreak in the still light. He sees the spare open in the far left corner. Arches his shoulder, turns to lever and strikes up. Noses the cue direct. Rockets the second. Hard with the third.

Scuffs the fourth.

Shit. But lucky this wasn't eight ball. Thankfully, it wasn't; he was playing alone. To play alone – that was something. To come down here, dressed in a beaten-up hoody and punished sneakers, styling stripes and spots into playful geometry. There's smoke too. An illegal, silver coterie hung above the tables. He doesn't drink. Or he shouldn't drink. Though tonight, on the kickstand by the table and a high bar stool, draping his hood and minding his fags, is a pint of beer. There must be music, but he doesn't hear it, refuses to listen. He doesn't need to take sides. These balls are his.

He can take free aim. A strike at whichever one impresses, chooses for difficulty, the toughest shot. Long time since he played tournament level. Not the best. Not the worst. He takes a sip. Eyeing the middle right pocket, he knocks a seven ball near sideways. The thing fidgets in the pocket, nestles. He gets baited stares. Him being alone. A young man. Working the table with deadly efficiency. But he's learned to erase any pressure, to enjoy his concentration. Several balls need potting. He goes to work, lumbering round the table, rifling sequentially. The cue aches hot. The maths of the next shot and the one after make sense to him. Stillness. He pauses to watch, to cast his eye over the table. His concerned gaze, mapping expectation.

People envy to watch, to take notice of this guy, on his own, as he sinks ball after ball. It's a run as good as any he's had. He can't miss. Pings a four ball into the opposite pocket: drops a spot. He anticipates the black, the final strike. By now a crowd has nosily gathered, mostly boys, a couple of men. The black is open. He curls a six, pendulum-style, into the side-hand pocket; on a turn he draws aim. The black. His strike is fluid. Hard. He watches the ball tumble over itself, pick pace across the green, plump full into the sack. The crowd disperses. Pretends not to be impressed.

He limbers up, set to break. Brings his elbow high, ready to crack the cue. Swoosh of ball. Whiteness. Vague as a bird. The knocked balls scatter. Impact ignites movement; they spark off the other, a chaos for the back pocket. Cue hitched between finger and thumb – pointed like an arrow, he assesses the situation. The balls are clumped like clouds. The beam from the overhead light looms heavy over the game. Making the shot cools him. Eagling from side to side, you can forget yourself like this. On to his eleventh pint of Stella, the taste's weak and carbonated. These days he can get by this way. Doesn't like easy. Worried playing alone might become a chore. Four, five, six games gone without missing, without coming close. The easiness of the game upsets him. He likes a challenge and begins to chase the toughest shots: balls that are virtually impossible to pot, to risk his own record.

There are days when he can't be bothered, not even to play pool or get out of bed; grey long days he can't look forward to. His war is the absence of fight. No resistance, no enemy to be alert against; he's over tense, always on guard. But glad to be free from the bullshit of army life, the discipline and the people. The Snooker Centre has become a haven: where he can collect his thoughts, gather momentum, thrash his white hot cue ball into packs of red and yellow balls. But today his peace has been disturbed by his own ability, and the gang on the table alongside are aggressive and irritating. Over confident. They don't see his worth, how they're in this together. They fucked me over; they don't give a shit about me neither. He's in that dizzy place between drunkenness and darkness; nights you can't remember in the morning. Chunks of memory lodged between headache and heartburn. Nights you'd prefer to forget, if only you could remember. Hangovers are half his daily activity. Why he tries to quit the booze. He can't get enough; more makes him thirsty. Veiled beneath his heavy, pinstriped duvet with the knowledge you've fuck all to do, there's a sense of progress beating a hangover.

His fatigue doesn't show. The ease of the game has made him angry. He stabs at the balls. He wants to see how much force he can control – how much fight you can drive into a shot. A voice. Urban and forced:

'Check out da showboat. Playin wit himself?' His lobes burn and he see another guy join the table. Bling. Sportswear.

'Only wenna think o you.'

'You sick.'

'Maybe. But you were watchin.'

'Fuck-ing nobhead.' The guy breaks the word in two: tongues apart each syllable.

'Maybe yow boys should shut fuck up? Eh? Maybe yer should shut fuck up before I come over theh and stick mah fist through your fucking face. Little fuckin cunt. Fuck off.'

'Easy. White boy. You starting? We'll eat you up. You hear? Fucking eat you. Who the fuck you think you are? Cunt. Calm yer shit down gora.'

'Fuck you. Dickhead.'

John goes back to his game with his heart a jackhammer, knowing he's being watched, doing his best to find a rhythm, but the pressure skews his play. Goes to shit. He loses focus on the game in hand and knocks the cue ball off the wrong cushion. Misses a sitter. If this were Kabul, Helmand, or Kosovo he'd have his boys; they'd take care of these cunts. Still his knuckles contract, grip the cue tightly, veins rippled green. Five crowd round the next two tables. Loud, piss-taking, banter that tightens his gut, pricks his ears. The kind of talk you get in the mess or hear during dull days on patrol. He downs the last of his pint. They speak street slang. From the front of the mouth, a stylised drawl, loosely enunciated. Fuck it. He's through with this civilian bullshit. Trying to play by the rules. He breaks his cue across his thigh, bulk of knee, and thrashes the biggest first, drawing blood with the cherry wood shards of cue. The guy's down with a bloodied face. The others tend to him, scared kids staring up with the angry whites of their eyes.

'Yow fucking come near me and I'll fucking kill yer.' John shouts and they know he's serious. His starry-eyed expression makes him look crazed. He turns on his heel and heads to the bar where the barmaid, Francesca, this twenty-something with a pert body that fills a white t-shirt and plaid skirt, leans onto the bar and leafs though the pages of a trashy magazine. John sets himself down on a high stool that wobbles under his weight.

'Who woh those twats?'

She looks up, taking her eyes away from glossy pictures of snow boots. 'Excuse me?'

'Those guys. What's the crack?'

'Am sorry, but maybe yer might want to rephrase yer fucking question?'

'Fuckin women. Christ almighty. Those guys. Who the fuck are they?'

'Juss regulars, Rambo. Guys who come in here every fucking day of every fucking week.'

HE HAS HEAT under his steps: on the way home from the club. Rough-stubble face coughing on a cigarette. Divisions. The streets are always alive round here; with the immigrants driving taxis, and the busy drug dealers and students going out all the nights of the week. A chalky brightness. The resins of fireworks in the sky. He has been renting a place for a few weeks; the bay window lurching into the garden and his key gets stuck in the door, unlocked.

On the communal landing, he can see through the grey dust of the hallway distancing the dull light of the kitchen. Fried food. The fumes of stale oil.

'Big John.'

'The doors unlocked?' Carter is standing topless in the kitchen: his bald head and rippled muscles.

'Sorry mate, just popped out for o fag.'

John's eyes are stern and voice slow, 'No worries.'

'You seen the new girl upstairs?'

'Nope.'

'Teacher. Pretty fit.'

'I'll have to say hello.' Carter laughs; John knew this would make the right-thinking man laugh.

'You got your housing sorted yet?'

'Savings.'

'Yeah, but yer wanna top up?'

'Am not o charity case.' Turning up the stairs his thigh screams. The jagged edges of a bullet hole. He gasps, growling through his teeth; his body a relic, remembering the days of war. When he wore camo gear bullet-vests, and ultrasound helmets. His apartment is what they used to call a bedsit: a large bedroom in an Edwardian house. A kitchenette and partition round the back of his bed. A Sony portable TV stood up on a chair. All of his clothes are pressed and folded, neatly, in a suitcase by the bed. He pulls down the blinds: the slattering catches of midnight streets.

Sleep is quick. Suddener than it has been. He sleeps right through the night without dreams, half-wrapped in his duvet. Thinking with his mind's eye closed. When John wakes up at half-past midday, he kicks himself out of bed. Mattress springs slumped and creaking: makes himself a coffee, flosses tobacco and blood out of his teeth. His belly takes the brunt of his drinking; his vain eat fatty, absorbent foods. Now it burns in the morning. There's a creaky headache, aching like the weight of an elbow crack on his sweat-glossed forehead. In his white vest with his black self-inflicted tattoos on either shoulder's front (a griffin and a spider) he thinks about whether or not those Pakis were gonna come in and chin him. Whether they knew who he was, where he lived? When he was a lad, it was football nobheads he got into fights with; but they were minted now, making a packet doing gardens, building houses, on worksites, putting their fists to use. Every fucker has to have his day at the bottom of the pile. Now it's John and the Pakis Enemies in direct competition for piss-on patches of land. Women. Space to do your own thing. In ten years time they'd be new guys at the bottom of the pile: those who don't die or get fucked up get lucky, and it'll be John making money in the next big thing. That's what he tells himself, thinking, Balls to it; I'll get myself down the club.

THERE ARE THE REGULARS, the lone men with pints of Guinness and Racing Papers who have laboured over a few drinks all day. Some of them have started coming in more often, he's heard, since Francesca started. The four old men will study their pints all night and won't talk; if they do, they chunter to themselves, moaning about the news, the horse that didn't come in, the wife. There's a hardness to old men that John enjoys. Big ears, thin lips, white tufted ears, slowly drinking. Big Fat Carl knows how to get the punters in. Getting a girl like Francesca to prance about behind the bar; she grins after hearing John's name for the first time, John Usher, with the stark shushing S sounds. Just as quick as her smile grips her lips it slackens into a pout. She falls into a cradled slump hiding her face between her forearms with her elbows.

'No fighting tonight, mister. OK?' She's a cocktail of acid and interest, twirling hoops in her hair.

'As long as yer promise not tuh hit me.' John deadpans, enjoys his self-parody; his expression asks her to study his rough-hewn features. Grizzly when he's hungover; grey-faced and square-jawed, bashed about features. A scar zigzags over the bridge of his snub nose. Dark hair tossed sideways. He hasn't shaved and stubble silvers his cheeks.

'What did yer do that for? Jus when yer were seeming OK.'

'His o got me had a not got him.'

'Bullshit.'

'Iss pre-emptive love.'

'Doh Carl catch up wi yer?'

'Fuck Carl.'

'Carl bovvered?'

'Eh hate them, those lads. His alloss banging on abaht em.'

'Thass worra thought.'

'Luvved it wenna heard. Lapped it up. If it woh up to yim, half folk in here'd beh

barred.'

'So am reet?'

'Yow owe him for brokken cue. Thass another thing Evelyn woh going on abaht.'

'Fuckin cue?'

'Yeah.'

'Owt else?'

'Noo fighting, am not kiddin yer.' She gives a stern look with her left-eye. A look that must be her mother's. Wrong on her face. He's getting to know her coming in here every day. Knows her shift patterns and the perfume she wears. He uses a different tack, pet-lip protruding; switching emphasis.

'Amount I put behind bar am probably keepin bloody place open me sen.'

'Thass woh Evelyn said.'

'Owt she ant said?'

'She's o mouthy cow, int she? Carl's o shit, but iss not that bad workin forrim. If he didn't slap mah arse every ten minutes, he'd beh fine.'

'Dirty basstad.'

'An your not?'

'Reckon yow dirtier luv.'

She smiles and notices a regular standing the other side of the bar with a handful of coins, exact change. John waits for her to come back, enjoying talking to a woman after so long hanging around with blokes. Wanking over centrefolds. High-definition, pixelated breasts. Dopey grins. She strides, unfurling hair that curls down her back carrying a charge of advert-shimmer. Gleams in the smoky light. Her walk punches and bounces and her buttocks to and fro as she takes those leftward, rightward strides. John groans, snaps his neck back, gets backwash and fizz.

He shakes his empty glass, kidding. 'Bulleit, cheers.'

'Doht you be dooin that, yer twat. Yull be mekkin yourself too comfortable.'

'Too late for thah.'

'Thell be back, those lads you scrapped wi. Yull soon be out of ere. Yow shud luk after your sen.'

'Ave sin worse.'

'Nowt to brag abaht.'

'Doh worry, chicken. Ave got more than empty space in

here you noo?' He taps his head, 'Wise.'

'Bet you are.'

'Things to talk abaht.'

'Snore.'

'You, me lass, ah cruel.' Her Portuguese looks, the grey shadows beneath her eyes, her dimples when she speaks in her snappy Leeds accent. The cold air has brought her nipples out as pokies in her t-shirt. He gets up, leaving the flirting, he reckons, on a cliff-hanger. Picks a table to practice his break on. But it's not long before he feels weary, over the table when he draws the balls for a sequence. Voices. Arabic. The language brings back memories, flashbacks: blasts in yellow scythes of light, the brightness of the balls, his panic like a chaff grenade over the mint green tables and the smoky style of the club. He stumbles outside to get some air and falls through the heavy-duty fire doors into a white square of streetlight. His skull pounds. The world tilts, goes vertigo. Cobbles and asphalt, his face slugs the ground. His friends are the boys he fought with in Basra; those mad cunts who rose up oil ridden rivers and he sat in choppers with; the guys who would rib you in the morning, take the piss out of your mother, your brother, your wife, then stick their neck out for you in the line of duty, in the heat of the Baghdad sun. Playing football, being bored off your face; on patrol, nailing a raghead's drug palace and building schools. Nothing can compare to the sense of family, the sweet chaos he experienced. He's been in touch with a couple of cranks from school and a guy he goes to the gym with on Tuesdays and Thursdays; but the banter, the sense of purpose, isn't there. John thinks he'll tie a knife to his ankle in case any of those Arabs come back for him. He feels faint. The car park is littered with shattered glass that twinkles in the powerful halogen glow making sure the CCTV gets everything.

He wants a coffee and a biscuit, and a kiss from

somebody worth kissing, but he feels rough, unloved, lost and angry. Feels the turn of the world, the night coming fast, the fog of bullet fire and bang of explosions, he sways and spews heavily. Cold sweats rinse your pig hot body and you're on your knees, dick and elbows trudging through the oily mud of Basra on your way to secure a target under a hail of fire. The night sky's black as hell and the Cobra choppers wolf over for support. All you've eaten is a bacon sandwich and your lads are struggling to get supplies to you through a no fly zone. You've never been so hungry in all your fucking life and you wade your knees through the mud, a hundred fucking pounds of bullshit strapped to you and you feel the threat of enemy fire with the silver flares of light striking in the distance. The explosions of grenades thrown from guys you know but you're still shit scared and you feel your finger firmer on the trigger, bloodless, pale and wonder why you spent months training for this? You hear the shush of Milan rockets and the doors collapse on an enemy stronghold; then you hear the groans and aches of pain. These weapons you've longed to play with are deadly. You just killed a cunt and a bang goes off dashing gravel from a ditch and the jar judders through your metal acorn of a helmet and fucks up your head.

WANNA HEAR A JOKE? He can hear Carl from the bar, laughing too loud, the heaviness of his bulk rasping on his throat. 'O Muslim walks into o bar. No-one survived the blast.' A round of hyena laughter. Carl has a tendency to entertain: there are days John spends here, alone, standing over the pool tables, twelve-pints to the wind, and days he watches and listens. The shape of faces laughing has always scared him; baring teeth, devil eyes, paranoia. Exerted, Carl stands behind the bar defiantly tapping a brown-leafed Hamlet to his lips, his black pool shark t-shirt and a smile that does nothing for him. He annoys Francesca and ogles her as she bends down to face-out the fridge. When Evelyn crosses the bar, giving the surfaces a second wipe that looks designed to wind up Francesca; he stops and stands, tapping his cigar. Carl has a punched in, embryonic little face. A button chin stranded by excess weight; his cheeks bobbled in stubble and his lip trussed with a wiry black tash. Francesca puts up with the petting if he keeps leaving her in charge when he and Evelyn aren't around. They don't tell Evelyn. John puts a quid in the jukebox and strolls over to the bar with Thunder Road as his entrance music. Today feels good, so far. Though he is still on guard, stalking the violence.

Carl offers Francesca a series of instructions, going into intricate detail about how he wants the crisps stacked and what display goes where. John grunts and gets Carl's attention, ignoring Francesca. She buffs her chest, grabs a firm hold of herself and nudges her breasts fuller, crossing her arms. Sulking like a girl. John grabs Carl's bigger hand and wins the test-of-strength handshake. Silent competition.

'Nah then. How you?'

Turning John smiles, 'Sin better days.'

'You were back on form t'other night, want yer? Banging up those Paki bastards. Al tell yow summit for nowt – we've had right trouble wi thah lot. Fuckin Pakis. Abaht time someone giv em o good hidin.'

'Doht take shit do I?'

'Been meaning to say hello, but av bin down brewery o lot lass few week – iss all toffs running pubs now. Wanna turn every half-decent boozer into o glass and steel shithole. Look ah me runnin me gob. Still play yer snooker?'

'Bit o pool nah and nen.'

'Yow could o med it big.'

'Woh juss o kid. You doht realise then.'

'Mah lad's seventeen, likes o game.'

'Good days, weren't theh? Good luck to yim.' Carl calls out back for Evelyn: excited to introduce her as his wife. She comes out wearing the head to toe black and cue ball badge of the Snooker Centre. Everybody wears black-shirts. In his Jonny Cash denim and black, John could be a colleague; they watch her slow walk, finger scratching her nose, head down. She comes into view, slimmer, better dressed, and eyes suggesting the decade since he last saw her.

Carl's hand on his back, relaxed and gripping.

'Look who it iss.' John says as Evelyn's face, papery in the pale reflection glow of her make-up. Spots of days. Things you wouldn't ever notice if you saw her everyday. We all suffer mission creep. 'Bin a long while since o seen you.'

Carl butts in, 'Yow two know each other?'

'Yeah – went toh same school. Bin years since ave seen yer too Evelyn love. Hope this fucker's treating yer well.' John laughs nervously and slaps Carl's chubby arm.

'Yer sorted out those Doritos love?' Carl shouts at Francesca, suddenly shifting tone and expression; she huffs so hard her tit peaks out as she begins vigorous packing.

'Bin four years, me and Eve.' Carl puts his hand around Evelyn, his stocky forearms, locks her tight. She wanes under his size. The pressure of his personality. John feels his biceps cramp: he wants to undress his strength.

'How abaht you, Francesca? Got your sen o boyfriend?'

She shrugs, 'Woh makes yow think I wanna fucking boyfriend?'

'Juss way yeh look at me.' She gives him the finger and Evelyn uncouples from Carl.

Carl goes off on one again:

'Ave had soo many problems keeping thiss place decent. Coppers doht care. Every night's a cunt.'

'Crazy.'

'Iss wrong, John. Nowt crazy abaht it. Juss plain wrong

way things are. Glad you gave them pakis a hiding. Time someone did.'

'Juss defending me sen.'

'Them's rapists, yer know? Gangs of em raping underage white girls. Them's bombing us. Is all in't news.'

'Rape?'

'Theh drive round in a Land Rover theh call Rape Rover.'

'Those guys I hit?'

'Who fuckin knows. Am pretty sure.'

'Now I feel home. Can I have o pint Sergeant?' He mumbles to Carl as they drift over to the bar. Carl pulls on the Cobra font head, releasing the honeyed, gassy liquid that quickly forms a white head in the glass.

'Iss on't house on one condition.'

'Wassat?'

'Yow come dohn tonight n play pool.'

'Thass it?'

'I wanna see yor game. See if you still have it the way you used to. What o yer doing nah? I mean to get by, for money and all that?'

'Goh meh savings. Thass abaht it.'

'Dole?'

'Fuck dole. I woh go on thah till I yav teh.'

'Well pop down.'

'OK.'

'Another thing.'

'Yeah?' Carl's face is near the bar, opposite John's and he husks a whisper. 'I hear one o mah barmaids has o thing for yer.'

'Fuck you.'

'Silly bastard.' Carl breaks out a chesty baritone laugh. She's playing with her hooped earring, Francesca. Leaning against a magnolia pillar, eyes downward, lipstick red. The energy of noise throng the tables as young lads banter and play badly. Scuff shots and cock up. It's a minor irritation to see the corked combinations of wrong-fingered cue strokes and the angles coming out boss-eyed and slanty on the table. John stews over what Carl said: his stolid features, slant eyebrows question the possibility as she scrambles from her slump, watching.

New leaves shimmying in the whitening rain. Head down, hood up, the rain glides giddily down his neck. A weird atmosphere in the club. It's like a soap with Carl and Evelyn staging an awkward relationship. His muscles have come loose from their usual firm, booze is making his face pale as goose-skin, his eyes grey. It's only been a few weeks. There was talk of him going on some return to society course, but John couldn't be bothered and didn't like the sound of it anyway. Sat like a twat in some classroom being lectured to by a dickhead who knows nothing about what you've seen. The shocks in his head. This is not for talking about; pouring yourself into the hands of a shrink. You make your own way through the valley of the shadow of death. The light is the grace that finds you. The street where's staying looks good from a distance: the superficial trellises and bowing trees, then you get close up. The cracked windows. The vine-green weeds that thrive. He knows the sloshing sound of gravel underfoot will be heard by the other people living in the house divided into flats: they'll have their own ideas about who he is and how he lives. He opens the door and sits alone in the dark. Things are fucked. Rows of shops he used to go in every day have been bashed through and renovated, made into student doss houses, mini drug and fuck emporiums for the dirty little middle class mother fuckers taking gap years, taking dosser holidays as working class oiks. They call this downwardly mobile.

A Billy big nob on telly said it was a good thing: The end of class snobbery. There are Indian families and white single mums. There are gangs of cocky students and chavs in shell suits and Travis Bickle haircuts. No blokes about. All the dicks are kids. Then the rain's white splashes are sharply sudden. At home, locked in, slippers and a vest, he sits in this dilapidated shithole that costs him more than he has coming in each week, in his candy-striped boxers watching cartoons of muscle men. Now the rain's nightlong whisper.

BASRA was before Baghdad. The flight in and you nearly shat yourself under the thrash of a rotary wing – a new city, surrounded by desert and yours for the taking. The first assault on Saddam's Iraq. Oil towers and square fields film-like through the chopper's open side: orange desert and black smoky skies. Nervously a spot edges its way toward a pocket, caught on the cushion.

'John Usher?' This cocky voice he knows. 'Shit, iss been what? Six year?' He lifts his eyes, if somehow able to follow through his next shot. 'Still o jarhead, Jonny boy?' Ronnie McDuffy. The biggest gobshite in Leeds. The same lean build and queer legs, topped off with a big head. Italian nose. He was a gobshite through school. Made acned days pass easy with Ronnie beating on the geeky kids – preying on weak teachers and twanging girls' bra-straps.

He balls cocaine into a Rizla skin and necks it. John goes for a note – the Queen regally up his nose and snorts the whole bitter tingling line. Crisp breath. He's never done coke and won't risk doing what Ronnie did – packed into a fucking ball, exploding, sloshing around with the beer. The pink muscle of his booze-worn gut. Why do that to yourself? Grenadier used to be his favourite word. Sudden, like bullet holes, Ronnie's pupils grow druggy wide. Aggressive and friendly. He talks business. Money. His four-year plan. Upbeat.

Some faces, in white vests, are looking. Nobody cares. He feels his heart's massive gun-shot rhythm, cracking staccato, the vertigo of his pulse.

'Good shit?'

'Thass strong.' The sudden dizzy blast of coke, he bullshits, 'Better than't last stuff I yad.' He sniffs again. Fluffy, chemically white.

'When woh that then? Must've been time ago, can't get much charlie in't forces? Iss drug o professionals; the middle-class have got right on it.'

'Typical.'

'Thess all sorts on't go nah. You got Mcat and Ketamine – everybody's going nuts on that shit.'

'Int that oss tranquiliser?'

'Yeah, and Mcat's plant food.'

'Fuck me,' John laughs. 'I've bin missing out'

'Not really, mate. Iss boredom. yer have to get off yer face every week, juss to rest yow ed. Heard abaht your scrap other night too, yer wanna take it easy.'

'It'll be alreet.'

'Juss sayin, watch your sen.'

'Will do, mam.' John puts a pound coin in the slot by the side of the table and the balls clatter onto the green; he counts them out shining under the light and they blur, his vision fogged by the cocaine. Colours brighten. Empty belly. Blood sugar low.

'Am not playin yer.' Ronnie raises his eyebrows; his glass tipped toward John and his pose creases a face that John knows women are strangely attracted to.

'C'mon mate.'

'Doht wanna spanking, do yer?' John takes it as a victory: there is a rivalry between them. Somehow Ronnie has a way of making everything he does a show. Makes John rethink his proud years as a soldier, his service.

'Hey,' John starts, 'd'yer remember when yer pissed that Christmas telling everyone Jack had shagged that lesbo in a bin?'

'No?'

'Yer even tapped her on't shoulder. Fucking funny.' These people in John's past have merged into one: a film reel of laddish faces, fight scenes, sex scenes. The fiction of his life. The same distance as he feels in his eyes when he talks to people he knows. Has lived with. Grown up with on the same rows of red-brick council houses and downbeat boozers. John bought booze for some girls in the park the other Tuesday; they asked him if he'd get them a bottle of vodka, he could keep the change from their twenty-note. They had waiting eyes. Kiddy tits. Come five o'clock, turning this way on his way back from the gym, he saw them sprawled on the grass alongside the swings. Doll faced and barely conscious surrounded by vomit sloshed magazines and dog-shit. Torso of the Week spread out and soiled. Something inside wants to fuck them. Sixteen. Seventeen. Cutely dressed. He almost knew the thoughts that made them rape on tour. Kabul. Baghdad. Basra. There are forces bigger, darker than we control. Something else? It felt redeeming, an underwhelming desire to put them to bed. Morality snookers your thoughts. Rules are Mondays are always dead in the Club; he's keeps his mental record. The peak's Sunday when the football's on. Otherwise rugby lads off the estate drop in for a pint after the game. Then it's Fridays and Saturdays that are the only time this place gets busy. This is a war they cannot win. Decline. No chance they'll pull in the student crowd with paint blistering from the walls and dried beer stains marched into the carpet. John won't question Carl, too lazy to give a fuck. Too distant to flag up the four-foot wide HD TV hung like a Van Gogh. Who the fuck is the brewery? Does Carl have a live license? These questions are too legitimate; the sort of thing ask if you gave a fuck and reads newspapers and wore cardigans. These tedious little people who always have an opinion. Something to say for themselves. That's not John's way. Ask when you need. See what you see. These things happen in other pubs. Only so much you can do as a landlord, but it's a risky game. John never puts money on a bet he's not overconfident about; good odds and unlikely to lose.

Ronnie talks about things and John's not sure how to answer. His face wrinkles into doubt. False smiles. Office talk. Money. Double-dip recessions and stagflation. Boring. Dad talk. Grown up since he's been away - John drifts in and out of conversation - Francesca stealing his attention. He likes her spirit. Lucky glimmers in the corners of your eyes.

'Got owt planned then John?'

'Fuck all.'

'Thass not gonna last you?'

'I've not been without work before, have I? Never been owt except part o army. Juss out to have mi sen o good time. A mercenary.' His lumbering body shifts, led by his graceful hand. He rests his face, gob on his knuckles, 'Got no GCSEs, qualifications, none o that.'

'What abaht skills? Thought you'd have equivalence? Thought o lot o the stuff you learnt in't the forces would be transferable?'

'Woh just o bog standard soldier, employers doh wanna go near yer. Yer sound like yow at work now.'

Ronnie has crackles a horselaugh. He has gold rings on both hands. 'Wunt o little security job beh right up yer street?'

'Goi'n from't front line to guarding Tesco's? Thass lark going from't Premier to Unibond.'

'What else you gonna find, as o civ?'

'Al know when I see it.'

'Sem again?' Ronnie points at an emptied pint glass, swilled with lacy-froth. The coke loosens John, along with the alcohol. The crick in his neck. Conversation with

Ronnie is bringing him round. Reminds him of days with more violence, the fug of bullet-fire, a sense of mission. The heat of the sun. That's another thing he misses. The sun in England is small, roundly pale, stuck atop the sky. The muddy tan darkened into his skin. The lads joked they'd come home pakis and be beaten up by skinheads down the pub. John nods in answer to the question, mind wandering between cravings for a cigarette and another drink. An urge to piss stringing on the end of his nob. He's taking part in this conversation third-person. His body doesn't belong to him, his words spoken as if his jaw's slackened, pumped with painkillers. Suddenly Ronnie's chatting to a blonde at the bar. John secretly hopes he'll crash and burn. The bar has begun to fill and swell with the end of the working-day. Diehards, gruff and manly, silverbacks of negativity; people he's never seen. The guy's he gave a crack to the other night, he knows from school. The Asian faces. The college uniform. It was faction and gang back then. He drums the beat to a song he murmurs on his lips. Some lyrics are missed, replaced by whispers of air. Dark shit runs through his mind, on repeat. Vague as a bird. The Raven's beating wings across the horizon. Other people.

'Here we go, mate.'

'Cheers.'

Froth moustaches their lips. 'Got any stories?'

'Stories?'

'I've seen news, looks mental being out there.'

'Had iss moments.'

'If yow don't wanna talk abaht it, thass fine.'

'Am not bothered.'

'Must've enjoyed it, out there, to stay soo long. Thess no times yer busted in some stronghold with an AK and kicked fuck out of everyone?'

'Thass all Hollywood.'

'So what did yer do?'

'Not o lot.'

'Yer must've? I don't believe yer.'

'Jobs o job.'

'OK. OK. Must be some dark shit. I won't say no more.'

'Lot o not doing o lot, honestly.'

'There's no courses thell pay for?'

'There all shit. Find summit on me own.'

'It's o tough job market though.'

'Maybe so, but iss no war is it? Fuckin' country makes me sick. Don't know what I woh fighting for. Come back and tossers are running the streets.'

'You on Facebook?'

'Am I fuck.' They talk some more, less seriously, old gags – the jackass stories of people they once knew; who used to make them laugh. Ronnie attracts Francesca at the bar, distracting her from her magazine. She struts over to the counter and puts her hands firmly on her thighs. Sideways on, sitting at an angle. The round curve of her breast like a trophy in white cotton. He wants the pouring curves of flesh in his hands. To suck the chorizo-meat of her nipple. Ronnie orders a round of lager and double whiskeys. Francesca gives him a dead eyed stare: the currency bulges his wallet. The gold rings on his fingers are working like thieves in his pockets to exact the change. John finds a table and slings his jacket around a stool, racking up.

'Shis mardy?'

'Alloss is.'

'I lark that though, John. Gotta love that. Think we've two tickets tuh fit city there.'

'Shis not easy.'

'Not into that?'

'She's not o slapper iss what am saying.'

'I call that o challenge.'

'Not o chance.'

'You got o thing for her, yer can tell meh? Uncle Ronnie's not gonna say nowt.'

'Anyway, where's everybody?'

'No fucker comes in here. Am olly down here because I've nowhere to be since Katy left me.'

'Surely thess someone?'

'Phil's about, but he's o weirdo. Couple of others. Then everyone else has either fucked off to uni or they've got married and had kids. '

'Not old enough for all that.'

'Me neither. Are you having o laugh?'

'Get yer cue.' The coke wears away - slackens his confidence, though anger fresh, grows inside. Stands, regally, at the head of the table: strikes a dispersing break that pulls the balls through different forces of opposing motion. The four green cushions face one another. John sinks ball after ball, plods round the table, menacingly. There's no chance for Ronnie to even get a shot in. He stands by the side of the table, hair twiddled. Gold-tooth smiling. They played pool in John's garage when they were teenagers; talk about the girls they liked, what they thought they'd do to Kelly Brook if they got half the chance; when they could, they'd drink bottled lager they'd nick from Ronnie's old man's supply in his cellar. John beat him every game then. Ronnie would think himself lucky if he got beat by two, or three. John played pool like a professional snooker player; that special polish, that control over a game, what occurs.

Guys like those from the other night walk in but it's not the one John cracked over the head with the cue. One is a gangsta wannabe called Malik, who's a small-time drug peddler skulking in an Adidas tracksuit; the other a pointy elbowed lanky cunt styling out a New York Jets shirt. Ronnie gayly pats Johns back.

'Easy, they've not sed nowt.'

'Doht lark way they move, theh eyes.'

'Leave off, Clint.'

'Theh watchin me, look.'

'Probably want teh see what all fuss is abaht, thell have heard baht yer.'

'Nowt else teh talk abaht?'

'Not round ere.'

'Jesus.'

'Look mate, clam the fuck down. Al stick this,' he waves the cue, 'up their fucking arses if theh come near us.'

'Keep yer head on, would you?' John spits out his gum laughing. Malik and his crony take a table about twenty feet from them, they trade stares as they set up. Behind the bar, Fat Carl grabs Francesca's arse, whispering into her ear and observes the tension, pulling himself a pint of smooth. There is a thrilling rinse of shame that has the shock of gunfire. Crusader. Ronnie has the break this time around and noses a spot into a pocket. He misses the next shot with the cue scuffing the scalp of the ball. When John takes to the table his concentration is shattered, he drums his fingers hard, finding the rise pose for the bridge. Nameless songs tumble through him. Choruses he's heard without listening playing on repeat. Malik plays three tables parallel, working a sequence of pots as good as John's in the last game. The cue strokes are different. John's puts a nimbler, subtler curve through the shot, like a flicked wrist. Malik drives the ball forward with a jabbing from the elbow, power generated between the shoulder blades.

Francesca brings over the drinks Ronnie ordered. Foggy tumblers rocking with ice. She goes eye-to-eye with John and he realises this is the first time they've stood like this, as two people, without a bar between them, three foot of green zone.

'Wass going on?' She whispers, 'Noh trouble, yer got thah?' Her eyes brighten, insist that he ought to do as she says and she glances her palm across his stubble. OK. John goes back to a game that has lost its energy, and for him, it's excitement that gives him a reason for trying. A cue ball leapfrogs over Malik's table. Struck too hard it thumped the floor, moving steadily along the parquet where John stops it with the black sole of his boot, the crony approaches.

'Ball?'

'Ere yer go.' John rubs it against his shirt as you would a corky, 'Yow tell your Malik if he wants teh play, am over ere.'

'FIFTY QUID?'

'Double it.'

'Ok.'

'Double it again. Those mah terms.'

'Rack it up, motherfucker.' John leans his cue against his shoulder. He twists and trawls his tongue through his mouth, stopping under the gum. Sweat glosses under the electric light and John wonders whether Malik remembers who he is; whether he knows the guy he got into trouble with the other night? The gangs at school? If he does, he's not letting on, not yet. Not giving any clue as he lines up the balls and plays a heavier game than John; shots charged with power. Blunt strikes. Shots explode. He doesn't like the finesse John plays into his game. Malik's cue play is bullish. The clap he gets on the break bosses the whole game. His heaviness changes John's plan, the way he sturdily charges round the table. Malik's thick winged scapula pull back like bows and extend powerfully into driven shots. He pots a red. He pots another. Misses the return, struck too bluntly. Bobbing between cushion and pocket the ball teases over the green rim and black hole.

'Mean tuh doh that?' John jeers as he takes to the far end, where with the green well lit he sees shards of light break from the cue, the flashy tops of polished balls. He goes about his process, but the motion, the timing is different. It's not like playing alone, you can't measure the same way, and your apparatus is affected by pressure. A tricky opponent. Scrotes who giggle in the distance, nosing in on his game. They're beginning to grate. Tougher to plant shots knowing the other guy will make his own amends. The laughter and the mockery. He'll get on your back for every mistake. There's a no smoking sign plaque on the table, another on the bathroom door with something about 2007 legislation written beneath. Nobody gives a fuck. Not when the police don't come down here. When nobody complains. So the smoke, the cumulative drag, curtains the table. Violet, grey, the uncertain drifts of tobacco smoke and John knocks out a long diagonal that shuttles the length of the table.

'Not bad white boi.'

John doesn't reply, unable to hear, his face, tension, as he vigorously eyes the table. From up close, zoomed in, the balls are huge spheres. He imagines round them, over them, under the turn and into the pocket. His mind morphing over space: the table, the collision, knots of probability. He hasn't been so involved in a game since he was wasting a day in the desert with a captain who had won regional Snooker prizes and played like every game was televised on the BBC and you'd sold out the Crucible. They'd circle the table dripping sweat and measure the others' tactics, their mentality, how far they were from cracking.

'I paid you o compliment, solja'

John smiles with his eyes, nodding he acknowledges. The thwack of varnished wood. He misses the side-pocket. The watching gangs' laughter exaggerates support for Malik and they chide their opponent. Deadly even, a stalemate, five balls sunk. Stripes and spots dotted generously, without much blockage, the rest of the game should be open with acres of green to see those final ones through. Ronnie has not said one word throughout the stand-off. One hand on his forehead the other taps his mouth. With the tension high and the air smoke plush, Malik plays on his own sense of drama and hurls his shoulders frontward to launch a vendetta against the balls. Frustrated by their loyalty to the game, their refusal to obey his force, his command, his cue stroke and certain eyes. Francesca bites her nails, and Carl agonises from the distances of the wooden topped bar. Malik cracks two. Three. Then scuffs the scalp of the cue-ball and a couple of his guys playing by the next table think about laughing at his mistake, but are overruled by Malik's stare. The eyes control. John comes back, on the offensive, light and agile, his cue play is effortless. He slings a couple of diagonals like he's Ronnie O' Sullivan, like he's the bloody rocket, does as he pleases. This is where he lives. These rare breaths. Best when he forgets his body. Daredevil shots flow with a fiery pace of direction. The subtle cue work. Only the black. Nemesis. He sees the arch of his leaning body shot through the white on the scalp of ball. Drawing aim like a marksman, sinks the black. Screaming over the table's rolling smooth the strike soothes the anxiety-jabber in his head. Thunder. The intensity of purpose. With the black resting on the curve of a pocket-full of balls, he can enjoy his victory and the bubbled malt of his lager's sharp, metal crisp. John stands straight and unlocks his spine, feeling a tight wrench and pop between his vertebrae.

'Think you owe meh some money, eh?' John daubs his cue with purple chalk. Malik squares up to him, chest-to-chest, their broad shoulders shadowing. There's a wash of posh perfume and John feels Francesca's hand tugging on his; knowing how she doesn't like fights. She said the last time it kicked off in here, she sat by the fire escape in a concrete stairwell, head in her hands crying. She lives with her head in her hands. Ronnie cleaves his shoulders between their chests, the fug of bravado: scattering fists. Pushing and shoving. Breaks them up. Malik gives a gap-toothed smile jewelled with gold fillings and pulls a wallet from his chest pocket. Slips notes into John's hand. He pulls on his shoulder. Hand around John's thick-neck, 'Good game. I know yow in trouble with some guys round ere. Watch yourself.'

'Think I woh lucky tonight.' John bellows louder and speaks to the room. 'Next time,' Malik says, nodding. 'Next time.' Next time. Then something happens. The ripe-raw memory. It's your second night in Basra – strolling about outside the building you seized today, with all the blast and mortar, as if nothing happened. Your knees are swollen from the crawling in the mud, sludge and gravel, and you couldn't see further than a few feet for enemy fire – now the bastards have sabotaged the oil refinery you were meant to take two days ago. The long plumes of smoke that you saw on Jarhead, except with the flickering orange embers, the long pipes black as the oil that swamps out onto the mudflats between the cracks of crater and dun brown desert. The thing's a mirage with its black stiff smoke and slow burn. You're on watch all night with your iPod playing Springsteen. Nebraska with its stripped back production, and you, standing and waiting, bored, wondering what will come of this; these burning oil fields, smoke as thickly black as you've seen, roaring up the sky. How long you'll be here, you don't know. But this is not what you came for. You can stand around anywhere in your camo gear and hardhat. Protected in artifice. You did that when you were at home. You want rid of your anger. Fight some Iraqis. Then maybe that blackness in your chest will go away? Hot noise, that quiet scream that doesn't let slip. That carries you through the night.

FRANCESCA WRIGGLES AWAY - freeing herself from herself - steering her walk with her brilliant arse - dishcloth in hand. The blue of her jeans and the sway of her arse. There's nothing can match this. Been too long since John had his hands on anything as good as that. Making do with those posters you pull from the centre-fold of Playboy, Penthouse, FHM; these girls who stand on a different stage to other women with their superhuman curves and swells, the orangey effect of digital touch ups and the tanned skin. She does the whole thing disinterestedly, Francesca. The way she carries her body through the movements of the day. She lounges around the place, ambling from table top to the Cobra taps. Ronnie's on another table, trying to convince some students to lend him cash for the quizzer he's just poured twenty-five quid into. Throws his arms high in the air; no doubt selling them a good word to one of his agents down the recruitment office. More to being a salesman than the job. They argue some more. John wants for Francesca to come back and he longs for the solace of whiskey. His dreams are of her body. Her love. Screwing his sluice tongue into her. Into acid-tang muscle, a storm of flesh over his face. Eyes heavy; the night preys on. He snuffles the nose with a cube of chalk. Looks through the bar to see who's where. The next mark. Swagger he looks for first. Brash idiots. Cocky. The sort who would bet a perfect stranger. For now he sets up his table. Francesca is being bollocked by Carl; she turns though he jolts back her by her trailing hand. John pulls out a white cigarette and grey smoke streams into silky shades of blue.

There are ways in which Francesca was ordinary: like other Burley girls with her bleached hair; the skimpy, short-sleeved, tight t-shirts. But seeing her trapped, trying to flinch for cover. John can only watch so as not to look too interested, too possessive. He weighs her portrait, remakes her behind his daze. Dressing and undressing, but failing to make a convincing composite, to x-ray beyond her clothes, her coconut skin. He pads Francesca on the triangle of her shoulder, giving Carl a pair of snake eyes.

'How's Evelyn?' John asks.

'She's out back, why doht yer go find her? She's doing my fucking nut in. Maybe yer can talk some sense into that swede of hers.' John goes into the back room where Evelyn's sobbing over a menthol cigarette. She's an atheist; her fingers were always bony and cold, John guesses they have paler bodies.

'We should catch up sometime.' Evelyn's eyes are on him as she stands to get up; she presses her hand onto the side of her hip and swirl of arse.

'Yeah?'

'Yer should see meh place, watch o movie.'

'That'd beh nice.'

'Everything OK with yer and Carl?'

'Fine.'

'Al not say no more.'

'His alloss employing dizzy tarts who can't do job properly.'

'C'mon, less get back out there. Carl will have o bitch fit if yer not out theh.' When they emerge, smoky from the backroom, straightening their creased clothes; John's hotly erect. Evelyn orders Francesca to mop the floor again. John scratches his head, halo of scalp, puzzled. During the daytime there's a sense of the evening that's about to come. The gloaming. John prefers to be here, among friends and their work. Better than sat at home watching TV and putting his rifle together, breaking it back down, only to make it back up again. Duty in the discipline. Yet some days he forgets to brush his teeth; others he won't iron, but he always ends up assembling his rifle. The one his granddad left when he passed away. A soldier. On a back wall, by the quizzers, there's a new game that's a speedball attached to a metal arm; you have to crack it hard and it rates your punch. The shape of your strength. John slots a pound in and gives it a right cross. The one he's seen knock out fifteen-stone men. The ball pounds into the inlay and the machine flashes LOSER over and over again. You're cleaning your socks in a kerosene drum. You're out of drinking water but have enough for your socks: rust-rotten, sucking dirt in the heat of the Basran sunshine. The guns are airy quiet now. Your company are down and out. Your sniper has rocked his spine and the medic's got second-degree burns from a surprise explosion. That's how militants fight. That's what you were told to prepare for when they gave the command to execute: kill on sight. Where you've ended up, as far as those second hand, eight-tonne Chinese tanks that choke on American diesel can carry you. So you're open to targets waiting in a clearing for support, for some fucker in a Chinook to help move your weapons and supplies. You know where the enemy is. Half a mile away in a grove of palm trees. You know they're waiting for the sun to rise, to cut off your vision, so all you see is sand and blinding white, and they'll come at you with all guns blazing. Those years of training, the equipment, your tanks, and you're up against the sun and your own sightlessness. The sun is rising. A giant, bigger than any you've seen yokes the blast-worn sky.

IT BEGINS TO RAIN. First there's percussion: a drumming. The battered ratatat on the roof. Infrequency between sound. Then progression, louder as the force increases. He kissed Francesca three nights ago and it seems longer. It can't be spoken about. He tries again to recall the feeling of warmth, to be nurtured, looked after by nimble fingers. Carl dresses a bottle of whiskey in a dishcloth winding round the orange base. His skin reflected in the strong light is bright pink; his poor circulation and sludge of blubber hiding his veins. The rain comes stronger, tapping at the windows, the water pressure of the night slows their moods. The luxury of being indoors. John hated sleeping in the rain - out there in a sleeping bag, the same shape as the body bags they used to bring home the dead. Between odd jobs, the daily grind; he opens a letter and sees his bank balance in classified zeros. Drops his mug of coffee. They call the dole Job Seekers. They pay your bills and your council tax; they pay your rent and give you cash; working for the government one guy called it, a jovial stranger in the customer waiting room. What kind of dickface would turn their nose at this? The thought of a mong job - cleaning toilets, shovelling popcorn, turning burgers; standing guard over aspirins and hair dye; the low-paid graft and the sneer of shoppers. Turns his gut. They will have their assumptions; and know nothing about him. His life. The things he has seen and the things he knows. Bad knees, two GCSEs, there's not too many fucking options. He thought he was a professional snooker player in his teens; and was going to be a sergeant as a back up. Discharged. As for the maths, he could earn more hustling and signing on than working full-time. Let those Poles pick up the slack. They'll work ten to a house living off Cheerios. Taking a head-count across the bar he can count four different colours: hear at least five tongues. The lucid rain patters. He eases his pint back onto the table: a beard of white froth and clinging bubbles.

Ronnie arrives and takes a seat next to John, wiping his damp forehead and putting his wet coat on the back of the bar stool and starts talking about his day in the office, a deal that's gone through, and John has stopped listening, choosing instead to watch Francesca patrol the bar. She stops to stroke a spillage, leans without knowing she's watched. Her body critiqued over the growing stain. Her cleavage grows deeper. The natural fall downward and together. Buttons undone.

John squeezes his glass; his temples are pockets of heat, warm as the throb of a headache.

'Out o yer league, mate.'

'Eh?'

'Pick yow chin up off o floor. Iss not attractive, yer know, drooling like thah.'

'Am just supping o pint.'

'Thass all, is it?'

'Iss her with o thing for me.'

'Lark fuck it is. Silly bastard.' There's a violent thud, and they look over to the punch-o-meter where Carl has given it a straight jab and got the record score.

'How's work?'

'Fine.'

'I mean, plenty o jobs, yeah?'

'Depends what yer wanna do. Iss office based, call centres, that kinda stuff really.'

'Mmm.'

'What yow good at, John? Less say this is an interview. You've come in, given meh yer CV, and am deciding whether we can help yow or not. What would yer say? Wass on offer?'

'I woh o professional soldier. I woh amateur snooker champion. Abaht six-foot. Single.'

'Very dry. Come on mate, go with this o bit. What roles would you be looking for?'

'I doht know. I doht even know woh jobs are out theh. Iss all IT and admin and shit lark that. Wass the work?'

'Plenty in't call centres.'

'Fuck that.'

'Worr abaht security?'

'Need mah badges, for o start. And like arr say, it's mugs' work. Another thing: av got o record. Someone woh tellin me you can't bounce with o record no more. Everything's all played safe, or outsourced to some third-worlder.'

'If yer change yer mind, or get stuck, here's me card. But one thing, yull work on that interview technique?' John tilts the eggshell coloured card, makes sure he can see the words between the glare and the green icon. McDuffy's Industrial Recruitment. He remembers letting Ronnie use his answers in maths to cheat and now he's going to be his employer. Ronnie's face appears suddenly gratuitous, animal, and heavily frontal: his nose birdlike, tough, sneering, without meaning to. His pearly yellow teeth are uneven. He's no looker. A charmer. He orders a double whiskey with a dash of lime, two cubes of ice, twitches with heavy expectation – self-imposed.

Ronnie fidgets. 'Am off for o piss.'

John watches as he goes. Francesca swivels her head, reins her body in as if to push away any glaring eyes.

'You alright, love?'

She grits her lip, quickens her blink. 'Fine.'

'Would yer like o drink?'

'Am working.'

'No 'arm in that?'

'Evelyn's on tonight. Sorry John.'

'She's o pussy cat.'

'She's o right old cow.'

'Busy this week?'

'Think so.'

'Saturday?'

'Am doing a shift-swap.'

'What about later?' John calms at the sight of Ronnie, zipping himself back up, on his way back from the bog seeing John in action and desperately failing; doing all he can to limit the damage, to salvage his pride. Wounds.

'Alright, love? Eh bothering yow agen?' Laughing, bobbing and waving at John: he gets Ronnie's elbow softly in his ribs. 'Yer can fuck off too,' she says.

'She's o bit lively for me, John. I'll be at table if yer need me, might need teh give her o crack with o cue, yer think?'

'Funny.' She answers. With Ronnie having started up a conversation with a fat girl, Francesca relaxes, has seemed herself all night; when she's anxious, she wears lower cut tops and more make-up.

'Wass bugging yer, Fran?'

'Money. Woht else?'

'Carl and Evelyn go away soon, doht thee?'

'Good.'

'Got two whole week.'

'For what?'

'Seeing how good am hustling at moment, and have o whole safe to play wi while theh gone.' John slurs a whisper. 'How abaht we get few bets gooin, put o bit in our sen, on meh playing Malik for o few grand?'

'You reckon I'll give yer the money from't safe?'

'Iss o stake. You gimme mah stake, and whatever I win, yer get fifty-percent. Cash in hand. Nowt Carl's not done before. Yull juss be borrowing it from't club.'

'Sounds dodgy.' With their heads lower to the bar, ears hear the whispers, Evelyn separates them and calls: 'Fran, have you got a minute?'

'Hold on,' she says to John, going over to meet Evelyn whose management style is sharp and awkward. She goes overboard that one, turning into a boss clone. Evelyn starts pointing her finger, vaguely accusatory.

'Could you be o little less friendly with locals?'

'We're talking.'

'What abaht the bar? How do yer think it looks if yer necking o punter while theh waiting for drinks?'

'Carl doht mind.'

'Well iss mah shift tonight.'

'Sos. Won't happen again.' When Evelyn stomps into the

back, Francesca targets John: their lips connect and compete with caresses tumbling from upper to lower pinks. John's tongue weaves through hers. She smooth lolls a motion through her teeth. He peels back a length of her hair beyond her ear. Then pauses at the flats of his fingertips. She feels them, softly inert. Her pulse radiates through his grip. Their eyes close. Sweeter this way – the climax of tease and longing. His kisses snicker her jawline. Quickly down the white of her neck, tenderly on the jugular. Her eyes flutter upward. A sole fingertip defining of her boundaries; between what is and what is not. These territories of skin. She rifles through his coarse stubble, in her girlish grip. Spiderwebs of saliva link and unlink; connecting and breaking, watery ribbons. The fluids of DNA, all gob and spittle.

Their lips press apart.

'Back on't for Saturday, I take it?' John asks.

'Not quite.'

'Sorry.' Her body's usual, argumentative posture goes limp. The creases on her white vest don't show as she slumps. Her eyes slowly. She goes about her work, subdued, under the constraints of a heavy schedule and an unwell child; a lot of people's favours. The complexities of getting through a day. John's excitement won't let up. The fact of its happening. She can see it glow in his features. A sheen and swagger. Warm saliva creasing from his lips he takes away his pint away to a small table and sits under a TV blaring highlights from Stock car racing. Tweaked estates and souped up Audis zoom by overhead.

Francesca hitches up her bra, untangles the low strap from her tanned shoulders and thinks about texting John, who she sees in the corner like a lost boy, his size shrunk around the table, head bobbing over booze. Waiting. You're still waiting. With your socks drying on the lip of the kerosene drum and your mouth drier than any hangover.

Still you have room for a smoke and light up your favourite brand and suck deep, drag hard. A Scimitar tank has arrived to give you cover and you arm a Milan rocket post, praying for back up, for the Scimitar to be followed by a couple of Challengers, and pray for a GR4 assault. But you wait. Nobody speaks. With their desert storm camo gear and heavy machine guns held snug to their bellies, this is what you waited for, what you wanted. That old song joining the navy and all you ended up seeing was the sea. It plays through his mind. No sea here except the wilderness of yellow desert. The heat. The damning heat starts to burn. The way your body warms and winces sweat. Then dries.

Thick-cast.

Francesca. With his arm straightened, holding himself over the table - a vantage point of thirty, forty feet, John catches the bounce of hair. A squirrel's tail. Up and down. Down and up. He drank too much last night - celebrated a night of wins. Two hundred pounds up. The best since he got back from Basra. Pulled a big-titted barmaid too; Stephanie, she came back to his place after a lock in. They fucked on the staircase and stayed up late to watching black and white TV movies.

His pint of Beck's flickers like eddies of wind through sand. Hypnotising to watch those vague drifts. The living world around you. He felt the need to get out - to move. This afternoon when he'd watched all his TV on Catch Up. Checked the football rumours. Seen two or three pictures of nineteen year-old girls and their natural breasts. Silver smoke mists about knees and shins. He takes out a cigarette. SMOKING KILLS. Enjoys the message more than the product. Death. Francesca's wearing a vest that squishes her breasts closer together, curved inwards, like hillsides, like the rolling thoughts of his cock. How it riles him to see those guys at the bar, stealing glances while she's not looking; caught as she bends, or when her arse wiggles as she walks away. Their filthy eyes across her body. He slots a quid releasing balls that quarrel onto the table. He rounds up: dead still, trapped in the old geometry of a triangle.

'Nah then.' He recognises the voice. He turns and sees the face it belongs to – Ronnie.

'Alreet, fella.'

'Frigid.'

'Shame.'

'Where's yer lass?'

'Francesca?'

'Fit one. She likes meh.' Ronnie smiles deep, deeper. There is a catty silliness to his face. Eyes too round, too broad.

'Haven't seen o CV from yow?'

'Yer wouldn't o done.'

'How come?'

'Iss not for me. Noh yet.'

'Dosser.'

'I'm a shark; thass enough.'

'Iss not though, is it? Look at yer. Yer struggling to keep shoes on yer feet.'

'It'll pick up, trust me.'

'Buh you got skills?'

'Woh good o they?'

'Better than playing pool with bums.'

'You start.' Ronnie brings his anger to the table, bridging his fingers and cracking a break. Only one ball moves, the rest stay static. John takes over where Ronnie has left off. Pings a three, four crack shots and annoys Ronnie when he strikes low through a red. Grinds a fifth with plenty of screw-back.

'I'd back yow. But thess not enough payback. When yer loss. You loss yer confidence too.'

'Your shot.'

Ronnie tries bobbing his head over his chest like John

does. 'Be good to see yer with a job, some direction.'

'Yeh sound like meh fuckin man. Eh can look after me sen.' He looks at his battered slip-ons, turned up at the front.

'Iss up to yer. Offers there.' Ronnie flukes a shot and misses the second. Shit. He forages for consolation, crosses his forehead with a palm.

'Malik ses some of his boys have a hit on meh.'

'Not surprised.'

'Dickheads.'

'Thass my point. Yer need out. Longer you hang around here, yull end up with half scum in this town after yer.'

'Money. Thass woh thee want.'

'Mecks world go round. Allos has done. Allos will. Money. Money. Money. Iss a religion. And it delivers.' He laughs, entertained, half preparing a shot he strikes stupidly hard. The ball chips spinning off the end of the table. Carl spots them and trundles over.

'Ronnie, hope yow not playing for money? John Usher. This man's Ronnie O'Sullivan o this town.' They laugh, all of them. Carl has a presence: a way to possess space. Stand and gesture. 'You had any more bother off those Pakis?'

John forgets his game. 'Been told so. But 'ad no trouble so far. Be o load o bullshit.'

'If owt kicks off, I'll have yer back, yow noo that.'

'Pleased to hear it. Cheers.'

'Good to see yer playing again, anyway. Yer get any games while you were away?'

'Still pretty sharp.'

'You got yer sen o stake oss?'

'Noo, he bloody hasn't. Skint he is.' Ronnie interrupts.

'Some things aren't about thah.'

'Works for me.'

'Thatss trouble. Every cunt wants to make o quick buck – get rich now and pay later. Every shitbag's at it, from't bankers right down to students and dole scum.'

Ronnie backs down, 'Woh only kiddin.'

'Still o stake oss, Carl?' John asks.

'Be up for that. All lads who play in ere – they're too green, not witty enough for't hustle.'

'I might have o game lined up.'

'Who with?'

'Malik.'

'Fuck me, John. Do you have a death wish? That beh riot, not o pool game.'

'Wunt be up for it?'

'Ad fucking love it. But doht expect any winnings out o summit. Iss a crazy fucking idea. It'd be o right scrap.'

'He's not so bad, he'd pay up.' John sticks his neck out, needlessly.

'The man's o cock. He's been coming in here years and he's o gobshite. He's a fucking Paki who wishes he woh black. Thinks he's fuckin black.' Ronnie gives John a bemused look who shrugs. Then Carl goes red in the face. Francesca's been watching from her vantage point at the bar, wondering why John is ignoring her tonight? His glare, the energy is what makes a slow shift pass. She stops dead. Quizzing her lips with fingers. Evelyn comes out of the back with a crate of glasses boggling her face, clatters her. Smashed glass. The bar hushes and then the ironic cheer.

'She's pretty, but pretty fucking useless too.' Carl has assumed control of the conversation; any disagreement will end in fighting, and John won't; it's not worth the bother, the hassle; it'd be every time he speaks. Always urging agreement.

'You'd sack her?' Ronnie turns his head shocked.

'Evelyn can't stand her. She's late every other day. But she does bring punters in. Hey John, thass not wrong is it?'

'Only reason am here.' He answers.

Carl chuckles. 'Something to think about.'

'Give her some slack. It was Evelyn who walked into her then, dint yer see?'

'She's me wife. Even when she's wrong, she's right. Can't budge there.'

Later, in the dusk you can hear the rain. The milky twilight. The energy of your body at 4am, weaning you off the booze. Joints tights with energy and head full of bad ideas. The DVD player has broken. Knocked off shit second-hand from Ronnie. That man knows how to make a quid.

THESE MEMORIES of war, still here, still inside him. The darkness outside, the light pollution, the night glare surges bright colour and clear thought. His room becomes outside, difficult to recognise in the twilight. His heart pounds and his head is bathed in a white lather. Watery-sweat. A dollar. Money is American now. You're thinking of war films. Platoon, Saving Private Ryan, Jarhead. Where did you get your ideas from; the hard-man lifestyle? Rambo was your fucking hero. A ten year old boy who used to shoot Coca-Cola cans in the garden on halcyon summer days. You used to dab your cheeks with charcoal and hide behind the bushes to shoot your mates who had water guns and Nerf arrows. Now you feel more like a Samurai: patient, scared, thoughtful. Your head heavy from the cold of a long chill night, your hands welded to your gun, knuckle-stiff, waiting for the sun to rise, for the enemy to come. The enemy has you on the back foot. Delayed by a sandstorm, an ambush, and the slowness of those second-hand Chinese tanks. You're stuck here in the open. Had to set up camp half a mile from that olive grove riddled with Iraqi soldiers and their guns and their slaughter. Now the enemy waits on an Iraqi Sunday morning. A sixty tonne Challenger tank rocks up for support and fires a hail of white phosphorus smoke rounds that collapse a bride to the township. The olive grove the enemy thought was so fucking clever has been swarmed in our slag of grenade smoke and the Challenger moves on. Sixty tonnes of killing power and you follow the trails of smoke in position, a series of gestures and the bobbing jog toward bangs, sooty smoke and blood tips your gut. You're ready for this. This is what you came here for. The smoke and the glory. You kick down a door with two blokes for support and there's an Iraqi with an AK47 slung around his neck and before he can lever the thing up to shoot you get him in the face. This is your first dead. The smoke. The glory. The first guy you've seen die. Women and kids in the next room shivering with fear and you fucking tell them it's alright, calm down, there's nothing to fear.

The heat under the bedsheets is way too strong: he kicks, twists and yodels – to no effect. He cannot untangle himself. He needs a piss. He needs drink. Fancies a fag. The night chores are back. There's an unread message on his phone. John, I've done something silly. Are you awake? Xxx. He won't reply; there's no compulsion; he thinks she's slept with Ronnie. Certainly. His hair has thickened into unkempt streaks.

He picks up his phone, an old-fashioned clampshell with the Star Trek flip screen and calls Evelyn.

Groggily, she answers, 'John?'

'Yeah.'

'Iss two in't morning.'

'I know.'

'What d'yer think yer doing ringing me? Yer lucky Carl's not back from work yet.'

He chokes back tears, 'I juss need to talk. To.'

'OK. But in future, we do coffee? Or do summit lark normal people – yeah?'

'Yeah.'

'Wassup?'

'I don't know … I shouldn't have said nowt.'

'Don't give me riddles.'

'Iss juss, coming back, iss not what.'

'Are yer drunk?'

'No, Eve. I miss yer.'

'Yer know who am with.'

'Am not saying it lark that. I juss miss seeing yer. Not in club, yer know?'

'Iss been good seeing yer again.'

'Thanks, luv. Glad someone is.'

'And thes Carl.'

'He thinks am summit am not.'

'He'd do owt for yer.'

'I know. I know.'

'A better go.'

'Hang on, Eve, listen. What do yer think would've happened if I'd not gone away?'

'Night, John.'

'What d'yer think?'

'Goodnight.' He hears the smiling edge of her voice.

'Night, night.' The line goes dead: he's not sure if she heard. The only way he can get to sleep down is to wank himself, sedated. He thinks of Evelyn, the generous dip of her curves. Her hair, dyed tickles against his face. Eyes closed, her hand cupping his stubble-puckered jaw, moves in for a kiss. Oily tongues. Stubs his crotch. His jeans swell. When they were teenagers, John took the lead and made things happen. She was shy, unshowy, pretty, virginal. Spot-ridden and lanky, John fancied his chances. John undoes his belt, unzips his fly and tucks his legs quickly through descending briefs. Imagining Evelyn's breasts in a lilac bra, reminding him of a butterflies. Ageless.

He drops kisses down her convex sternum. When he reaches her silky belly, he draws his tongue around her naval. She begins her many-fingered grip of his cock and strokes past wiry black hair. His blood-blushed cock is rudely exciting – glossed with pre-sex translucence. His middle finger works her petalled cunt. Her hands are tiny and her coy fingers work quickly; faster as her arousal shivers through the elephantine cavities of womb and ribbed gorges of female encasement.

Her breath's hot vapour in his ear. Dirty words. Rhythms falter as she speaks. Varies pressure. Marbles his scrotum. Licks and tramples the base of his penis with her tongue. The clotted swirls of ball sack. Tasting leathery and sweaty. Her lips spill over his cock. Her head at his crotch, uncannily close. John holds her hair, bringing her face to work lewdly between his legs. His mouth sucking on her sodden cunt flaps. Quickly, she groans through the stages of elation. Her eyes flutter like moths. He swells into her: shimmering resins of spunk caught in the mitt of his hand. He mops himself with a dirty pair of boxers and turns the TV on: settles down, returning to a classic Steve Davis championship match from the Crucible, the Nugget's still got it: balder, slower, failing better and trying harder.

JOHN FEELS through his junk-mail. Crappy shite in bright print:

Start your own business today and earn £2000 per week on your easily won commissions

Shakes his head; knows if he wanted, he could win three times that a day, on the circuit, with a backer, a bit of bad money behind him.

Your local government is the greenest in the region
We recycle more waste than any other …

Eyes brighter than the cheap typeface. He doesn't care whether it's the greenest fucking constituency on Earth!

Whether it's the MP for fucking Eden on message. He wants warmer summers. Their could be scope for him to start a vineyard. The whole world could change. Holiday makers on their way to Leeds to get pissed up on synthetic beaches. The weather is too cold. Sniggers. His attention transferred toward a bank statement. He reads and rereads. Clarity through repetition, like a poem. Some fucking phone company has been doubling his direct debits, another has taken out insurance he hasn't asked for on a phone he no longer has, no wonder he's skint. He dabs his cigarette into a yogurt-pot ashtray. A hangover. Snaking the pit of his skull. Suspicious. Paranoia follows him through the day – a dark penumbra around his thoughts. He tries not smoke before it gets dark. It's one of his few rules; designed it to ward off daytime depression, sitting around with a fag and coffee like a single mum. But he can't help it, as he slinks another cigarette out, securing it with two fingers that are gradually smoked yellow. SMOKING CAN CAUSE IMPOTENCE. He flicks the lighter and texts Evelyn. Runs water that sparkles daylight into the kettle. The bin stinks and has attracted two flies jigging flies. He woke up with Evelyn today, under the lemony sunrise and a desert of clouds. Leaflets are delivered through his letterbox, more takeaways that all do chicken, burgers, pizzas, kebabs and curries. He can't trust a place that spreads itself so thin. Jack of all trades. Master of none. More bullshit comes through – this time a St George's cross, invitation to an EDL demonstration.

Slogans like a shopping list are written on the back: no surrender to Al-Qaeda. Bring back Great Britain. Ban the Burkha. In twenty years the population of the UK will be unsustainable. Islamification is inevitable. Say no to Sharia Law. Stand up for Britain. March for England. Politics is anger and street level hurt and pen-pushers and big nobs and nothing ever fucking changing. Not for real. Power is stretched across massive space, a chain of command, losing energy with every rung. Politics is dreams for the mindful. Unreal. John's days are about not getting whacked or found out; about keeping clothes in your back and food in the fridge. Cigarettes to smoke. Booze to drink. Women to fuck and some kind of cunt to tell jokes to. Every prick needs a prick. There were politically-minded guys who fought with him in Afghanistan who thought they were there on a mission to change the world order, export democracy; but John didn't get involved in those arguments. Either/Or. He was a solider. Some people bought every word that came out of Tony Blair's mouth - had been waiting for a noble war all their lives. All soldiers want to see action until they see it. He understands now why his granddad never spoke about the second world war. Nothing to say. How can you explain the carnage? Speaking the words re-lives the memory. The gory sights of blood and bayonet. This kind of thing, this march would stir up some trouble between the whites and the Pakis and John wouldn't mind being there when it all kicks off. There's a war on the streets. The old and the young. The new and the old. His arms tanked full of adrenaline and with his arse-kicking boots on, he could have a field day and knock the fuck out of everybody. Carl says there's civil war going on between Muslims and non-Muslims. His fat fucking arse will be on the march and he's got Evelyn to reluctantly make banners and posters. Propaganda. He takes out his rubbish, the first time in eight days, the big bag heavy and warped by yoghurt pots, plastic trays, beer bottles, pizza boxes. The leftovers of his weekly free-for-alls. Bin men still on strike. Lazy bastards. He lobs his black bag onto a cairn of five others. John closes his eyes, still touching the still-rough pattern work of his gun hewn fingers; the palms deviled by soot and fire. The furnace of shellfire and sunshine. You see a flock of Unmanned Aerial Vehicles fly by overhead tailed by a pair of Gazelle helicopters heading toward the centre of Basra, toward a six-storey building like the one's you get anyplace else. Glass. Steel. Reams of white plywood and filing cabinets and aqua-tinted windows that cushion the noise of the Challenger tanks behind. You realise what this is all about. Here in the heat and noise and your boots blotted with mud and the dry blood of the damned. You run with those bloody shoes and the get-up. The weight of the baggage and your mind carving you up with chaos and disorder. You shoot to kill. When you reach the building that the Gazelle's have launched a glut of HOT missiles at and you see those polished aqua windows shatter into noise and a thousand pieces. Westland helicopters these. You charge forward, probably live on the news: with the Challenger tanks behind you into the chaos; coming up with rifle fire and shouting with your squad, Motherfuckers. C'mon you little bastards. Four insurgents come out dressed like soldiers and you and your boys fire your assault rifles and the others come out those that don't die bow their knees in mud and surrender.

Blood and dust. The melding of the bodies. Weapons and gun-fire, rockets flying from behind make sure you. Where to look? Sounds are movements. Dying. Life cleaved from the body. Your heart beats. You take aim and shoot. Your rifle gets heavy, ten minutes in, hot with rapid-fire. You hide around a corner, shivering; listening for commands, shooting.

RUNNING. Not seen anybody for days. His head is smoked out with niggles and inner fears. He works a boxer's step over the paving stone and the tarmac filler; nimbly light on his feet. The ache in his knees starts like a keyhole, his pain is shapely, a shrill point of contraction. Running uphill. The streets are laden with rows of red-brick terraces with small yards where in the Summer his mum and aunt used to sit and talk to the neighbours; the old guys who lived here when he was a boy are all gone. History. People from another era. Names like Walter and Hilda, wearing tweed and flat-caps. These folk were real. He is breathing hard, already. The body loses its conditioning so quickly. He was running twenty miles a day not too long ago. Every day. Some of these houses are occupied by students now; their rubbish in the garden the overfilled bins that never get taken out. Others are single-mum's and their litters of kids. The eldest acting like surrogate fathers to their brothers and sisters. Left up the street up along the bobbling road underlain with yellow cobbles. The Gledco factory you were afraid you'd end up working. A lifetime of packing carbon and graphite products. There are some professionals in these houses; small-business owners, forty-something's in plaid shirts and sandals, home-owners. Spray-paint on the garages, and the pavement and the sheds. A Mercedes parked outside the factory and John slows down his run, checking his sweaty bathed forehead and the shape of his pecs, how big his arms look in the narrow curve of the window. Above the sky are white cunning clouds and temporary blue. He tries to run faster, get more from his thighs; take some of the pressure from his Achilles and shins.

Fast, yes. Faster. Along Argie Road: the thickets of bushes overflowing and metal railings on one side and the redeveloped houses on the other. Formerly the bakers and the fruit shop you can just about remember. Some houses have been kept alive, looked after with well-painted doors and neatly tended gardens; others are concrete drives and cracked paint. Tended to whenever the council can get round. Dodge the dogshit. You get to a junction at the rump of another factory: here the houses divide from the back-to-back to semi-detached terraces. They have back gardens and occasional porches. Swooning downhill, the landscape picking up some of the pace; his legs are dull and leaden. Breathing has become strenuous. Then Grayson Heights and the tower blocks your old man used to live in. Where the lifts are stinking of piss, and you can see out over the whole city. The privilege of height. The shitty council decorating jobs, outsourced to some cowboys. Yellow and blue and red block colours of handrails and doorways. He stops, hands on his knees. Panting. Eyes slide from the kids on bench across the street. Thirteen year olds smoking Lambert & Butlers. He's breathing hard. The air is cold and sharp like ice. Evelyn says he's paranoid because he thinks twisting his torso and picking up a pace again, that everybody is out to get you. A vast conspiracy is railing against him. Down Kirkstall Hill and the thicker bushes and more factories with no manual labour, ran by a couple of people behind a desk. A work-force of robots and expensive machines. Further down. Downwards is lighter on his legs. Opposite the council building is the burnt out shell of a shopping centre. He tries to rebalance the shifting of his weight; brings his feet closer together and tries to take shorter steps to stop him bounding. The shock percusses right through him, ankle to jaw.

Now onto Kirkstall Road running alongside the cars and the cycle lanes. Heading toward the big city. The final stretch. Past the massage parlor that's a brothel where some of your mates shagged Paul's mum and the dinky bookshop that nobody goes in. Adrenaline. Willpower has taken over. He is running on autopilot, thrilled with pain. The sky breaks and cool droplets of drizzle line his forehead; and he is grateful, pointing his tongue to the rain. Acidly. He closes his eyes, focusing on the rhythms of pattering feet. The scenery dissolves into white pain. The dedication to keep moving, the determination to end.

THIS STAGE-MANAGED VISIT to Evelyn's mother's British Rail bungalow by Headingley Station takes them back ten years. The place never changes. The same sixties décor and smoky orange-brown tint to the coral lampshades and retro kitsch furniture that John thought old fashioned when he was younger. Evelyn thinks he needs to get out of his bedsit, beyond the club. Meet real people. There is a world to see she repeats. Every ten minutes the trains that Evelyn's soot-faced Archie once drove throttle alongside the bay window.

They're sitting on the sofa opposite Glenda, who is small and old and round. 'Iss lovely to see yer again, John.'

'And you Glen.'

'Thought yad lost yer mind going out there. Naughty boy.'

'What else was there for me?'

'Want our war luvvie.'

Evelyn interrupts, 'This is o bit heavy.'

'Am juss pleased to see him, love. Right as rain. Every time I turned on news I yad him in mind. Am so glad yer made it back, all in one place. Not with no legs missing or nowt.'

John tries to turn the conversation away from Iraq, and into something more neutral: 'Lots changed since I've been away.'

'This little madam has. Mind, yer can't knock Carl.'

'Always been good to me.'

'He'll do right by yer. I was worried about age gap at first, and his lifestyle, but he's got o heart o gold.'

'He has.'

'Mind, I allos liked you John love. His still o looker now isn't he Evelyn?'

'Mum.'

'If I were thirty years younger.' She laughs in her chair, the joke going someway to exhaust her.

'Well, Glenda love, if I were twenty years older.'

'His o cheeky one this lad.'

'Do yer remember that time you two set off down't shop wearing each other's jackets?'

'Ooh I do. We did have o laugh.' In the kitchen, Evelyn slips away to make another round of teas and coffees: John doesn't like any less than two sugars and Glenda has the teabag left in the mug. Whenever she brings company Glenda has to grandstand; make her innuendos and tug at Evelyn's patience. Except these days she's generally too tired, and tonight is making a special effort for John. They've had these conversations before. Like listening to an old album, or a childhood film, the amusing stories are effortlessly rolled out and belly-laughed over. Though they have tears in their eyes, these stories are never quite as funny as you remember. But, for John, this is traveling back in time. To a place before adulthood and responsibility; before war and shame, the broken nature he carries with him, in all its vagary.

This is different to his own parent's house. The glupey talk of his hotshot brother; then the arguments and the shouting. He hasn't spoken to them for years. And he will never again. In the action of a laugh, the full horseshoe of gob, he sees Evelyn goldenly warmed by the fire.

At the porch, they have said their goodbyes to Glenda. Skin still warm enough from the beating fire, in the cool wind.

'Thanks for that.' John carps.

'She loves you.'

'Was good to see her.' The stars are amulets of fire a million miles way. 'Feel lark myself again'

'Iss been great having yer back.'

'Rather here than there, love.'

'Yer so wooden.'

'And, erm, you know? To see yer.'

'Me too. Away from the bar, and Carl, and Francesca.' She shivers girlishly, bending at the knees, 'I want this.'

'Yer can have it.' A smile wears at John's face. Increasing, unfolding the usually tightly-strung muzzle of lips.

COME ARMAGEDDON, COME. These nights in the Snooker Club blend into one. All late night boozers and then back on it in the morning with a Bloody Mary or Whiskey and Apple before moving back onto the lager and the chasers. He doesn't want to get too close to Carl. Kindness comes with conditions and expectations. People spend their lives this way. Sitting in the same bars with the same people. This seems to be a version of hell to John who watches the Queen's rugby team strut into the bar. Big chests and arms. Thicker and oval solid; denser than John's ever was who spent most of his time running over hills and mountains with a kitbag and doing press-ups and bodyweight, endurance exercises. Time moves slowly, liquidly in the Snooker Club; the stale air. Where nothing ever happens and nobody changes.

The overhanging lights sway over the groups of drunken, yellow-toothed men hunched over the bar. There are quiet tensions and the thick stale flavours of cheap aftershave. John eyes every woman he sees. His knob works. His dick's still got oomph. He feels as though he can chat-up any woman, whoever may pass, except Francesca. She rears up, pearly eyed.

'Woh can I get yer?'

'Woss Carlsberg like today? Tasted like o badgers arse lass time. Carl not getting yow to clean barrel these days?'

'If yer gonna be lippy I won't serve yer.' He can never tell if she's seriously angry, or that she likes to go deadpan; he stares at her for clues.

'Lippy?'

'Sometimes iss like yer think world revolves around you.

If yer happy, everyone has to be happy. If yer in a mood, we yall have to be in a mood. OK?'

'Alright. As o customer toh bartender, I woh letting yer know yer beer woh shit.'

'Doh drink it then.' She lays both her palms on the table and smiles, she's had him again.

'I'll have o Stella, anyway. Think o could use o bit of wife beater. Might come in handy.'

'Very funny.'

'Yow hard to impress.'

'I doht lark guys who try.'

'I doht lark girls who doht.' She leaves John without a pint to stew over their conversation; she knows what she's doing, a flirt. Not to be trusted. Like Evelyn warns. She pulls out a tulip glass out the dishwasher and pops a cocktail umbrella in his Stella before passing it over to John.

'Thass on't house for making meh laugh.'

'Good girl. Listen,' John taps a two-pound coin on the bar top, his tone heavies and Francesca holds her posture, defensive, 'are yer still up for the bet?'

'It'll go bad.'

'Am odds on to win.'

'Nothing's certain though, is it? I woh certain I woh going to model, now look o meh. Juss another single mum, working minimum wage in a shithole.'

'So woss there to lose? Nothing's certain, truss me on that. But odds o good. Believe in't odds, iss probability. Maths. I beat Malik, I'm better. We noo that. I can step up meh game. I've got more in't tank. Every day I get sharper.'

'How do yer know Malik want bluffing?'

'Cos he want.'

'How doh yer know?' She's playful, wrestling with John's words to put him on the back foot.

'We yav a safe full o cash, a top-quality pool shark and nothing to lose. Those o kind o odds yer can't refuse.'

'But thess everything to lose, John. I yav bills to pay and rent and Jake.'

'For how much longer?'

'What o yer trying to say?'

'Yer not wrong about Evelyn. I doh understand, but iss like yer say, you don't get on. She yas Carl round her little finger.'

'They're gonna sack me?'

'Juss how it came across, thass all am saying. Iss how it woh said. But yer need to look out for your sen. Carl's o cock anyway, touching you up. Why not stick it to em, make o profit while their backs are turned and give yer some security before yer get out. Save yourself some face.'

'Did he really say that?'

'Am not o shit stirrer, yer know that. Iss something he said and summit yer shud know.'

'Convenient for yer?'

'Yow twisting things and yer know it.'

'Am quite hurt.'

'Because o job?'

'Well, that, and way you have o breaking bad news. Thanks John. Thah woh really nice. You've made meh feel really good.'

'Am trying to offer you o way out. I wanna help yer Fran, yow know that. You know that.'

'Juss gimme a minute.' She pulls his cheek hard until it sticks red and John knows it's time for him go find some other amusement; he could see tears showing in her eyes and understood that the cheek grab was a bluff. Working a shot on a table between rows of other lads playing sloppy games with loads of missed shots he sees Malik through the yellow light. The glow of green baize. John thinks it'll be somebody Malik knows behind the window: being smashed, him being followed home on two or three nights and the dog shit delivered through his letterbox. They're waiting to break his legs. This is the politics of the street. But before they do, he wants to beat them on the table: be good for something other than fucking up their faces.

'Soldier.'

'How's it going?'

'Juss heard some guys coming to duff you up.'

'Fuck it.'

'C'mon mate. Think about it.'

'I welcome it.'

'Fuck?'

'Yer heard of Audie Murphy?'

'Cut crap, what yer got for me? Wanna rack up and get your ass handed to yer?'

'How about a rematch – real cash this time? Get a bit of heat behind it, momentum. Odds.'

'Bollocks.' Malik stops sudden to check his pocket for a text. The rumble lit up his Adidas bottoms.

'For real. Yer better start by getting out o ere, right now. Juss gotta text saying boys are on their way down this place.'

'Am staying put.'

'You crazy. You got o death-wish?'

'Av got a drink wish.'

'Serious. You a nasty ass motherfucker.' His tongue licks over his teeth, as he laughs and tastes malts of cheap whiskey. There's a trembling in his hand that Malik sees when he racks up; the balls seeming to take an age to mosey onto the table. American-style. The wobbling shuffle of white stripes and acrylic shine. Yorkshire voices thinly in the air, touched by the smoke of a hard day's work. He knows when they arrive. The noise-level decreases. Whoops. American style. Malik's boys are five brown faces staring at John. Skin-colours are opposition strips. Whites. He's feels wrong: Pakis. He's not Carl. Us. He waits for Them on his mahogany table drinking Guinness, snacking on greased-dry roasted peanuts. Slightly burned, the taste on his tongue is wooden and dry. The people in the bar know what's about to happen, what's going on. He won't use a pool cue this time; he'll go down fighting. He's called from across the room, 'White boy.' But he doesn't listen, stays in his seat. Two burly hoodies hook his arms from behind and another bitch slaps him; he wrestles one-arm free, twists to crank a wrist-lock. Then twats him across the face with a right cross, cracks a tooth. Some other cunt fronts him up. He waits for him to speak, throws a right as his mouth opens. His jawline open, strings of ligament snag, crack in two. Fuck you, you motherfuckers. Fuck. Impact. Dark. Some fuck's crocked him with a knuckle-duster. He's beaten down by a guy with a bloody fist. His body, undefended, now belongs to them. There is no time, no sense of self, or seconds passing. There is pain, of varied strengths, volts through his body. His face takes the blows, the skin burns, the bony protrusions pounded rare-pink. One takes a cigarette to his face, the others hold him in down. They scorch an 'O' into his forehead. The butt hisses into malleable, blistering skin. Malik's voices calm protest. They turn and leave, as guys from the rugby team run over from the other side of the bar. The whole event lasted a minute. A dizzying, drench of pain. Bruises creep to his ribs and chest, spidering his vulnerable spots, underbelly, cartilage. The cigarette mark has crusted into a violet swell on his forehead. His bollocks are sore. He's helped to his feet, humiliated. He has never been beaten up in public before. Another window gets smashed and John starts to come round, thinking of explosions, mistaking the Chelsea tractors outside for hummers and the people trapped inside, as refugees. He forgets himself slipping into reveries then steadies, refusing to be helped to his feet by the rugby players. Stammering upright, he orders a triple whiskey. If those rugby lads weren't about, they'd have fucking killed him. These streets play by their own rules.

Double-whiskey downed, he a third. Francesca has left the bar unattended to watch CCTV in the back office, thoughtfully smoking a menthol. Hates violence. Every time it she's near it she hates it more passionately. John will get his own back, he promises himself. He swears on his mothers' life, squeezing his fists tight, into balls. Squeezing his chubby bulge of knuckles. Eventually, like a walk on cameo, emerges from the back with a First Aid kit, 'You're o fucking moron.' She measures a plaster over his forehead and swabs his cuts with vodka dabbed onto a make-up removal pad.

'How we gonna go into this together?' His arm follows the curve of her waist, he feels strong.

'We've nowt to lose.'

'Good girl.'

IRAQ is behind the daytime, behind the kitchen counter. A mirror-world living beneath the shadow of his soul. It breathes for him. Looking into the mantel-piece mirror he counts his heartbeats: Machine gun chatter. Glow of chaff. His bullet-rattled fingers shocked to calcium bone. Rareness. You understood a soldier's routine. The twenty-four hour clock and your day drawn out precise as a diagram, two-dimensional. Soldiers belong to the job. Rip out time and you get chaos - a thriving chaos of sex, hunger and violence. Now his day is stretched out pointlessly between mugs of tea, commercial breaks, walks to Tesco, waiting for the vodka to freeze hard in the fridge. Evelyn still hasn't said anything about where she thinks they're going: about what she wants from their relationship. Boring conversion, but on the cards and inevitable. He hopes she knows he's not serious, not in the way she'd want. He doesn't want her to leave Carl, although he feels himself growing closer. He depends on their routine. The way she cares for him. Her probing glances grow into gazes. Studies him like a book. These new skills she's learning. He rests his weight downward on his two hands pressing onto the sink, peers out the window at a blackbird bobbing in the garden and chavs monkeying down the street. White trash they call them. They can say what they want about the whites. There are people out there who want his reputation, his blood on their fists. Loves it. Bring on the fucking hatred. Nothing excites you like an enemy. A reason to get up in the morning.

When he was in combat, his bollocks answered all the questions. Glands. Reflexes keep you alive. Rifle in hand. Covered by his camouflage gear, he was a soldier, out to ambush a country breeding terrorist scum, led by a dickhead who killed three-quarters of a million. Remember the stats. The numbers. The reason you're here. Your rifle shots bring democracy to a bloody, foreign country. He didn't care for the cat and mouse about WMDs, not really. Part of him believed in Tony Blair, he listened. Saw his role in the operation. He had watched him on cable, on the parliament channel, saw the Tory faces gawp and the sense of History, big things were happening and it connected Blair to John Usher to the sand-swept fug of bullets and dead bodies. Blair impressed him; made him believe, and while he was out there on patrol, or standing guard, thinking of home, he was proud to be doing Blair's work. He kept it to himself. The lads would rip him. They were in it for the laugh, to fire guns and drive tanks, some of them. They said it was like a club. Never had anything like it. Even three or four pills, twenty bottles of lager and a big bass-line on a Saturday night, which was the closest thing to it. Incomparable. John knew what they meant. The thrill of murder. We are the enemy now, the West. John's Granddad - before he died - told him straight out that he thought it was a bogus war that no sod believed in. War is no glory.

There's an ambush and only you and two other lads saw it coming. You splashed off the bank of the Shatt al Arab into the green water and hear the chatter of machine-guns. The bombs. Explosions. The fug of smoke. You're swimming breaststroke with the weight of equipment on your back and your helmet tipping down over your eyes. The water cools your sweat-hardened, sun-baked head. You're safe round the back. Get the nod and lob a couple of grenades over a white brick wall and leap over the bank, behind knee-high walls. The smoke of your grenades. You've maimed a rebel machine-gunner. You kick him in the head. Stand on his nose. With the butt of your gun pressed to his chin: you shoot and there's a spurt of blood. Your lads run back through to join the company and you stand with the dead man underneath you. You know you're a fucking bastard, a right cunt, tell yourself you don't care. You're alive. You think you mean it. But you hate yourself. Draped in camouflage, face bursting, and your body aches, knackered.

AT THE BAR John swings his body round to a couple of gobby, middle-aged regulars; he's open to conversation. 'What you two losers up then?'

They laugh, looking at one another. Checking to see how to take John's trespass into their private world.

A Yorkshire voice, brawny North, like his Granddad's. Not watered down like all these chavs who sound like Mancs, or the stylized drawl of arse clown gangstas. 'Some old, mate. Nowt to get excited about.'

'His o big head, Len.' Carl interrupts laughing: these gleaming yellow teeth. A mouth full of them.. 'His allos bin lark it. Ant yer John? Why yer had to go and join army while rest of us were content to graft at home.'

'How'd yer mean?'

'Lark these gap year shits. See the word? Theh ant even sin their own back yard.'

'Yow ever bin anywhere?'

'Nowt to see.'

'How'd yer know if you've never been?'

'A with Carl on this kidder.' The other, fatter man says; his eyes creasing to open like a puppy, leaning over the bar. 'Olly place a wana go is to past. Be twenty again. By eck.'

'Ah lark getting older, me.'

'What foh?'

'Am only twenty odd. But yer old enough to know your sen. But am still young enough to get me end away. Eh?'

'Av got o missus. Av shagged her before - why would a do it again?'

'Seen it all before.' Carl bellows. Smoke rises to curl and ribbon his white cigarettes, orange-tipped, smoke fingering his dry throat. The ribbons are always the same. The legacy of smoke. The way smoke moves, glowing swirls. He used to watch his Dad's Lambert & Butlers. There's a clampdown on smoking he's read in The Sun. Yes. He agrees; the forceful simplicity. But this is middle-class big heads in fancy houses and well-trimmed gardens finding ways to line their pockets off the working man. Nobody like you speaks for you. This is Carl's gripe, he thinks. He remembers the way Francesca looked at him the last time she served him a pint. The toll is straining his belly: the cherubim rolling fullness of his sixteen stone body. A soft-skinned vehicle.

'Aye up dick face.' Ronnie rocks up with his usual arrogance, busy eyebrows, the machination of his face.

'Rambo.'

'Yer coming to sit?'

'Can do. Meeting someone soon though.' He says with this school boy sincerity. He's wearing a grey and yellow jumper with zigzags and boxes.

'Wass with theh get up?'

'Iss nice, you shit. I bought it today - in't sale. Thess

loads of stuff dirt cheap. We can go tomorrow if you want, got day off. Get yer dressed in something thass not a black bloody shirt.'

'Not my bag.'

'You'll never snag that barmaid dressed like o vicar. Need to get yourself some new threads, something that someone would wear in this century.'

'Got myself plenty of women already. And I didn't have to dress up like a spaz.'

'Game?'

'Go on, ant beaten yer in a while.' They make their way over to a table next to a tiny black woman and a fat guy in a New York hoody. John isn't in the mood for a game and thinks about Evelyn, whether she's working tonight – twitches his head every two minutes, expecting to look at the bar and see her. Ronnie notices his reticence; plays the break confidently, enough to pot two colours before a third with good screw-back.

'Who's yer bird then?' Ronnie asks, handing over the only available cue to John who analyses the wood-work, sees that it's cracked in two places, and answers. 'She's married.'

'Fuck me. Are you crazy? You mentalist! When Carl finds out yer are in deep shit. Brilliant.'

'Glad to entertain yer.'

'Iss not that, iss just stupid. Shit.'

'He woht find out. But iss Francesca am worried about. Been trying to put on my good guy side, and if this comes out – thass it. Game over.'

'My lips are sealed.'

'Theh better be.' John waving the cue to the rhythm of his words wags like a finger. He hits a sequence of five balls in quick succession. The blur of their colour flashes across the table. Ronnie jumps up and down shouting in mock fury.

'So how'd this happen?'

'She came round mah place.'
'Thass it?'
'Well, things look like they're in the shit for her and Carl. She thinks he's having an affair with Fran.'
'Unlikely.'
'I noo, but things are bad. We had a little chat t'other night and I said to come see meh. Then you know how it is, it goes in stages. The Usher does his thing.'
'Romantic.'
'Thass right.' John passes the cue to Ronnie who despite having a good game is being pasted by John.
'Is this o one off then?'
'Who noos.'
'Careful though. I've heard stories abaht Carl.'
'He's o fat bastard.'
'Yeah, but he's nuts. Doesn't matter how fat you are if you're gonna do someone with a baseball bat.'
'Things o getting interesting round ere.'
'That they are.' They laugh and John takes back the cue to slam in his last balls and moves onto the black, which he pots by turning away from the table and winks at Ronnie as the cue slides past his back one-handed and pots black. John goes for a piss, and in feint buzzing light is amused by the commentary of the graffiti on toilet doors. Allah Almighty. He sees you shitting. A voyeur. A porn-maker. Further down by the gambling machines: Fuck Off Pakis. Somebody has drawn a St George's cross with black sharpie and on the other side reads my shit stinks. John pulls out a thin-pointed sharpie he uses to jot records of his hustling and writes Ronnie's number on the door, with the caption ring for good time. He pisses and uses the mirror to readjust, pulling his black jacket free from his belt buckle and unruffles his black shirt. Life's about fucking and fighting; we're animals. Some guy told him that as they wasted a day smoking on an outpost near Tikrit. He had

struggled against the heat, wandering into the orange sun. Sand beat down his face, the wind corkscrewing through the desert and they laughed, happy to be alive. Outside, a thug is trying to borrow money from Ronnie who can't quite refuse, can't get rid of him. John rolls a finger across his knuckles, checking to see how well they've healed and clocks the strangers stare, faces up eye-to-eye, the intensity strong enough to ward him off.

Silence, like when the RPG went bang behind your precious head and you cannot see and you cannot hear. When vision returns, the whole place feels underwater, slowly without noise. You're on the roof of a square building in Basra, stone-deaf, and the troops are firing mortars from behind a tanker that has exploded. Black smoke billows up through the side-streets in baking dusk. You have your chemical-protective kit with you. Your rifle. Your bollocks. The militant bastards are good today and have blown past a couple of soft-skinned vehicles carrying supplies. Your ears won't work and your dinner is on fire. Gunshot. Fire. Gunshot.

IN THE FOYER there's the noise of trailers, scrapings of pick and mix, the chat of customers, and John in a purple shirt looking bored. There are punky kids who look like they've been standing by their tills all day today, and yesterday.

Hand's sore from the popcorn scoop. There are four of them, all standing by flat screens, punching in orders from time-to-time, trying not to look too disinterested. There's a queue over twenty-two feet long. A sock of popcorn's emptied into a warmer. Hot-dogs cock-slapped onto the grill. Management have taken position outside the box office, and stand in an important circle stroking their chins. The neon signs above have never glowed more brightly. Somebody's wandering around with a dustpan and brush.

John would prefer to be having a cigarette. He finds a seat on a metal stool and sees Evelyn arrive through the glass double-doors. Her face ten years younger with the polyfilla of make-up and bloody lipstick.

Tickets in hand, their queue for the film crisscrosses the queue for the popcorn, soda and hotdogs.

'What did yer choose?'

'Some RomCom.'

She punches his arm, 'Really?'

'I lark em me.'

'D'yer think anyone will see us?'

'Nope.'

'Why not?'

'Thass the answer yer wanna hear.'

'Hmm.'

'Anyway, what's there to see?'

John gives a wink to an Asian security guard he knows from working on the doors. Evelyn adds, 'Don't play silly beggars.' One last glance through the glass double-doors; the world is miserable outside. The silverline of sky and mercury rain. How can this be the sky that nearly baked him alive in Baghdad? In the screen the seats are tombstones of padding and plastic; with a broad, flat, girder of immoveable hand rest that divides the pair of them. He may as well be sitting next to anybody else. They decided not to buy any overpriced food from here, Evelyn knowing the mark-up. But John envies the mouths grazing on buckets of popcorn all around him, stuck in their seats. A loose Malteser skittles under legs beneath them rolling all the way to the black curtain skirting the large screen. An usher has a seat affixed to the side of the room. Sitting gayly, cross-legged. Before the trailers, the cinematic adverts come on with the flickering scars of film you don't get on TV and the steroidal, surround sound.

The enigma of unpurchased items. The strangeness of

things you haven't yet bought. It's too dark to see her facial expression, the violet liquor of movie dulls her face into a generalized, female shape. Down the stadium seating are couples and situations, the ferreting dicks and stomachs churnings of worry over a false move. We're all the same, deep down. Somewhere. Carl's face occasionally pops into his mind; but he's surprisingly guilt free. Cold. He cannot picture them together or understand how Carl would react. He is one of the many other men who have enjoyed Evelyn's body. Just as he did ten or twelve years ago when they were teenagers. The shocking gorgeousness of her big black bush; the disgrace of rudely pulling out his cock, dolphin leaping into broad daylight and the whore glimmer of her eyes. He likes it when prim girls go wrong, turn dirty.

He knows why they're here; it's easier them having being lovers or that they are familiar with one another, their privacies, how they belong in the world. He can't see her doing this with any other man. The film is dragging on between scenes. He can't concentrate on this fictional set-up when his mind is racing with thoughts of Evelyn, confusions. It would be easier to give up. He sees the papery, vein-rippled back of her hand and tucks it in his. She stirs rigidly in her seat. Takes it off. Scolded, the cold like ice water. It would be easier to sit at home wank yourself to death, than try and attract a woman, keep them happy, keep them from straying. Then there's the loneliness. The human longings. Letters from home. Only the other soldiers received them. The scent, the mannerisms; he's remembering her, why he loved her. The cobwebs around his eyes are coming free. The depression lethargy. Dead Man's limbs. It all works out in the movies. That's why we come here. The reassuring lies. Cinema is another religion. The film ends. Lights up. A mob of ushers armed with bins and brushes ready themselves for the sticky clean-up job.

Outside, somehow, it has disorientatingly become night. Dark as a bat's wing. Dark as the tyres on Range Rovers rolling out of the multiplex car park back to the tree-hedged suburbs. Evelyn says she loves coming out of movies at twilight. Something transforms inside her. Elbow slung round her waist. Evelyn loves his gentle, manly grip. He squeezes her proudly stopping as quick as he started suddenly edgy and alert, aware of who and where they are. Publicly visible. The conspiracy of eyes. The nosy old buggers who twitch their curtains. She's on a blood-type diet. The tubby layer of puppy fat and the roundness in her cheeks has been ruthlessly starved. Symptoms of age. Somehow John is younger than everybody he knows. These years, he can remember everything. She only drinks white wine. Her favourite TV show is Coronation Street. Her bra size is Double D. He prefers her curvier: the longings he has for her arse bulging in tight-fitting jeans. The nasty ass. Losing weight: losing the natural Botox that eases out wrinkles with glowing fullness. It's good to see her again, like teenagers except already trapped by life, the bounce in their step's gone heavy, eight years ago he was only seventeen and dreaming of being a Snooker Player. Footsteps. Eight years ago. Slow down. Evelyn was two years older, the shy girl next door. At that age it was a longer stretch of time. She felt like a woman. The memories are quick and vivid; he can smell them, alive. She walks quickly, in a rush, in a hurry. She was a geek at school and everybody thought she'd go to University and become a doctor, lawyer, teacher. Professional. But she married Carl. Stuck between what she wants and what she thinks is real. The long straight Roman road is dry, stonewashed gray. The streetlights glow in a conjoined mandarin sequence of orange circlets. Cars parked unevenly. Women drivers. They reach the street where John's living now, five streets from his Mum's old place. They walk through John's yard and Evelyn tuts at the crisp packets and ripped-open bin-bags. Foxed and burgled. He asks a question to deflect attention away from the stray packets of ready-made males, milk bottles and brown envelopes.

'Film woh o bit shit want it?'

'Iss a curse.'

'Yall allos see a shit film with meh'

'I can put up wi thah'

'Want gonna say nowt, too slow though want it?'

'Thah guy behind too with white man afro? Wunt stop kicking meh chair.'

'Thought yow'd o said summit.'

'Couldn't be bothered.' Evelyn takes a seat on the sofa and gives it a sniff, as if to check it. She takes a look around – the giant John Smith's ashtray, the greasy pizza box left half open on the floor and a picture of John's Granddad, after the war waving out of a steam train. John's in the kitchen pouring himself a whiskey, topped off with tap water. 'Wanna tipple?' he yells through to the living-room.

'Any wine?'

'Ang on love.' Without thinking, John runs out to the mini mart and leaves Evelyn alone. She could use a drink. She's sure Carl was having an affair last year; and the way he carries on with Francesca, he may as well be with her. They nearly broke up two years ago when Carl said he wouldn't have any more kids, didn't want the hassle. It's part of the reason she never went on to Uni or got a decent job – she wanted to be a Mum, decided it's what she wanted most. She takes a round mirror from her handbag and redraws her lips in wild red stroke. She doesn't know why she's bothering, John's not fussy. He should open the windows more, get light and air in. Too awkward without booze. John feels alert and it's difficult to talk to Evelyn. He feels boring. Sure that she can be more spontaneous with other people. Somebody who is not him. She counts thirteen cigarette stubs in the ashtray and pours herself a glass of water. Conversation with her is all procedure. When was what and who is where. Tangibles. Jackboot steps before the door bucks open and John rinsed in a wash of drizzle and sweat pours wine jerkily into plastic beakers.

'Doht have any glass glasses.'

'It's alright, didn't expect you to.' They sit with their drinks without touching, knee's distanced, guarded, Evelyn still has her jacket top on; a green girly thing he doesn't have the catalogue knowledge to describe. Everything is words. Words you know, words you don't. Evelyn mumbles, 'I think we should call it off.'

'Call what off?'

'Am not gonna sleep with yer.'

'Dint stop yer before.'

'Carl'll find out.'

'Iss that all yer bothered about?'

'Mostly.'

'Has he found out yet?'

'No.'

'So wass worry? Where is eh any road?'

'Preston, on business.'

'Wass that?'

'Beer tasting, new ales.' John goes for a piss and then cleans his cock thoroughly under the tap and forgets to flip the blinds, someone out there will have seen him cleaning his snake. It's a sort of kindness, to Evelyn. He smudges the head with his thumb: the cool tickles his balls, collects droplets on his hair. Two minutes later he announces, obviously, 'Am back' and takes a long sip of his drink that rattles his teeth with cold, stroking Evelyn's cheek, smudges mascara.

'Av started o course, Open University.' Evelyn sits upright, her palms primly flat on her closed thighs.

'Doing what?'

'English.'

'Yer speak English … What yer wanna learn that for?'

'Don't be daft.'

'Wot iss it? Shakespeares and that?'

'Nothing wrong with trying to better your sen.'

'I juss watch films, when theh come out.'

'Iss not same.'

'Reading hurts me head.'

'Yeah but yer think don't yer? Yer not the meathead you pretend to be. Yer so easy to read you.'

'Yer gonna get a new job with it? Sit around talking bollocks and supping lattes?'

'Don't get so defensive.'

'I jus hate pretentious twats.'

'And am not one. I juss want summit to do … For me.'

'Wass Carl say?'

'Not o lot.' Her eyes suddenly dispel their excitement: the thought of Carl slows her movements, kills conversation.

'Am not kiddin you know?' She says.

'Abaht what? Yow hard tuh follow tonight love.'

'I can see yer eyes; am not sleepin with yer. Arr want us to be friends – forget owt else. Friends.'

'Iss not me talking about it.'

'Yeah, but a know what yer lark.'

'Am not gonna lie Evelyn love. All always try to shag yer. Thass juss way I yam.'

'Hmmm.'

'Do yer remember those neon condoms I got once.'

Smiling, she giggles, 'Yeah.'

'Yer never anybody's but your own, John.' He turns on the TV and Evelyn steadies herself, watching him, his big hands trying to dab the buttons on the remote; the way his lower lip hovers when he's between thoughts. He's pretending not to pull her, just laying off the offensive, is enough to pull her round. The threat that he might not give her any attention.

'Yer doht have to sit over theh.' She tries not to spill any tangy wine as she budges up, 'Iss getting cold over ere.'

'Shudda said.'

'Arr did say.'

'Yer know what I mean.'

She sees his silver crucifix, hanging on the mantelpiece. 'Yer not in to all that are yer John?'

'Not so much.'

'You are sentimental.'

'Me?'

'I thought with things you've seen, well.'

'Sometimes yer juss need to hope.'

'Thass not enough for me.'

'Iss good to see yer, thass one thing. Good to see o friendly face for once. Someone who can hold o conversation. Them down club, thee all idiots.'

'Don't I juss know.'

'Now yer doing o degree, yull probably have no time for barbarians lark me.'

'Iss olly a bit o paper.'

'Am proud of yer, I am. Seriously.'

'Come here.' She kisses his lower lip, desperately pulling back on it, exposing the gums, his teeth. John carries her weight upward, bringing her face level with his. Paws at her bra-strap whilst twirling his bobbled tongue to brush with hers, vining their mouths together in a tangle of tongue. The Prime Minister Gordon Brown today visited Basra for the first time since . . . The news is ignored. The first time since he got off his fat arse. Busily undoing her buttons, excited by the captive breasts, he nuzzles them. A space of flesh, he pushes his face snug between their curves and kisses upward. She remembers their first kiss together; spring, years ago under a tree in a park by a dual carriageway. Classy. John smiles, fumbling underneath her shirt with an adolescent excitement and lodges his hand between her belly and belt. His hand is stifled by tight denim, hot belly, his knuckles crackling under the button – his fingers reach out in a pair, a smooth V against her lips, her wet furs. Belly-to-back he rodeos his rhythm against her. Upstairs in the darkness, Evelyn takes off her lace knickers and curls like a cat under the bedsheets. The fangs of John's fingers ease knuckle-deep into her fanny fluids, the gripping wattle of minge. Evelyn rolls his foreskin back and foreword over his cock's lilac head. When John enters her he glides close and deep, until a rhythm develops – she scratches his back, he's getting it right and he thrusts slowly. Exhales. Big bellows of breath. Screams at the backs of their throats. Orgasm shudders her middle like a powerful birth. Rocking through her ribs to the swell of her clit fucking makes Evelyn's eyes close and her middle-aged breasts jerk. Moans. Knees shudder. She feels the hollowing of her cunt. Under the bedsheets, the night dark as Guinness and violet clouds above.

This Sci-Fi pitch of black gets him thinking about Space, the nowhere darkness that clots the stars. A Milky Way. In Stephen Hawkins robotic tones he hears half-remembered waffle about physics and the processes of the Universe. He doesn't need maths to confuse him, when life is tough enough. Life itself. God used to feel like a hand on his shoulder, a sense he bigger than he could describe. The Holy Ghost. The ceiling. He takes a piss under electric light, eyes strobing to the halogen spotlights Carl has obsessively stuck up in every room, adds to the daze off staring at the night. As a kid he was obsessed with Space: he was wondered what was at the bottom if it, like he's looking down a well. He had a poster on his bedroom wall of stars and he made a solar system out of polystyrene balls: they glowed neon at night. Primary School was obsessed with professions ... Who do you want to be when you grow up?

An astronaut, John said. Up in the ether his neck cranes to see: there you are lad. Everybody wants to live in the stars. There are benefits not having to do anything, free from pressure. But most of the time he can't relax, not without cigarettes and (or) alcohol. Playing pool and shagging all the fitbags. Never the fitheads. Glance in the mirror at his mug shot is the beaten-up face of who he used to be. Gray stubble. Deep sunk eyes. Heavily-lined forehead; the rivet nose and russet face. Punkish bed hair and boozy eyes. Back on the sofa thinking of jobs and pool. Tomorrow. When Evelyn goes with Carl to Leeds-Bradford the airport, he'll play Malik for big money. The thing he's been looking forward to, the thing that scares him. A nice little earner. He slaps his pillow with a gentle backhand, pushes his eyes shut, surrender for another day, the grey light to rising. All the bullshit thoughts of all the bullshit things he doesn't know. We know more than we can say.

A dog barks, cataleptic. Head is too heavy for pillows, he stacks them three at a time. Still his head sinks deeper, and he aggressively pats and pads the duvet; then turns the other side, feeling hot. As though thoughts are rushing out the top of his skull, spraying onto the quilt. Sweat glimmers. The green-spored tap drips-drops. He shuts his eyes, sees the blackness, he could be anywhere; near sleep, close to his aboriginal dreams, his memories are deft and vivid highlights of random events; some from yesterday, a decade ago, memories that merge into convenient truths. Then War. The memories he separates in his head, light and dark. Backlit by Devil's of shame. No man is good. The TV is sullen, dead without its flickering bank of images and hardcore noise. Buzzing off a cigarette and sunrise not far away, he lets go, feels his body's weightless plunge into selfless sleep. Rheumy darkness. A bang. Square-walls. Ruffled noise on the carpet upstairs. Then voices. Neighbours in harsh whispers. Throbbing pain in his head:

the stalks of his eyes. The ceiling. Smacks of noise. The click of the bathroom light and a piss that comes tumbling forcelessly, a steam of clashing water.

A SWIRL OF SMOKE covers the table. Malik toys with his cue, twirling rotations. John's pose is stiff with worry. He sees the white of Malik's eyes: the gathering concentration. A crowd encircles the table. The slick cue strike. Then the rolling out of the balls, the dizzying laps around the table both players make: sure to weigh up every angle, every opportunity to see something they may have missed on their opponent.

'Not bad.' John says, first to speak, to break the tension belonging to silence.

'Tut tut.' Malik exclaims through the clicking of his tongue, ready for John's mind-games. Refusing to be distracted by his banter.

'Clever boy.' When the fear, the worry has reached its highest point, John becomes anxious. The inflated pressure spurs him on. The risk. Adventure. He sees the openings created by Malik's mediocre break. The way he doesn't like to play safe, all or nothing. John has Ronnie and Francesca in his corner. Before the game began, Francesca squeezed his hand tight whitening his knuckles. While Carl and Evelyn will be squabbling over cocktails in a Spanish resort, John has got into their safe and borrowed himself a stake big enough to bully Malik. Interested to turn the game into something more lucrative, like those old black and white films about cocky hotshots who play big money games running long into the whiskey-glazed night. John has cash wrapped in a bank bag in his back pocket. The presence of heavies makes for a stand-off. A suspension of violence. Kettling them in with the whites of their eyes. Pakis and Slapheads. Eyes slide. The music has been stopped. The televisions are turned off. Ronnie's eyes follow the reverb of every shot.

John is four for four with Malik, even as he weighs up a straight across the green. One stripe is blocked by two stripes and a spot. He has a way: but the line has to be perfectly struck, without compromise; he shoots straight. The gluck of a ball swallowed. He starts to sweat. Malik's unconcerned and his entourage is oddly quiet. John goes for a stripe freed up by his lucky shot. He bobs the cue before striking, methodically, cracks hard. He shoots, scuffing the centre of the cue ball by about two millimeters. Fuck. He swings his head round to gauge reaction, eyes beaded with worry. Francesca's face creases pain, the crest of her hair falling over her nose. Malik takes to the table, striking low and hard. Then long and winding: makes the shot twice. He shrugs his shoulders, cracks his neck sideways. First game over and John's not playing to his best; any slip-up and Malik will get him. He's good enough to make it count. But John's better: he has the edge, the fluency. Malik becomes immersed in a crowd of his own people exchanging low-fives and hip-high handshakes.

Francesca slaps John flat across the face, shouting, 'What the fuck wer that? His embarrassing yer … I thought yow said yer could do this?'

'Iss not over yet.'

'John, get yer act together.'

'Relax.'

'I can't, not even watch.' Her anger cools him. Convinces him, oddly enough, that he still has control. He's not given up as quickly as she has, and without her prodding, it'll get easier. He fuels himself up with the rest of his pint, locking his teeth, tightens his jaw. He regains composure for a moment. His previous coolness has been replaced by a steady panic: his forehead's warm. Body rinsed with watery sweat. His fingers tremble as he clasps the gloss of the cue. Malik finds it funny to see John ruffled; his people behind him watch drawing long drags of weed. Green tinted smoke distorts their faces. Seeing Francesca's nervous face – imagining what would happen if he lost the game spooks him. John breaks, tentatively; the pressure forces him to play safe. When confident, his drive would explode the pack, he makes sure to hit the middle-side of a ball about a three deep in the huddle. The balls settle far enough apart for him to think the break is OK. Pleased. He drops one into a pocket.

John slants his head round to glare at Francesca with her hair twiddled and ruffled by angsty hands. John gives her a shiny wink. Ronnie gives him a thumbs up. This is what he wanted. The chance to impress. To play chance for his money, to dare a lifestyle. Fuck the dole. The hand-outs, the dead-end jobs. Moping about and feeling sorry for yourself. Drinking yourself to distraction. John grits his teeth: lowering his chest parallel to the table – he surveys the game. Calculations wriggle through his head. It's beyond thinking and he can't measure it, the possibilities of strikes and counter-strikes run through his mind. He grips the cue hard at its base; shoots flat and dull and hard. Sends the five stripe in the corner thumping into the middle-pocket.

'Any time yer wanna give up, let me know.' Malik's harrying him along.

'Yull be sorry, yer silly bastard.' A rapport has developed. Friendliness through rivalry, he senses more to Malik. Craziness. The good kind. Doesn't give a fuck. Take bullshit seriously. Malik turns in two easy pots one after the other, followed by a tricky long low diagonal, which he thrashes arrogantly.

Malik overshoots.

John, sensing luck, urgently takes his cue as though if the moment passes, he'll have missed his chance stabs a ball firmly in the open pocket. He feels the game coming back to him, the momentum fixed, coursing through him. The force that operates his scapula that chooses which ball to hit and which to miss, that feeling of talent, he believes is the fluency of winning. As the black becomes the only ball left for him to pot. He grins at Malik, drilling the black with screw-back. The pressure drifts away, temporarily. Once again the balls are dug out of the pockets but the break belongs to Malik who piledrives the cue down the middle. The balls scramble. Retain energy. Rattled. Throng.

'Easy on't poor buggers.' John says, hoping to disturb Malik who he can see is busily working through every ball on the smooth baize. John snorts a line of coke off the table's metallic rim. Malik is seven ahead. John can see how he can find a way back: tap the nearest six, and then attack the eight in the far corner. Depending if that works he can zigzag between Malik's blockade of balls, leaving the pesky black. He pots the six. Snaps the eight. But strikes violently when he only needed to work the ball inside a slender gap. The force staggers the cue ball. Knocks it off track. Nudge. Foul. Malik now has two shots. He breathes heavily. His eyes work the table. He clobbers a curve ball, sideways. Yet somehow pots it delicately. The black is pushed deftly, falls easily into a pocket bundled with other balls. Francesca can't keep her hand from her mouth, her long fingernails mesh and disfigure her expression. Her eyebrows jagged, crease her forehead, and John knows he's in trouble. Ronnie says nothing, does nothing. Slugging his pint to the bottom of the glass. Cunts laugh. Malik waving his cue around like a saber jumps up and down on springy, athletic knees. John gnashes his teeth, pushes his tongue forward in his mouth, trying to break past his teeth. His breathing staggers, slow and deep, then quick and hacking. Drums of his clockwork heartbeat. God. This shit is fucked. This is a first class fuck up. The sow skin of his lobes burns. Francesca, first to console, grabs him by the cuff of his neck, a fist-full of collar. Hair. She lodges her head between his shoulder and neck, crying. John pushes her off: seeing Ronnie in the distance. He doesn't want her sympathy. He sweeps his arm across the table, knocking off the few remaining balls that bounce densely onto the parquet, rolling on the square tiles toward the sticky carpet.

Fucking moron. You missed your shot. His temples moisten hot with sweat, his stomach tightens, John counts out the money he owes – slaps down every note while Malik's boys jeer the skinheads and snigger in their logo branded hoodies. John shakes Malik's hand, gives him his winnings, patting him on the back as he takes his jacket, lights up a fag and heads home for a bottle of whiskey and a manky sofa. Food-stained. The world falls around him; like he's looking up at a cathedral, a tall building, something toweringly immense. He can't look Francesca in the eye. Ronnie chases him, pulling at his sleeve and John bats him off elbowing away and gets to the Exit ignoring riot and chaos.

You try to listen hard. Listen, intelligently. Yesterday when the sun was up and you saw your lads playing football. Not yesterday. Your other life. The boredom of the daily routine. Listen to what the something inside is saying; now you remember the suburbs; firing mortars into the open distances? That they can hear your destruction. You load it and Dicko fires. You load and Dicko fires. On one the firing pin gets stuck and you grope and handle the metal edges of the shell, ripping it, tugging it with your hands, desperate, willing it to work. You stare right over it like a dickhead. 'Don't lose your fucking hands,' Dicko says and you get the pin out and sure it up for its massive arc. You think of free-kicks and five-a-side. Bored of the heat and the flames of the fire. The endless chaos of noise. The fucking RPGs and buildings taking a kicking. The sun wears you down hard. Thick with dust and sand. Listen to the noise.

II

JOHN DARTS his orange tab end into the gravel on the bluish road alongside what he thinks is Carl Brown's car dealership; he recognises the place, before it was Paddy's it was a drive-thru car cleaners, before that a service station. Behind the portacabin acting as an office, the River Aire oozes along snagging trolleys breaking into white waves over juts of rock.

There are rows of second hand cars: Saab, Nissan, Subaru, Ford, Mitsubishi, Renault. None of them British. Funny. Carl. Through the small square window in the cabin he sees Carl's triangular heft of back and round-broad shoulders, wearing his favourite black and red hooped polo shirt.

Approaching the blue door with gashed with splintered wood, John knocks loudly and shouts 'Carl yer fat twat, let us in.'

'Yull wake the dead you will, you Squaddie cunt.'

'Was walking past and thought I'd pop me head in and see how you woh doing. Evelyn said yer might have some work?'

'Canna get yer o drink?'

'Whiskey, cheers.'

'Fucking whiskey o this time? Are yer Irish?' John has heard Carl's question, but he holds his fists and answers tight, somewhere between the swelter of knuckles.

'Two old maids on a beach, streaker ran past, one had a stroke, the other one couldn't reach.'

Carl stares laughing until you laugh with him. Here's another he goes on: 'I don't believe the Scots are as tight as people say, but I did hear that when two taxis collided in Glasgow recently, 48 people were injured.'

'Good one.'

'Tell us o joke then.'

'Have got none.'

'Yer didn't banter with the Squaddies?'

'Yeah, but iss all piss-taking, character stuff.'

'A Scouser went to a prostitute. She said, 'Do you want a blowjob? He said, 'Will it effect my dole money?'

'Yer fucking nuts. Wass with all foreign merchandise Carlos? Doht tell meh you of all people's employing foreigners?'

'Iss industry. Yow want me to sell British when you can get a nippy little Jap for half price and half mileage? Capitalism iss what it iss. What fuck can I do about it? Would you work for minimum wage round here?'

'Was thinking more sales, admin.'

'You'll be lucky. Car washing's all I've got.'

'Cheers.' John clasps his mug of water and looks at the pictures on he walls: A3 print outs of Ronnie 'The Rocket' O'Sullivan at the Crucible; a picture of young slim guy that looks like Carl in a Leeds rugby shirt grinning toothily.

'One minute yer playing for Leeds Rhino's me mate. Next yer knees gone and yer out in the cold.'

'Yer still have any involvement?'

'Am the mascot sometimes, but thass o secret. The little kiddies love it on a match day.'

'Brilliant.' John peers out the white double glazed window where two young Asians are washing cars with yellow foam brushes. Carl strips a cheap cigar of its plastic covering.

'Who are those pals out there mate?'

'Saj and Rikh.'

'You got em on't cheap?'

'Theh work like trojans for fuck all.'

'Business good?'

'Down on lass year. People got less money for new wheels. No credit. Thes still o market for ol' bangers lark these. On some models I've had increase, yer know?'

'Sounds abaht right. Who can afford a BMW these days other than wankers like Ronnie?'

'Posh twats. Bankers. That lot.'

'Exactly.'

'Between you and me, how yow getting by?'

'Playing pool. Ronnie gives me o bit too for helping him move things, keep stock. Keep quiet abaht some o things he's up to. Got me savings. Got jobseekers and waiting for housing to come through. Bottom of list me being a bloke and that.'

'Am looking for o lodger.'

'Evelyn wouldn't mind? Another bloke in the house? With you and your lad?' John's face tightens as he tries to work out whether Carl actually knows anything. He pushes one foot forward and brings his bulk nearer his desk, examining John.

'You get on, and we could use o bit of money for a few month to be honest.'

'Not got much choice.'

'No, you've not.'

'I'll have o think. Thanks anyway.'

'Don't be pissed all time, or bringing women back though. I know what you're lark.'

'Promise.'

'Unless thes one or two for me.' He laughs, 'Wanna here another joke?'

'You wanna sack yer writer.'

'What's the difference between o nigger and a snow tire? A snow tire doesn't sing when yer put chains on it.' Carl brings his arms behind his head, sits deeper in his chair and clasps his fingers. His arms are huge triceps and big boned elbows. Nasty. John fancies his chances. Would love to go toe-to-toe. Just to see what the big fuck has going on. Long walrus face; boozed ruby. Big cunt thinks he knows about violence.

'Yer met Simon?'

'No.'

'He's o good kid. Look after yim.'

'Uncle John.'

'Thass right.' The phone rings and Carl pulls the receiver toward his face, angrily, the plastic coiling like a pigtail. The tone for business is forceful. John gives him a wave mouthing goodbye, silently. He's thirsty and has been dreaming of a chilly pint of Becks all day; the kind that comes out the pump jumping, frost chilled to the glass. Hops, the life of the pint clean on your tongue. Carl speaks clearly on the phone with deep Bradford vowels, bringing his punter round with man-to-man honesty. John stares at the glass-framed A3 print of Ronnie O'Sullivan and wishes to God that it was him leaning like a gunner over the mint green baize, eyes concentratedly, preparing the kind of shot that goes down in history, the kind of shot that makes you groan with envy; he remembers a game, five years ago, Ronnie 'The Rocket' O'Sullivan, the best player in the world.

Out in the yard, three white guys who look like the hundreds of Albanian or Kosovan passport pictures he's eyed are wiping down the cars with yellow sponges and suddy water. Thick white foam spills cleaning over the cars; sodden before the two rounds of polish. A smoking Bangladeshi speaks into a blocky Nokia. These immigrants are about ten years behind. Living off the hand me downs. The sky is duvet white gives the day a sullen dullness. Round the corner they've built a shopping centre with a Morrison's and sports shops on what used to be playing fields; further down the road the other way, playing fields have grown into a multiplex of a bowling alley, cinema and low-rent nightclub, full of coke-sniffers and fourteen year olds in slutty skirts. That's where the gypos trespassed when he was a kid, nasty buggers. John broke his tooth fighting one when they tried to bully his gran into getting her roof tiled. The fang came free like husk and iron-edged blood gushed through his mouth. He walks along the main road, sampling the air and reading the new style graffiti. Burley's not the quiet little place it was; every street has its own drug dealer, set of students, single mothers, foreigners. Everybody is foreign. A community of strangers. Funny thing to miss when John spent most of his life trying to get away from here, the small-minded bleakness of inner city cunts. Everything is bad. But nobody wants to do anything about it. Nobody packs their bags and rides out to the promised land.

Further down the road, again, there's town and the skyline visible through cloud at a three mile distance, viaducts and the shorter, squat buildings of the inner city. He's headed toward the distance, toward skyscrapers with red signals warding off aircraft and student flats – a city within a city. A coliseum of cunts.

LEEDS UNITED are fucking shit. John borrowed a best goals of Leeds United DVD the night before, watched the likes of Gordon Strachan and Harry Kewell play their hearts out for Leeds; and thinks about what a bad fan he's become since he went away and Leeds went down; like the pair of them are connected, cats in a bag, Leeds United and John Usher. If Francesca ever caught him thinking this way, she'd rip the piss out of him and that's what he likes, what he needs.

When Ronnie comes round (the front door busts open, every time, he refuses to knock) he invariably brings in shopping bags full of knocked off shit, multimedia and games he's picked up here and there. It's as if however much Ronnie gets into the white-collar thing he always has something dodgy on the go.

'What yer been up to? Sat ere all day wankin?' He sneaks two bags behind the sofa.

'Been looking for work, ant I? Getting o bit desperate with rent due and nat.'

'Fuck-in-hell.'

'Cheers.'

'How much do yer wanna borrow?'

'Two-hundred, juss until Thursday.'

'No problem. What yer doing after thah?'

'Carl and Evelyn.'

'Really?'

'Gotta do it. Iss only short term. While am inbetween places.'

'I'd love to say yer could move in rahd mine, but iss o one bed place, mate. Really. And I can't have yow on't floor when am bringing back bits and pieces I pick when am out and about.'

'Doht blame yer.' Ronnie joins John on the gingham sofa; the Leeds United DVD has played itself round and back to the beginning again, now onto a menu page with a picture of Billy Bremner embedded behind the options.

'If Leeds had any sense they'd never o sold Cantona, Ferdinand, David Seaman, Denis Irwin.'

'Fuck off.'

'Am serious. They've been o selling team since Don bloody Revie. And I can't even remember thah far back.' Ronnie's still in his white shirt suit with the collar unbuttoned and the cufflinks off, easy smile and slick shoes. He doesn't have to keep having a go at Leeds United; dirty Manc bastard.

'Can't all be glory supporters? Can't all be like you Ronnie mate. Got money. The talk. The team. The car. Shame abaht looks though. Respect. Nobody respects that.'

'Must've touched o nerve. Yow big gay.'

'Juss cut meh some slack. Thass all am saying.'

'Dint realise you were so uptight, these days, this park life must be doing yow in. I see em every day at work. Blokes who've sat on their fucking sofa for six months, a year, even longer sometimes. Thee go mental.'

'Seems like everyone else is mental to me. Working yer arse off for't man. Getting your sen all worked up and in debt to wear right shit, to full your home up with right shit, to eat enough good stuff so yer can have right shit. Iss bollocks. Everything is o load o fucking bollocks. Shithole.' John pushes into his thighs to help him off the sofa. All Ronnie's talk of wasting away comes true when he feels his legs straighten, knee's creak, and lumbers toward the kitchen on the lookout for another beer. 'Want one mate?' John calls into the living room, listening to Ronnie who says he does. John pulls two Budweiser's from the fridge. Long. Slim. Bottle-brown. He knows Ronnie will complain because it's not some lairy, German lager. John loves the cool mellow lightness of American beer and as he wrangles off the cap with a tin opener, all the life in the drink rushes forward as a gasp of foam, heady and blissful. He brings in the beers with a box of nachos and sits back down next to Ronnie who has the remote in his hand and is trying to tune the Freeview into a classic Snooker game on an obscure digital channel he didn't know he had.

'Who are these twats?' The TV shows two Snooker players from the seventies one with a handlebar moustache and another with a ginger afro, playing on some Northern Gameshow.

'Jesus.' Ronnie gasps his mouth oval into a bright smile. He lights a cigarette. 'What yer gonna to do with your sen John?'

'There's that prick down't Snooker Centre I think weh can sting. If weh can raise some stakes, that'd be o decent enough payoff. I think he's stupid enough to take bait. If we get o few o us putting money up then we'd be alright. I have to get Francesca her money back before Carl comes home. Been looking at factory work – but fuck me.'

'Francesca?'

'Yeah.'

'Why do you allos say her name with that look on yow face?'

'Because she's o nice girl.'

'I've noticed.'

'Maybe you have. But something else you've done is really screw this situation up. If yow want me to, I'll go lend her money myself. Fucks sake John, she could be out o job and your way to fix all this is to make the sem mistake again.'

'Cheers Ronnie mate. If yer could. She deserves o bit more than a fuck up lark me can give her. Poor lass. '

'I've not much choice.' The pros on TV are playing the game like it's a riddle, strolling round the table, cerebral. Unable to pot anything or get a run going, they snooker one another into a stalemate. John cracks his neck with a sideward flex and burrs a flat note down the glass bottled Budweiser. He should close the curtain in case any scrotes come past in the dark and glare in again and pull faces, banging on the glass like they were last Sunday; white faces in the dark. Rain climbs down the window in clear dashes; John watches them while Ronnie is going on about the economy, the types of people he works with. All digressions end up with self-congratulation. The snooker show has cut for some messages; he's picking up American lingo, watching TV so much these days. The two men stare at the screen as a woman comes on practically orgasming over a fucking Boost.

John leans away from Ronnie, turning his body outward, open, 'Would yer be in?'

'On what?'

'A rematch.'

'You av to beh kidding.'

'Seriously. Malik's been lucky so far. But av got o sense o yim, I know where he's weak, how to get o yim. His due o defeat.'

'Woh if he's hustling yow?'

'How can he be hustling me bah beatin meh?'

'His clever.'

'But his not player I am. This is perfect chance for't pay-off. This is how game works. You don't lose o bit then walk off; yow lose to up stakes then come back for't pay off.'

'Iss not just o game though.' Ronnie has become serious and his eyes have sharpened, you can see how he must be at work, behind a desk, when he's not being the wide boy down the pub. 'Iss not a game. Not when yer got other people's money, other people's lives o stake for it.'

'Iss not o risk, we'll win.'

'Yer fucking mad you are. Yuv lost plot completely.'

'Am better thah yim. Thass o fact.'

'Yeah, maybe. But woh abaht yow bottle John? Woh abaht as soon as pressure comes, o crowds watching, yow stiffen up?'

'Nerves.'

'So what abaht that?'

'I've got past that. Truss me on't this, I know what I yav to do and I'll do it.'

'Iss too risky for me.'

'Av taken bigger.'

'Woh does Fran think abaht all this?'

'She's not really speaking tuh meh, but as soon as I apologise, get cash back wi interest, then shell come round. Am sure.'

'How many beers yer had?'

'Eight.'

'And yow talking out o yer arse. Get o job. Get o normal fucking job and shag Evelyn. Thass your road to recovery, right there.'

'That's not woh I want.'

'Then maybe yull have tuh adjust.'

'Am not giving up on it, not yet, thess something I can do mah way here.'

'OK. But doht pull us down wi yer.'

'Have o bit o faith.' Ronnie channel surfs and stops on a music channel with a blonde girl dancing in a cage and singing as her hips thrust, bobbing, she wears a skin-coloured Lycra outfit. John shuffles to the kitchen: his palm against the fridge, feeling his triceps ridged hard. Groans.

'So yow moving in with Carl?' Ronnie shouts through from the living-room.

'Looks thah way.'

'Juss lay off Evelyn then; but get o job.'

'I no, I no.'

'Another beer?'

'Goo on then.' He pulls open the fridge again, hears its puckered crack and the beers are running out and there's nothing more than the bollock of a lettuce in a juice-struck tray.

JOHN USHER curls his coat round the head of a tall bar stool with metal legs and a swirling wooden seat effect, crafted for arse comfort. He only sees Francesca's forehead and pulled-back hair. Then the tops of her eyebrows and disgruntled face. Cracks his fingers, pulling thumb across index, popping the joints.

'You know thass rude?' She rises to her full five foot eight; with her back straightened. Proud tits.

'I've never got thah. How can clicking yer fingers be classed as rude and so iss getting yer arse out? Rude seems to cover o lot o things. I think yer t-shirt's rude.'

'I'm not serving yer.'

'Why?'

'Am not gonna to spell it out.'

'C'mon.'

'I feel lark o fool.'

'I know yer do, and am sorry. I look like one too. I look like o right bell-end. We had it all to win, it woh right there.'

'Oh yeah?' John reaches out his newly cracked fingers, feels them loose and free, and extends, wiggling toward Francesca over the bar. His pink blur reflects in the clean sheen, his fingerprints gloss glaring smudges.

Francesca's hand doesn't meet his, and she moans, 'If we had nothing to lose, how come it feels so much lark we lost? Thank God for Ronnie.'

'Yeah, thank God for yim.'

'Why be so sarcastic?'

'Am not, am serious. Iss juss that, well, I think iss easier to be the good guy, the hero when yow rolling around in it.'

'I think iss easier to slag off successful people, sound lark what you're making out John?'

'Carl is going to sack yer. Iss on't cards. Before this even happened, you were on your way out. We'll get thah money back. Together.'

'Soon as his back, he'll find aht. His not as stupid as yer think and then thass it. Game over. What ma supposed to do?'

'I'll fix this, truss me. Am not kidding around.'

'How much did yer lose?'

'Fuck me, Francesca.'

'Don't get all defensive,' her head jolts back, her finger points. 'Tell me, how much? Yer lost more than I put in, didn't yer?'

'Something lark that.'

'How much?'

'Everything,' His eyes are steady, fierce and his eyebrows arch into his forehead, 'Everything, OK.'

'John.' She lurches, reaching out to cross fingers with his outstretched hand, she releases, 'But it's only what you deserved.'

'How can yer blame me? Think I wanted this to happen? You had o choice.'

'You made me trust yer, you made me.'

'Don't be lark this.'

'Yer not even sorry, you're o cunt.' For the first time John is offended by a woman swearing – the word too heavy for her. Oblong on her lips. Back straight: her posture's as prickly as it is dismissive. John knows when he's beaten. Cracks his neck left and right and slums in at the bar – big thirsty sips of beer and something ulcerous in his belly – like spaces of absence. Malik walks into the bar with a tall guy with black wavy hair shining under artificial light – needlessly smug. Small-timers. Too much swagger in their limped walk. They set-up a table and slot a pound coin waiting for the balls to bumble out onto the table, slipping down from the see-through plastic side panel. This other guy seems like a stooge for Malik: racking up for him, taking the triangle and placing it over the stray balls. He sets them down into the rubix cube simplicity, necessity, of what goes where; the small 'c' at the bottom right hand corner of spots. John watches without moving his head (turned agape, backward from his body) his eyes following the movement, the curiosity. John can't resist not to give them a crack: to rise up from his chair and slap four-knuckles between their eyes, spark them cold.

'If yow hit em, John. Thass it between us.' Francesca says sternly, although he's not sure if he imagined; either way, it sounds sensible.

'They need o good hiding. Look at twats.'

'Olly one I can see.'

'Dunt suit yer all this.'

'Maybe not, but iss what you deserve.'

'Al make it up to yer.'

'Start now. Leave em be.'

'If thass what yer want, thass what al do.'

'I want you to want that. Am not going to be like Evelyn, being sympathetic. Yer need to get yow act together. For you.'

'Owt else?'

'You owe me three-fifty for't pint.'

'There.' He groans, pulling the last change from his deep pockets, somewhere in cotton nowhere, he finds the shrapnel, squeezes it tight in his palm to lodge the hard corners that leave jagged marks and hopes for a starry imprint. Behind him Malik is playing like Fats Minnesota, knows the game without looking, can hear the way he drives the cue, dull thwack of balls ploughed deftly into one another across the green. These are moves designed to spite him. On the bar in front of him is paper mulched by spilled lager, the newsprint hovers over the liquid, paper as the ink blotches bolder magnified by booze.

THE MOON is covered by thick clouds blackening the sky. The moon is a cue ball. On the pool table of the sky. God is a shark. Past the aisles of redbrick houses and the village green, the autumn's cool is refreshing and shrubs sway in gardens, like necks. Copper-shot leaves in the park where the daytime's make-shift cast of single-mums bring out the kids, dogs shit in the playground, panting happily across syringes and condoms. Kids bunking off school smokes on the swings. Unemployment gives you the time, too much time, to see the world as it's happening. Without you. He was going to ask Ronnie about work. Couldn't bring himself. There's no hard graft on the books that would be worthwhile, not like when you're serving; the tingling cramps in your muscles, your head full of swagger and purpose. The power of death over life, the chasing bullets. You work minimum wage and lose the safety of your benefits. Pay higher tax rates than a billionaire. It doesn't suit him not fending for himself, but where's the incentive? What's Ronnie's job anyway? He wouldn't mind shipbuilding, going down a mine, plunging himself into something psychical and brotherly. Something to make you sweat. He has troubling reading: the word and the pages blur. The words come to him in the wrong order. He can't see himself in an office. The women would make him kick off – brutalise photocopiers. Give the water-cooler a good fuck. How the mighty fall. He's not done. Not down and out. He thinks he can still make a few bob hustling locals down at the Snooker Centre, a movie-character lifestyle. Everybody round here is pretending their somebody they're not; the afro kids with the gangsta walks and the wannabe hard-men with their shirts pulled over their heads. Guys like Carl who think they're in the fucking Red Army. The clouds swirl into the cosy dark like dolphins leaping over swells of water. Funny to catch the sky changing colour. Nature doing it's work. The electric throb of his heartbeat. He didn't expect to lose the game: he didn't expect to put so much against a second-rate scumbag like Malik. He paid all he could and bolted, leaving Francesca's stake to pay, and then some. He has no money to pay his rent; the savings from his sixteen grand a year in the forces have been dwindled away on by booze, fags and long nights playing American pool. John has the film poster of Rambo: First Blood on the wall. They sent him on a mission and set him up to fail. But they made one mistake. They forgot they were dealing with Rambo. A young Stallone, with taut biceps, ripped pecs and wild dangling black mullet. He used to love Rambo. More than Rocky, Die Hard, Alien, Mad Max. The gulf war was one of his first real memories - the daily broadcasts - of well-to-do BBC journo's with their slick hair and cream shirts reporting from the blaze of heat and sandstorms. Those burning oil fields. It was his choice to join the army. Now he daydreams of Francesca, her forgiveness, making up in the bedroom with a kiss and cuddle without their clothes, without the shame of that night, two weeks ago. He reconstructs their first kiss - this time with the special effect of nudity and plays it over and over to himself on repeat. His hands dip into her jeans, nuzzling beneath the round studded buttons, bustling and finding rough wetness. The garden gate creaks. Evelyn walks through the door with a deep tan startling John on the sofa.

'Managed to slip away.'

'Good.'

'But not for long.' She says, pecking John on his forehead with a sweet kiss, rushing to close the curtains and gather piles of his scattered rubbish; the crisp packets, stiff socks and tab ends that are the vagaries of a lifestyle.

'Good holiday?'

'Sun, sea, sand, Carl.'

'Lovely.'

'You wanna see him, he's black.'

'Brilliant.'

'I know.' She smiles, crafts a tongue between their lips that wets John's stubble: he's stayed in all day watching motor sport and a cramp of ache runs down his back and creaks at his knees; he has that daytime gloss, dazed by boredom, stuck in his own thoughts, stumped.

'Cuppa?'

'No.'

'Am gonna make one anyway. So there. What's on TV? We can put o film on if yer lark?'

'I'm not feeling it.'

'You can go to the club?'

'I'm in thah place too much.'

'As long as you know that, you'll be fine.' She cuddles his forehead in her long fingered, nubile hands. Nudges his nose.

'What you been up to?'

'Not o lot. Working. Looking after Carl. Thinking about what I'd do if weh broke up.'

John doesn't know what to say. 'Yer can speak, yer know?'

'Am not looking for nowt serious ... Not now. Me heads not in't right place Eve, love.'

'Get over your sen. Am not asking you to marry me.'

'Av not got much food in. Thought weh could get takeaway if thess owt yer fancy?'

'Yer really know how to treat o lady.'

'Shurrup.' He laughs: Evelyn is pushy, he's not used to her like this, so different from the shy and spotty girl he lost his virginity to those years ago. She rests her cheek on his chest. She's wearing a cream woollen top that gives her breasts a smooth, long curvature, a cosiness. Accidentally, for the first time, he feels like she's the world's wife. They're saddled there on his sofa and she nudges his crotch, his mouth muffled by her caresses. The news is banging on about some shit in the Middle East. The arsehole of the world. Those places no different from the other: sand, sun and gunfire. Tribal leaders and warlords. Drugs. Simple lives. The West. He's on the other side watching through the parallel universe of the TV: where the focus is on split-hairs between generals. The dynamic with the government; what the public think. Professional opinions and then grunting soldiers. All this footage the journalists report looks Hollywood staged. He channel surfs semi-nude music videos and thirty year old movies he can barely remember seeing when he was a kid and before the bombs and the sepia: greyness, the black of his own understanding, the char and the bone. Nothing so useless as a Mother's tears. His tea slowly goes cold. A chill that ripples stretches through him, turns him over to his side. He needs to stretch, to scratch something that doesn't itch; though Evelyn won't give in, tickling at his hairy gut, kissing him, loving him, doesn't give him a break, let him be the miserable cunt he longs to be. Glassy eyes. He shoves her. Big palms in her back and heart beating fast, lump in his throat; then surrenders. Holding her is giving her himself. He takes her fully in his arms, a firmer grip over her body; the tactile flesh. They lay on the sofa. 'I do love yer, I do.' He whispers bass-baritone. She's wearing a frog-green dress as long as her legs. He can't leave the jabbering idiot of the TV on for another minute. The synthesised noises. In the dark room without the flickering footage, light becomes greener as it filters through the ribbed curtains. They'd do this when they were teenagers: a first love, they had not experienced anything like it before, a few weeks, a handful of dates seeming epic, longer than it ever really lasted. She's filled with age. Her arse has more shape, as do her breasts and her eyes are beginning to crease. His own body has deformed. Swapped daily drills for pints and his muscles have quickly given up their strength, firm: and his belly has been the first thing to balloon. She scratches at his ribs with her small fingers clawing closer like a child.

'Has Carl been OK?' John asks.

'Why yer whispering?'

'I don't know.'

'Idiot.' She punches weakly.

'Last thing we need, is.'

'Yas no idea.'

'About me moving in with yer?'

'His been keen on that for o while.'

'It's o really shit idea.'

'I'd pretty much agreed with him. Eh woh adamant and

it woh before us. Juss for a week or while, while me benefits come through and that. '

'You're kidding?'

'Iss that or some shithole.'

'What abaht Ronnie?'

'His place is two bed, but he ses he has o bird.'

'Does eh?'

'Eh ses so.'

'Thing is, it would be nice having you around, and we do need a bit of extra income. But that's impossible.'

'Nowts confirmed.'

'Shit.'

'It'll be fun. No need to creep about.'

'Don't be there too long though? It can't.'

'We'll look for o place.'

'Really?'

'Really.' They soon loosen the grip on their hug and the kitchen light comes on as Evelyn tends to the kettle and John makes brown sauce sandwiches. It's rate for Evelyn put her foot down though when she does she can't be persuaded, even John thinks the idea's stupid; but where do you go? When your cash has ran out and council waiting list for houses is jammed up until Christmas: and you're a single man, able to work, without kids and you're not an asylum seeker; you're just a useless bastard with nowhere to go. This mood Evelyn has gotten into turns John on. It's good to see her spiky, self-important, forceful. Her hands on her hips. Carl generally gets back from a close at the Snooker Centre at about 1am and they know that they'll have to have sort themselves out before he gets back. She wants to eat up their precious time together with a nap afterwards.

The evening gets late. Sky blackens swirling mauves and tiredness reaches for their eyes. They climb the stairs together, footstep to footstep on the creaking floorboards. John should've washed the bedsheets but he can't ever get them back on, and there are covers hanging off and bare mattress exposed. Evelyn has to sort out the slackness before they face one another, pull off their tops and clap out the bedside lamp. Smearing lubricant on her lips, wiggling his finger, he slowly opens her. His hard-on wriggles into life, like a tadpole. She is dryer than other girls he's been with. And her long nipples in his mouth are salty. Pulls back his foreskin, over a violet head and bends to lick down and upward against his glans. John cups her nape and her mouth surrounds him with soft-tongued, sucking warmth. Each stroke improves his sensitivity and he eases her away, casting his tongue down her belly, licking at her buttery thighs with a stiff tongue. She yawns delight. He knows her body and his cock eases downward into her. Smoothly together he thrusts steady. Without a condom a warm pressure pincers and eases their traction, encourages her to claw him inward and for him to drive deeper, imagining the pink nowhere, the womb, his penis pushes further and she wants for him to fill her and her body to shudder in contractions, take his thrusts and eventually wilt, explode orgasm. John moves with his mixture of serpent smoothness and porn-star know how though can't enjoy the action, the intimacy, when he's doing Fat Carl's sloppy seconds. When John comes he doesn't care that there's no condom and sperm skewers out of him absorbed and lost in Evelyn. Never uses condoms. Gets himself down the Sunshine Clinic. They clamber under the sheets tired and sweaty. Evelyn sets an alarm on her phone and they take their belly-to-back clutch, holding tight, and fall deep into sleep. Moonlight gives their faces a silver glow. Cars bullet past outside on the main road. The pay-as-you-go phone drills, collecting messages from Carl who'll be about ready to cash up at the club.

When Evelyn wakes, she takes her clothes that have been scattered in a bundle across the bed, her silky pants on the floor and fixes her hair in the mirror. John hasn't twitched, even with the alarm as loud as it was and he snores, cataleptic. She kisses his forehead, thinking about his dreams and makes her way out the door and down the road, to get into her pyjamas and wait for Carl who'll be moaning about Pakis, about how the yuppies at the brewery want to incentivise everything, turn his beloved pub into something gay and wacky.

CARL has jogging bottoms that match his zip-top, black hair that greased into strips, nestles his scalp. He smokes cheap cigars and John thinks of Del Boy. Frank Butcher. Ray Winstone. Greasy, lovable, sleazy men. He rests four fingers down on the broad mahogany kitchen table: fat, short, knuckle-haired fingers, flat at the fist. The house, semi-detached, is in the same area as John's, but junked out in cheap teak and tobacco smell.

'Cuban.' Carl says, levitating a long, unsmoked cigar across John's line of sight.

'Flash.'

'Not when yer can afford it.'

'But yer caht?'

'I noo. But money's relative, innit?'

'How woh yer holiday, anyway?'

'Beautiful out there. Majorca. Lark o postcard. I'd live out there if o could.' Carl's body's beach-tanned and he's put on weight: drinking too many sangrias by the poolside. He's known Carl drink thirty pints before, though he's settled down now since he married Evelyn.

'Al have to get myself out there, sometime.'

'You'd leave Leeds?'

'No problem.' Carl ushers John into the living where his dopey dog Dasha leaps up at him with both front paws, giant tongue drooling steely saliva. There are pictures of Evelyn on the mantelpiece, on their wedding day. Her cute, rodent-like face popping up out of her ivory dress. There are others of Carl when he was younger, thinner with dark hair and front teeth.

'Take o seat,' Carl says, pointing to a sofa, 'Think on about t'other night. Pakis John?'

'Sorry abaht that.'

'Were yer gonna tell meh?'

'Yeah o some point. Today probably.'

'Yow brought Pakis into club, who I heard yow'd been scuffling wi again, and lost all yer money?'

'Thass right.'

'Olly one thing for it, fancy o whiskey?' John has a policy of never refusing a drink, no matter the time of day. He calls it a promise to himself. Carl has his own crystal decanter and John can't work out where his taste for gaudy shit comes from, it's not Evelyn. 'Cheers Carl. Dint want to go behind yow back, but two weeks iss o long time and it woh a big game. I'd overrun on meh rent. Yer know how it is. I thought I'd do him, his shit. But I fluffed it.'

'What happened?'

'Doht know. Iss lark Shellshock. When am under pressure, or whatever, I freak out. Me heads all over place.'

'You noo wot am gonna say?'

'What?'

'Let meh stake yer.'

'Yow sure?'

'Coarse I bloody am. We done it before.'

'Oh cheers mate.'

'If yer gonna do it my club, I want the profits.'

'Won't let yer down.'

'You better fucking win though.' Carl has a power with words, contained in his chubby body, he pronounces things with his elbows, brings his forearms into the conversation. Everything forthright. Bull-headed. Matter of fact. There's no joking around with Carl. The whiskey is good, better than the stuff they serve at the centre and the muzziness rises through his body ending up as a stingy blossom in his gut. 'But this goes beyond one game. I can stake yer regularly. Get round the city. And we can sting those paki bastards to. I yate them as much as you do.'

'Iss noh that simple.'

'Why not Einstein?'

'There o things going on.'

'Nothing I can't handle. Look. I know yer need o spot to stay so why not kip on meh sofa? Just till yer get back on yow feet and get your housing benefit through.'

'Iss o grand offer.'

'You're o gentleman, I lark that. But doh be afraid to ask for help when you need it. I know yow'd olly do same for me. Working-class. Thass woht it is. Guys lark us stick together, lark bloody Pakis do. Thass how thee get upper hand. Back scratching. Loyalty.'

'Cah really say no, canna? I'd love tuh, but Evelyn wouldn't want me ugly mug round ere? Another fella to look after?'

'She would.'

'Another bloke in the way?'

'It'll olly be o few weeks, and you and Eve get on.'

'We do.'

'Yow ever gonna go back out there? Iraq lark?'

'Thee woht have me. That side o me has finished. All abaht working out woh to do next.'

'Well, yer can't do that with no cash can yer? Struggling from day to day?'

'Yer right.'

'Anytime, bring yer stuff and well make you at home. What's mine is yours.'

'Be careful woht yer say fella,' Carl laughs, 'I've got meh eye on thah cigar.' John's eyebrows rise as if to meet: a furrow. He wipes away dust with his free hand. A mahogany shelf encases pictures of Carl as a young man lifting rugby trophies; his torso as slim as John's was in the forces.

'Come round when yer lark, get out of that shithole.'

'Just for a few weeks.'

'Could be for o few years for all I care. Now mate. Here's to o lucrative future.'

'Cheers.' Carl lights John a cigar and they take deep drags and puff alternate smoke rings. The first night is long and strange; he can't really get used to this grey light bothering the blue curtains. He can hear Carl snore. And he's bound in these pajama bottoms (he's not used to wearing clothes in bed, never) he plays with his drawstring, flat on his back, gasping for sleep. He was going to send Evelyn a text. But remembers his place, recognises the impracticality, and chooses to annoy Francesca instead. I'm still sorry, sorry I messed up. I miss you. Xxx. It was sloppy, sentimental, if at least, functional. He can hear the boy's footsteps trammeling the staircase: the soft, padded echo of his sole on the plush carpet. He can tell it's the boy, Popeye (Simon) because Evelyn tippy toes, daintily and fairy-like; Carl sounds like a moose falling down the stairs. The light-switch is flicked on and a sudden expanding beam grabs the kitchen. John outstretches his body on the single-bed in this cupboard of a room (only managing to accommodate three-quarters of his length) and bellows a huge, bearish yawn and makes his way into the kitchen for a pint of milk and to meet the kid.

'Evenin boss.' He heaves open the heavy fridge door.

'Hi.' While Carl is loud and purposeful, his son can't match his volume and reminds John of the captain of his under 13s football team, who's dad was the manager, always pushing him, rushing him into adulthood, a stiff and stereotypical manliness.

'Evelyn goes crazy if yer drink milk and iss not in o cup of tea or for breakfast.'

'Mad bastard, all get o new pint.' Popeye shakes protein powder into the last of the milk. Bubbles spawn and he flexes his measly triceps as he shakes, nonchalantly to impress John.

'So thee call yow Popeye?'

'Olly at school. Now everybody calls meh it.'

'Check out guns.' Popeye smiles, giving him a standard flex of his right bicep.

'Al have to teach you some things abaht training.'

'Am doing Sports Studies.'

'I can tell yow things they won't. I used to be o soldier, use to box o bit too. Played o lot of pool with your old man – as he said owt? He woh lark an uncle to me when I woh your age.'

'Woh he?'

'Eh looked after me, lark his doing nah.'

'What abaht yer dad?'

'He left. I woh too young to remember.'

'So yow never met him?'

'Av met the bugger.'

'You know how long yer staying?'

'Not long, doht worry kid. Al be out o ere soon as I can. Get me sen back on't straight and narrow. Giz that here.' He points to the mass weight gain protein powder and stares at the nutritional information. 'Iss all sugar this. Look. What yow want is some real protein powder, this is juss shit.'

'Lark what?'

'Casein.'

'Where do get thah?'

'I'll show ter. Amino acids, too. Get them. Will have yer built lark o brick shit-house before long. Anyway kid, am knackered, al get myself off tuh bed.' Through the window the sky has violet tinges and darker clouds skirt the horizon. He has woken again, more beadily alert. Dog hair plays with his nose. He sneezes a green bomb into folded tissue. Under covers, he gropes himself and begins to wank. His left-fist chugs under the sheets. Francesca. Eyes-closed. Time to dream. He works her hand over her cunt: a puppet for his fantasy. He has seen her in his dreams. Unclothed. But his imagination can't sustain his sleeping minds accuracy.

Roused, and drying his hands with tissues, he steps into twilight. Works his legs into a rhythm. Follows the straight long streets to junctions glowing amber. Night is a different world. He lights a cigarette and stares at the rigging on telephone polls. Every one a mast, ship-like. Night is where he belongs. How the air hangs fragrant as leafy evergreens breathe naturally out. There are orange and purple tints to tonight's' sky. He walks steadily uphill. His calves pinch and the pounds clumped round his gut slow him. Francesca won't ever want him. She never did. He would disappoint her. Sex is a different game for women. Evelyn must be used to fat blokes and does seem content enough to sleep with him. John feels sorry for her. Putting up with her fat bastard husband and a lazy lover who sleeps on her sofa and eats all her food. He has reached the One Stop that used to be a carpet shop. He steps in past a wooden door put in place after the ram raid two days ago. He heard in the club that it was a guy called Danny who he used to go to school with. Some chav off the estate. The electric light is strong and blonde over the pre-packed food in its sheaf of transparent plastic and belly bands of cardboard with pictures of models gobbing their food. There's a German beer he likes but they only sell it in the Paki shop he used to live near. He settles on a twelve-box of Carlsberg. Probably the best lager in the world. And goes to find himself some nibbles. His loneliness has really dawned on him. How heavy and dull his day has been and how he reckons, if he plays pool or football, even watches football, it'll get it out of his system. A blonde student wearing high heels and a floaty white skirt crouches beside him to look at the ciders. John brings his elbow high. He sees a guy he recognises in the queue. The same short back and sides, the odd shape of the guy's head.

'Phil?'

The guy flips round, grasping a tub of Persil. He takes a second to recognise, the penny drops, 'Fuck me. Wondered who it was.'

'Ant seen you in years.'

'Been a while. What yer bin up to? Caroline says yow woh in Iraq?'

'Thass right.'

'Good to see you – yer lookin well. Will have to catch up. Get mah number from Carl.'

'Cheers. Al beh in touch.' Phil slaps his groceries down on the counter and John takes a look around under the CCTV camera. Sacks of sodium and salt. Fast food.

John puts his supplies on the counter.

'Twelve pound.' A Bengali-looking shopkeeper says.

'Cheers.' John pushes over a note and a handful of change.

'Thanks.'

'Eh, fifty short?'

'No Sir.'

'I fuckin am.'

'No Sir, thass right.'

'Fucking int'

'Show me yer receipt. Look.'

'Give me mah change yer cunt.' John has grit in his eye. His broad shoulders firmer as his chest bluffs.

'Here yow go Sir, sorry. Mah mistake. Come again.' John picks up the fifty and lobs it between the eyes of the shopkeeper, 'Fuckin keep it yer cunt. Hope it woh worth it.'

When John gets home he pulls out his receipt and analyses it like a Sudoku, a puzzle or crossword he doesn't really understand. Those Carlsberg's were Export. Shit. More expensive than he realised. The Paki was right. He feels a brief sense of guilt and cracks open a can of Carlsberg and waits for the Champions League highlights to be repeated on ITV. He wants to sleep, closing his eyes on the sofa with the TV still on trailing in the background. Try to sleep. The cold reminds you of the late nights on guard. The rubbery darkness of the night sky. Your body won't untangle. You're in full-kit. Your pair of camo trousers and a snot coloured t-shirt. Your hair is buzz cut; the sweat swells out of your pores and you're thinking of home, of beer, of those cold fucking days and those radiated nights. You have lost the will to wank. The thought of a woman is too hard. You flash through all the women you ever fucked like a Filofax: try to remember the flavour, the sway of their breasts and the way you loved them. Adjust your limbs, twisting and turning. You read somewhere that in Vietnam there were Yank soldiers who volunteered to be undertakers, to fuck the dead. You wonder how many here would do the same. You need darkness of sleepless dreams.

RONNIE pulls up playing Duran Duran and tells John to get in. The car's a Tabasco-red Mitsubishi, only a couple of years old. John feels stuck to the cream leather upholstery, fixing the racing duty seatbelt over his gut. Ronnie keeps his eye on the road over the dashboard. The car steals through distances glowing ahead halogen bright – attracting admirers. Men turn their heads. The city plays itself like a hologram on the chassis twisting and turning through the semi-deserted midnight streets. The car feels expensive. He can feel his belly jut tight as Ronnie eases upward through the gears, and the seat cradles him fixed and secure, like a buggy.

'This must o set you back?' John glances round with a meerkat intensity for an ashtray. Speed and forward throttle brings out a taste for nicotine.

'It woh o good deal.'

'Must've.'

'You never thought o driving?' There's something robotic in the question, as he trips gear and keeps his face fixed, concentratedly on the road with the lapsing reflections passing by his face.

'Caht afford it, can I?'

'Still skint?'

'That game wiped me out. Gonna go for a second game and get myself back on't track.'

'Yow think he'd go for that? I mean, his on top int eh? Wass eh got to gain from another match?'

'His greedy – I know his type. Allos wants more than his fair share. His like you Ronnie.'

'Yeah well maybe havin more than yow fair share int such a bad thing. I yad to bail Francesca out.'

'Thanks for that. Suppose that means yer in there?'

'Noh really. Yer think she's that cheap? Juss put cash down and I've bought o bird.'

'Noo, thought she might warm to yeh. Didn't mean it lark that. Nah you've shown yow warmer, softer side.'

'Funny bugger.' The traffic lights are a row of green. Blurred colour on the tomato-red chassis – city light swims intricately across polished metal.

'I've heard this model is four inches taller than't previous one.'

'I think thass right.'

'No coach class either. This iss all top nick. And the torque – fuck me. Cars o beast. Not faster on't straights, but round bends. Wass hoss power?'

'Three hundred.'

'Fuck.'

'The tests ant been done yet, but they reckon iss at least three hundred.'

'Am not that big o car guy, but I could get on with this.'

'Can yer hear that?'

'What?' John plays the knock knock of Ronnie's game.

'Exactly. Acoustic insulation.'

'Wass that for?'

'Cuts down on't engine noise.' When John closes his eyes he can remember the cockpit of a tank, the sensation of power and security. They pass vacated road works and girls on street corners, trying to not look cold in miniskirts and long coats. On a deserted stretch of blueberry road Ronnie puts his foot down and accelerates murderously forward. The theatre of still things shift in the gallery of fluid motion. John could do this all night. Cruising the streets if just to feel the power surge of a gear shift. The smooth knuckling tightness swerving round stretches of road and corner. He likes the blacked out windows and the anonymity makes him feel important. Onlookers stare in other cars when Ronnie pulls up for red lights.

'Do yer still see much o Francesca?' Ronnie speaks out the side of his mouth: wrenches the gear-stick back into neutral.

'Not really seen her since o lost.'

'Still got o thing for her?' The red light goes through amber to green and somehow delays John's response, 'I got a thing for half the girls I see.'

'Thought as much.'

'She's not worth fighting over. Green light.' John nods glumly, making his feelings practical. They accelerate again cutting through a complex intersection then wolfing up the steady gradient of another road.

'Carl sacked her. Yow know that?'

'When?'

'Lass night.'

'Carl's o wankshaft. What o cunt.'

'Said it woh because o brewery, the crunch.'

'Bollocks. Am living with enemy nah.'

'Thass fucked up.'

'Right you are. Poor Fran.'

'What you need o nice little earner, but theh cutting jobs every day. Works lark o fucking factory these past days and weeks. Queues outside. And jobs! Why the fuck would yow want to turn in yer benefits to work full-time as o porter? O toilet attendant? Shit. Lot ov it. Anything yer do o Polak will do for't half money.' The sway of windscreen wipers tosses wash over the dashboard. At a crossroads, a growling car pulls up beside them. A jacked-up Subaru Impreza with the rally insignia that Colin McRae made famous. The '98 WRC model, with an exaggerated spoiler and lowered suspension. Ronnie slides a glance to John who gives a simple nod. Manly. They can't see either with their blacked out windows. When the light turns green Ronnie puts his foot down, hard, asking the best of his engine, stabbing the rough gears upward and releasing the gas. The tires scorch asphalt. The four-by-four Subaru, tearing through the straight streets, has the edge on speed. But when they come to a chicane, Ronnie rabbits through the space between a truck and a backlog of taxis, making use of the cushioning suspension.

'So theh sacked her?' John says meditatively – turns the conversation back down, away from politics.

'Got her notice. One weeks pay.'

'How is she?'

'Not taken it well, but she already got an interview with another bar. Iss more that they sacked her, she's taken it personally. Blames Evelyn.'

'Why would she do that?'

'Reckons she has o thing for yer, she's jealous.'

'How do I manage to fuck things up even when iss not me fucking things up?'

'Iss o kill.'

'Am o fucking voodoo doll, me.'

Ronnie's phone rings and he cuts the call off, 'Keep getting calls from queers wanting tuh shag me.' John cracks a cheeky grin and Ronnie flicks the switch on the radio. People with regional accents argue about tonight's game: a penalty that wasn't a penalty. Cool and silent in the burr of air con the Mitsubishi storms down the road rising a slight incline and Ronnie eases it into fourth; gets some real speed down, losing no traction, he puts his foot down again into the horizon, under street signs and high windows with halogen beams.

FOUR REDS played firm in their positions. John jerks his fingers and tightens the bridge, his hand stiff and lean. The cue strike is good, he's getting used to the full motion that comes through the hips, makes use of the body, his intentions played out on the table.

Living with Carl's not so bad; considering he's knobbing his wife and his kid always snooping about. In many ways Popeye reminds John of himself, when he was a lanky teenager, bony limbed and insecure, wishing he was a big man and could stand up for himself, like his old man. He'd pack himself full of protein and train like a boxer, gradually the muscle appeared on his body, dense and heavy, it gave him confidence and a steeliness that's still there beneath his thickening exterior.

He sups his pint, another two hundred-forty calories. Even though he feels like an inflatable, he's not as fat as he thinks. During the day the club doesn't get much external sunlight: there are yellow-blots at the high windows and what filters through mingles with the twenty-four hour electric light; it sanitises the place, brings out a forensic obviousness to the stains on the carpet, the dead stale stink of old lager spilled into the tables, the seats and the plush bar-stools. He is a man with nowhere to go, nobody to see and nothing to worry about, so why does he get these thoughts? Sudden and striking, crackling into the stump of his skull and bridging his neck. Reality too bright, colourful. Real. He wants to sit down forever. Those memories play like short films, like adverts with nothing to sell. He goes back to his pint, sweating, smothering his warm forehead and calms himself, gets back in the game. Practice. Drills. He has to beat Malik; it's become a vendetta, a way to test his self-esteem. It's about more than money; it's about winning back his bollocks. Carl has turned down his Eagles Greatest Hits and he can hear him blather on his mobile; his distinct throaty vowels. John's not sure he should get involved, with Carl so temperamental, his bullish mind-set means he could go for you at any moment.

Carl puts his phone down, twenty feet away.

'Everything alright?' John booms. He leaves his game in a static flux as he pulls up a seat next to Carl.

'Need o hand with owt?'

'Thanks for offering. Bloody brewery, al tell yow something abaht those cunts. If o have to rearrange this bar one more fucking time I'll go ape shit. I'll have myself o bloody coronary.'

'Wass up?'

'Between me and you, theh looking to close some sites. More money selling them on as property.'

'Yer don't think this place would? I mean, iss quiet during the week, but everywhere is?'

'Iss all costs. Bottom lines. Brewery owns o couple of spots near here. You know places. Sports bars. American style things and even they're struggling, doing better than us, but not by o right lot. We'll have to lose more bar staff, thass one thing.'

'Yow kidding?'

'Wass it come to when you can't keep o local ticking over in o neighbourhood lark this? Used to be pubs on every corner. The Lion. Fleece. Monk. They've all closed down in't last few year.'

'Sad. Good boozers those.'

'I got in shit for ignoring smoking ban too, but iss olly thing that brings in half punters. Francesca did too lark. But she was lazy. Not bothered abaht us. Keeping going. One time we'd have o door man on who'd pick and choose types to come in here, but we're having to let Pakis in because theh olly ones who'll spend any money. Rola-Cola is as much as a pint. Theh put o fair bit into those tables.'

'She was o good barmaid.'

Carl's face is fierce, 'If yer lark that sorta thing. Lazy mate, rubbed Evelyn up the wrong way. Yer know women.'

'O yeah.'

'Lark cats.'

'You thought o shit lark karaoke? Putting on o quiz night? That sort o jazz?'

'Tried it. Punters aren't bothered. All young uns are buying booze from't supermarkets. Wine bars. Clubbing. Theh all pill-heads. O lot who used to come here go tuh wine bars in town. Iss not how it woh.'

'Suits me.'

'Yow'd drink beer out o puddle.'

'That I would.'

'So what you gonna do? Where's Tetley's, I fancy o pint of cask?'

'Thass another brewery thing. They've got me balls tied in o fucking knot. They've got cheaper deals with lagers that doht take effort ale does. Lasts longer. Sells twice as much. I doht blame em. Iss punters who've let meh down. Fucking country. Why dunt anybody want to sup o good pint? Iss same all over, iss o twist. Why woht working man stand up for himself?'

'Doht know what to say.'

'Iss o cunt of o situation we find ourselves in.'

'Yep.'

'Ah know yer a quiet guy, John. Yer where allos a shy kid. But I don't know how yer can keep so cool abaht it all? This sewer o shit. Life.'

'Juss never given o shit.'

'I give too much of o shit. Thass my problem.' Carl shuffles his arse on his seat to conjure a burning fart, 'They've done nowt for me. Fort's working man. The lot of 'em. Fucking Tories yer expect it o them. Them's at war with working class. But iss Labour too. All them immigrants coming in and getting houses and cars and lot. Yer know we still had o toilet to share down bottom o road when I grew up? Theh wunt give me mam no money when me dad were sick because he had o good pension after grafting all is life. Meh cousin Gary, his got cancer and theh re-assessing him for't sick. If yer o fucking immigrant yer can walk right in. Done nowt for me. None of em. Shit wages. Higher taxes. No reason to save. Iss shite. Iss all Erdu this and Erdu that nah. Everything written in every language going and nobody speaking English. Yer tek o look out o window and all yer can see iss Mosques. Iss not o world I remember. Shite.'

Carl's face is red, volatile. Swimming on the swell of his anger. John sighs, 'I juss don't believe thes o solution mate. I never expect those politicians to do nowt for me. Am John Usher, am o fanny man. Thass that. End of. '

'O fanny man?' They laugh rocking in their chairs.

'Yeah, love it, don't I? Long as av got booze and o pool cue in me hand. Some totty to stare at.'

'Yull want summit more, one day.'

'Al keep away from that. Never wanted to settle down.'

'Thass what I thought ... Before Eve.'

'Shis o gooden.'

'That she is.'

'Yer know, in't army? We allos had plans, strategies, big meetings abaht stuff and all training. But how stuff happens is alloss different. Yer can never anticipate. Yer can guess, but never any more. Iss all guessing.'

'Will have to go fishing soon, down't canal.'

'Aye.'

'Do yer remember Angie from't down road?'

'Should ah?'

'Yer used to go out with her.'

'Oh yeah.' John snorts giggling, 'Thass right.' The phone rings and Carl answers, tugging at his polo collar, loosely at first and then tighter as his tension grows. The place does look tatty and needs several coats of paint: probably deep clean and new furniture. John drains his pint and places it on the table top. A creamy ginger head lolls at bottom the glass bottom, the distorting disc, stretching catlike.

POPEYE has this annoying habit of doing sit-ups, crunches and press-ups on the chiwawa rug in the living room in front of the TV. One. Two. Three. He struggles, counting his reps with the leftover breath of each exertion. 'Fuck it, kid. Can't you do that someplace else?' John says, trying to watch *Serial Killer,* a programme about murderers. This episode has John by the collar, all about some crank who tried to poison his work colleagues with thallium.

'Training, aht ah?'

'For what?' John shouts, ducking and weaving, bobbing his head past Popeye's body so he can get all the gory details.

'Get big. Project massive.'

'Yer not gonna get big doing thah.' The boy looks disappointed and finally stops heaving his body round the front room. He's wearing a sweatband and a white vest so old it's bobbled.

'How'd yer mean? Dad said.'

'Wass Carl know abaht bodybuilding?'

'He-'

'Shut up. Look. Come ere.' John tips up his sleeve and flexes hard, bulging the slothen oval of muscle that lays slack on his arm. Loose, overcooked, there's size and shape enough to make Popeye listen.

'Cool.'

'Yeah? Yer should have seen meh o few years back. I woh built lark o brick shit-house. They used to call meh Rambo. Yer know Rambo?'

'Course I do.'

'I woh roided up to fuck. Ripped and got good size too. Now o young fella like yow, with no fat on theh bones, why are you juss using yow bodyweight?'

'Press-ups make yer strong.'

'Wrong. Lifting weights makes yer strong. Progressive breakdown. Sets and Reps. Proper routine.'

'Can yer show meh?'

'If you get yourself out o way o that mother-fucking TV then maybe, I will.' Evelyn can hear their conversation through the bubbled glass on the middle of the white PVC door. She's worried about the way that John's started talking to Popeye. Like he's a Squaddie, a junior recruit and not the kid who's lived here all his life. Evelyn calls out to John ten minutes later and tells him to come into the kitchen. Scratches his balls. One hand on the remote to pause the TV. He makes his way in to see her. 'What?' He asks, with the blunt, disgruntled tone she'd expect from Popeye.

'Can't yow lay off him?'

'Who?'

'Come on. Yer know who. Popeye. You've been talking to him lark he's shit for o few weeks now. You doht do it when Carl's around.'

'I lark the kid.'

'So why yer so mean?'

'Am not. Iss just having o laugh. Thass what young blokes are lark. They take piss.'

'Iss more than that.'

'Whatever.'

'Yer can't take yer frustrations out on o defenseless young lad. He's just o kid.'

'Eve. I can't believe you're even saying this to meh. I caht believe it.'

'Are you ok?'

'Am fine. Everything is rosy. I doht wake up in't night with sweats, brain tricking me into thinking am in Baghdad. Am o grown man living on o settee. Am stuck. Fucking stuck.'

'Stuck where? What do yer want o do? What is it that you need?' John doesn't answer, putting both his palms on the fridge like he's about to be frisked and nods his head downward. A cold chill shivers down his body nervously, a blade-like twitch. His head aches as his temples slow to warm. The burr of the fridge plays dubstep, monotonous. Nothing has gone right since he's come back. His depression is the crystal flecks in ice water. The world has gone mad. There's nothing. He thought he'd get working someplace, buy some stuff, hang around with old friends, but so far not a thing. He thinks he's weak. Embarrassed now at flexing such flabby muscle at Popeye earlier on. His belly cudgels harder at the cotton of his t-shirt than it ever has. The twenty-something beer thickened gut.

'Where?' Evelyn tries again.

'I yav no idea. Trapped.'

'Come ere.' She nuzzles him in her open, embracing hug. But her body on his feels useless, an unwanted weight, dull sympathy.

'Don't feel so bad.' She whispers, stroking his overlapping sideburns from his ears. 'Thes summit I need to tell yer.'

'Yeah?'

'I've not had me period.'

'Yer kidding?'

'Av taken a test too.'

'And?'

'Iss positive.'

'Who's iss it?'

'Iss not Carl's.'

'OK. Alright. Yeah. Gimme o minute.'

'Am glad iss happened.'

'Yer mean, yow weren't on't pill? I thought all women these days were. And yer married? Do mean to say that yer and Carl don't ever?'

'Iss not Carl's.' She takes his hand and plants it on her belly; the burgundy sweater, her belly takes on a new meaning, there, his hand warm against her swelling gut.

'What we meant to do? Gonna need some time to get me head round this Eve. Juss lemme calm down. How's this gonna work? A can barely afford.' He grits his teeth, unconsciously to keep the emphasis and lower the sound with Simon in the next room. 'Am not ready for this, really. How can I look after theh two o yer?'

Evelyn takes a seat at the table, and explains herself diplomatically to John, hands expressive, 'I want o baby, and am pleased yull beh the daddy.'

'Are yer nuts?'

'Iss not abaht you, not now John. Put it away for ten minutes and listen to me. Am having o baby. Lark it or not. We need to get things planned – if yow wanna beh o part of it. This is what I want and what's going to happen.'

'What about my say?'

'Iss my baby in my body.'

'How can o do things right on your husband's sofa with no cash to me bloody name?'

'For now.'

'How can you stay so calm? Have they already got yer on't Prozac? My God.'

'I thought yer might have taken this better, might actually have been fucking pleased.'

'Yuv done this on purpose?' John is shocked, lips broad.

'It'll be alright.'

'No, Eve. How the fuck can it be?' Bares his teeth, in whispers, crescendos of movements stopping dead: 'Am trying to get me head straight. Me head above water. What about Carl?'

'We can get o place.'

'Are you serious?' Evelyn bursts into tears, sniffling through breaths. John, finger and thumb on both eyes motions clockwise, trying to ease the gusts of anger. He reels her head to his chest, tears singing, warm on his England shirt. Popeye, about to come in for a glass of juice, turns back behind the door.

RONNIE gets a double cheeseburger and John goes for a McChicken sandwich with McChicken nuggets and a litre of full-fat coke in a bucket that comes with a couple of cheeky portions of fries. They've picked the only table that hasn't been spat on and smeared with moss-smelling bacterial wipe. John aligns his pots of ketchup, brown and special sauce.

'Why do yer do that?' Ronnie asks, with his wrapping garbled loosely round his burger, high in the air he eats, with the burger level with his nose. While John puts it on the table, dissembles it and eats it like some cheap buffet.

'Always done it. Ever since I woh o kid and step dad brought me down here on't weekends.'

'Deadbeat dad syndrome.'

'No, my step dad. My real dad fucked off ages before. Guy couldn't get anything right. God knows how he managed to poke so many women. He didn't do bad for himself.'

'I remember. He looked lark o farmer, or a serial killer or summit scary, no offence.' Ronnie raises his hand in innocent protest, eases off the chewing, 'Like a wrestler. Daddy haystacks with that mad hair and crazy tan.'

'He did. Mam said she never really knew where he came from. Usher was an Irish name. But he didn't look all that Irish.'

'Am Irish - but do I look lark it?' Ronnie glances through the rectangles of glass, to the car park where his beloved Mitsubishi sits pretty on the asphalt. John has fallen in love with the car too and would do anything to take the thing for a test drive. To get behind the wheel - the studded indentations for grip, his foot revving the full throttle of a well-balanced 4x4. When they step outside, on a sugar high with meat sweats, the pale sun bastes the Mitsubishi's bonnet and grate.

'What else you been up to? Your old man still got his money tied up in that poxy retirement plan?'

'Yep.'

'Fair enough, I suppose. Those cranky old bastards are different class these days.'

'They've got more purchasing power and fixed capital than any other fucker. I woh reading in't Times other day...'

'Since when did yow read Times?'

'Since I got into business. James Bond read Times. If it's good enough for him.'

'Timothy Dalton was good enough to play Bond. Are you Dalton o business world?'

'Shit, no. You talking out o your arse. Nothing wrong with keeping up with goings on. I keep my nose to floor.'

'Thass why yer always smell shit.' Where Ronnie still has half a burger clouded in the crackling, polythene wrap, John has eaten his burger and nearly finished his dips.

'Yow never got anywhere with Francesca though did yer?' John presents his trump card, bringing his face into a sullen stare and only slightly twinges a brow. Ronnie's elevated hand twitters.

'How'd you know?'

'You'd have bragged be now.'

'Lark fuck I would.'

'Can't get everything yer want? I managed to kiss her once or twice. But that woh then.'

'Yer did?'

'Yeah.'

'Tell me more.'

'It woh no big deal.'

'Iss to me.' Ronnie says, his voice rising despite his best efforts to cramp his anger. 'I'm sorry. I'm just really interested, that's all.'

'One night. I leaned mah pretty face over't bar and she kissed me back.'

'Shit.'

'Woh o good en. Take what you can doht yer? I thought I'd lost it by thah point. But then there o some women. Some that can bring Lazarus back from't dead.'

'Yeh.'

'You OK.'

'Am fine. Was that it then? You didn't ever manage to fuck her or nowt?'

'What is this? I'd have thought you have a grade A boner for her.'

'I don't. Less talk abaht summit else.'

'You having that?' John points at a chip Ronnie has refused to eat and left out on the table, well-salted.

'Have it.'

'Cheers.'

'Anyway, Berbatov is the shit.'

'Yer are one dirty Man U supporting Tory, Japanese driving wanker.'

'Am not o Tory.'

'Sorry, I forgot. New Labour.'

'Thass more lark it.' Ronnie pulls out car keys from his pocket. They leave the table, groaning to their knees, heading for the brightness of the door. The suns javelin rays level out into the thick glass. In the car, Ronnie puts his foot down and levies the clutch as he pulls out the car-park without saying anything to John who's yanking down the passenger mirror to style his brush-bristle hair, square jawed. Sometimes he thinks he's like one of those comic book heroes: big and shaped in a traditionally manly way. Ronnie's spared no expense: oyster-coloured upholstery and teak trim. An iPod dock playing eighties synth-pop. Dreary lines of the road buzz and blur. Up a gear. Ronnie powers down the shark-grey streets and camera flashing byroads. Ronnie's side-profile – the hard ridge of his dick nose. Grooves of red skin where he's nicked himself shaving. Love bites.

'Who's lucky woman?'

'Hey?'

'Yow neck. Someone larks yer.'

'This?' He confirms the markings with his free hand, as if he hadn't noticed.

'Yeah.'

'Shaving rash.'

'Fuck off.'

'Serious.'

'Bullshit.'

'Honestly.'

'Bullshit.'

'Leave off me would yer, dickhead.'

'Yer can't bullshit o bullshitter.'

'Bullshit.'

'Bullshit.'

'Yeah. Certain. Am sensitive abaht it too. So if yer don't mind. Shut the fuck up thank you very much. Look at that.'

Ronnie diverts to the window but John can only see the rough foliage and shrapnel that collects and grows by the roadside.

'You know you acting pretty mysterious these days. First that cruise round town for no reason. Now all this cagey shit. I thought you were Billy big tits; that you wouldn't keep your gob shut if you had a fitty on't go.'

'Iss between me and her.'

'Aha!' John says, exhilarated, and Ronnie lets it go, flicking the indicator and getting in line to take a right onto the dual carriageway.

'You're right.'

'I knew it. No need to beh coy round me. We all have dry patches sometimes. Sometimes we shag a minger.'

'Yeah. That's right. Exactly that, mate. Well done for working it out detective inspector dickhead.' They hit a glut of traffic: side-by-side to panting cars and their rolled-up windows. Kids pull faces at them through tinted glass. The car in front has a St George bumper sticker and on the radio the host talks about tonight's TV. John rolls down the window jamming his elbow into the inlay, he thinks about lighting up and stops short. Cradled in the chassis, the thought of babies. Baby sick. The pink new-born skin. Speeding, they enter a concrete tunnel so long they can't see the end. Horns. White lights. Hard lines.

IN THE NIGHT John wakes and can't get back to sleep, turning and fighting the stiffness of his body, how it won't go limp and relax. Wing-nuts of elegant muscular aches knot along his spine. The lacing inside his shoulder blade snags, won't stop tightening and traps a nerve in his neck. The sofa cushions part form a divot and separates his body into two unequally supported parts: it pulls at his grey t-shirt and exposes his lower back to the cold. John's tosses and turns in the stiff cold, his head burning and thinking.

John pulls his headphones tinnily playing Black Sabbath from his ears, and he hears what he thinks is crying coming from the kitchen, sobbing in the midnight blue light. He throws on his joggy bottoms and walks topless into the kitchen, expecting Evelyn. There Carl sits, belly trapped behind the table, murdering a corned-beef sandwich. His thick arms stretch the fabric of his Rhino's rugby shirt as he lifts the white bread to his mouth and chews, slowly, mourning some thought. A distant idea. John fills a glass of murky water from the tap and pulls up a chair, 'You're up late.'

'Things tuh think about.'

'No good doing thah now, yull knacker yourself for tomorrow.'

'Why's life so shit? Yer work. Yer do right. Yer must know what thass like? Iss why we get on: we try and get by with our heads down. Got o shitty letter from't brewery today and theh sending some cunt from head office to 'assess' business. Iss bollocks. If iss not them iss government. Eighteen percent tax on lager. Eighteen! Crippling us with DDA regulations. Smoking ban. Iss as if they want us to fucking fail.'

'Sure it'll pick up. Iss o good pub.'

'No use with optimism, no good for us in the long run. Another thing, we let Fran go; Evelyn reckons she woh fiddling the safe. But she brought punters in. I pulled a few strings, got her some hours at a place in town.'

'Caht see her being on't fiddle?'

'I checked the last three months finances, twice. There want o penny missing. I'll tell you summit – John, she's not been herself recently. Doht know what Fran did to wind her up. Yer don't think she's seeing o fancy man on't side do yer John?' A burning flickers along the hairs up his neck and John cups his glass. There's no chance Carl is playing with him; it's not his style, to play mind games, not with his temper and heavy fists. He once saw Carl batter a guy with a cricket bat for telling a joke he didn't like. Carl's face fattens, square when he's depressed. His forehead a bulk above his downward looking eyes.

'She's not one to put it abaht.'

'Thass woh I thought.'

'C'mon, what we need iss o big pool game. Get punters in. Meck some money staking. They'd all be boozing, get guys in after rugby. Do some fliers. Get em in who haven't for o while. Get em spending. Turn our predicament into an investment.'

'Get Pakis in is what yow saying.'

'Money's money. Whoever's spending it.'

'Fact o life.'

'But yer doht have to lark facts, do yer? Whatever government is allos same. Working man gets nowt. Labour. Tory. Whatever. I've voted 'em all at one point or another. When me mam were dying we couldn't get care off NHS 'cos we had a nice house, that we earned. We struggled ten year to buy this. Then there's all those next door come in from nowhere getting full benefit, housing, schools, hospital, and they've paid nowt. Av worked all me life.'

'Things are different now though, innit? Yer can get benefits for owt. Yer can get compensation for owt. Yer borrow whatever theh fuck yer lark.'

'And?'

'Jus saying, things change. Yer have to take advantage.'

'Lark you, kipping here? Not taking dole? Anybody would think yer were stupid.'

'Am not dole scum, yeah?'

'Yer o good lad.'

'Whatever help yer need, big guy. You know where to find me.' They laugh: Carl leaden with sorrow. Skin azure in he evening's velveteen dark, eyes black as his rat's arse moustache.

'Should get myself off to bed. Thah woh another thing: Francesca made day go that bit quicker, you know what I'm saying? Bit o banter.'

'I know what yer mean. Been too long since I've had o bird. She woh olly one I see.'

'Lass next door is o fitty. Not chinkies. T'other side.'

'Yeah?'

'Student lark.'

'I'll have to say hello.' There are no stars in the sky. Darkly sullen through the viscous double-glazing. Reflections of the kitchen; the tubular light-bulb flickering neon lime. When the Snooker Centre goes under, that'll be John on the street. Outside a burger bar wrapped in a manky blanket with a charity box. He thought about signing on today. Can't fend for himself. Not an earner. Living off the state. Dole scum. You'd have to explain yourself to prissy cunts in beige shirts. Carl's dinosaur steps down the stairs ripple pulses in John's water.

TWO CUE BALLS slowly ache their way across the table. The chalky noses of cues held in anticipation. John over hits by a touch, the baize dulled and balding. Mottled holes and patches that have worn into the cloth are screwing up his judgement; it's his third game of the day. Been playing every night. Carl stakes him, Preparing him for a Pro-Am tournament and John's happy to earn twenty, thirty, forty quid a night on easy games; it pays for his booze and living costs. Carl's cue ball, luminously white, arrives at the back cushion. But his sloppy break is misdirected, his bridge wobbled as he struck and gave too much power to the wrong part of the cue. The balls absorb the impact and don't move except for a four ball that bobbles out, top-spun.

'Seen better.' John says, superior, confident. Approaching the table and judging the scene. His black jacket shines wet from his drizzly cigarette break.

'Cocky bastard.'

'Let's see.' John answers, like a doctor, evaluating the symptoms, like he knows the best way forward. Answers. He doesn't understand Carl, why he looks out for him, what he wants from John and who he thinks he is. Big twat. John has three or four inches on Carl, is broader across the chest and has a longer reach; a spider-web has been tattooed on the webbed skin between his thumb and forefinger in greeny-black ink. Evelyn watches from the bar, elbows on the counter and her face supported in her hands; she's been watching for ten minutes. John catches her, unsuspecting. She turns away. He feels her eyes on him, radiating over his back, flowing over his movements and reads things into the game. His mind is visibly at work. John angles his cue stroke from the side railing into the pack. Sparks movement. One rolls into the near pocket and he's off; build a sequence, had a few in mind but now he's going for the hardest. A flow that sees him side step round the table to bob down and take aim.

'Another two today.' Carl murmurs to distract John.

'To be expected, with o new offensive.'

'Makes meh sick.' John leans over the table, black jacket, his back spot lit by the glare above. Carl goes on, 'Should never have gone in, shunt be in there. Iss o distraction; keep our minds off state o this fucking country. There were no terrorists in Iraq. More terrorists living on meh street. Should be fighting Burley if they want o war on't terror. Bomb that fucking mosque. O stop funding fuckers for starters.' Suddenly loose-limbed, John pokes his shot wide and gives way to Carl who pots two easy shots hard and then finds himself snookered behind John's balls, acres of green and nothing he can pot.

'What would yow rather we did after 9/11?'

'Iss complicated.'

'Wass complicated abaht it? We were attacked, on home

soil and we went out to scorch earth. Send o message.'

'That we can't fight o war?'

'Didn't look that way from mah perspective. We brought hell fire on those places.'

'You know better than I do.'

'Thass right.'

'Yeah, and fair play to yer. But what I doht get is they've hung you out to dry and yow happy with that? Where's yer fight there? The shark I know?'

'What yer getting at?'

'What yer gained from it? Where's your reward for putting yer life on't line, yow well-being? Tony Blair's on't lecture circuit making millions. Yanks are swimming in oil. Weapons industry has had o field day. Private security firms. What abaht you? '

'I spent it, iss me own fault. Me, I did that. My fault I was discharged and me who spent money. The war cost millions too, costs lives o good people.'

'It woh establishment war by liberal elite. Iss all o twist, everything. The working man is alloss one who pays when it comes to expenses, immigration, bankers, war. We pay with our lives, our own blood.'

'Them wars were abaht freedom, peace, security.'

'Them were abaht oil. Fat yanks lacing their pockets. Political elites holding onto power.'

'Yow think BNP can do owt?'

'Thell have o go, shit em up.'

'Caht see it me sen.'

'I worry abaht yer sometimes, who yer think yer boys are. Wass been lost. Them and theh fucking smoking bans, their poxy wars, the fucking banks. Then thes guys lark us: good guys, gentlemen struggling to do right and get on. They hung yow out to dry and mah pub is in't shit, run by same Toff wankers who want to turn a profit, nowt else. What abaht community? What abaht our heritage? Yer can have o black culture, o Muslim culture, o queer culture, but what abaht whites?' The rain grows strong and patters like fingertips on the corrugated roof, loud sweeping waves. John analyses a cloudy mark on his glass thinking Carl makes sense. Why does it makes him so angry to hear what Carl bangs on about? He does believe in Iraq and bringing down Saddam. He has no choice. The place is shabby since they sacked their cleaner and only have one guy on during the day. Who has to do the lot - sweep the floors, stock up the fridge, clean the toilers and run the bar. There's a rumble in his pocket and John ignores Evelyn's text. Two students in skinny jeans and choppy fringes and thick glasses walk past. They're deep in conversation, speaking with Southern accents, the guffaw and drawl of the upper classes.

'Beat me, I'll take o fall. Make it loud.' He says to Carl who knows exactly what's going on.

'You hear about Paddy?'

'No.'

'Got sent down for assault. On top of other offences he'll be out in o month lark. Got into o fight with some mouthy kid, gave it o bit too much and there yer go. Can't even defend your sen. Slap down o spotty little kid.'

'What woh it over?'

'Paddy woht stand cocky guys, yer know what I mean? This kid woh giving him some jip, called him o cunt and it went from there. Silly.'

'Ready?'

'Go for it.' John pulls a shot, yells out loud and made sure to set Carl up for at least two returns. The two guys who recently walked in sit up and take note. When John loses he goes to the bar, standing next the guys and casually slaps out his wallet plush with twenty-pound notes, a Dayrider and a Snooker Centre card. That's when he challenges them to a game, ten quid on it, and hammers them both three times. Wind rustles on the boarded up window they can't afford to repair, hole-shot like something out of a saloon and John rubs a cue ball bright on his sleeve, thinking doesn't Carl fucking bang on? Nutty cunt. He won't stop taking things seriously, seeing politics everywhere. Everywhere it isn't. He feels a closeness to the pakis and the blacks; to the new immigrants, we're all drifters finding our way. Who gives a shit if they're in Britain or Baghdad? Like the guys in the forces, the Yanks who thought God was behind everything and saw him everywhere. People believe mad shit. The world is what you believe. Taking it easy with his hands behind his head on the other side of the room is Malik sipping on a Diet Coke. He wags his finger to acknowledge John.

Carl bull wiggles over and passes John a flier.

'Here's another demo.'

'Same lads as last time?'

'Looks that way, be o right one.'

'Iss o day out.'

'Iss more than that, there are things at stake. Iss abaht making o stand, letting em know weh not happy.'

'Yer think it'll change owt? Those anti-war one's dint do nowt.'

'Theh were ponces. Political elites shit em-selves when white working-class guys lark us take tuh streets. Theh call us fascists and white scrum – straight off bat. Yer can't say nowt abaht pakis or nig nogs, but yer can say what yer want abaht us. So fuck em. Thass what I say. '

'White liberation.'

'Am white Mandela.'

'Fuck me.'

'If yer not wi me John, al be disappointed, deeply. Far as I'm concerned this is o war.'

'Theh woh trouble at last march.'

'Thass the UAF's fault. Won't leave us along. Cunts.'

'UAF?'

'Unite Against Fascism. Load o posh pricks slandering us, when we had blacks and Asians ourselves. Iss not abaht race this, iss abaht putting o stop to it. Giving England away. Them liberals would rather give Britain away to Sharia Law.'

'Iss a mad world. Us in Iraq and them over here.'

'Iss all those at top. Elites. Hundreds o years they've been fucking working man over. Winds o change? Winds o fucking bullshit more like.'

'Yeah.'

'Yer doht see right passionate?'

'No.'

'Yer not depressed? Yer nerves?'

'Am juss not that political.'

'You wait and see. When yer realise, when yer see.'

'Want another drink?' Carl can't afford to give drinks away the economy what it is; John bumbles over to the bar and left cold by what Carl says, unconvinced. There are grains of truth in what he says; things that he recognises and likes Carl's balls out attitude. Head on the line. Carl's face buttressed with chins and neck bulge, and John texts Malik while he remembers, he could use some weed. The way your body hums asleep.

MALIK pulls down the tinted window in his BMW and John gets in: they cruise down the road through the black evening rain and into a warren of semis; the streets are deserted in the early morning hours.

'Twenty bag?'

'That'll do, got any rizzler?'

'Nah.'

'Can you drop me off at service station?'

'Woodsley Road?'

'Yeah.' They make their exchange, twenty pounds for a

polythene bag of weed. The BMW slants down Stanmore Hill and panthers down and up the wet tarmac, the windscreen wipers frantic like batwings or eyelashes. On the radio there's some gangster rap and the air conditioning has John cool, goose-pimpled and way too cold.

'How yer been?'

'Living with Carl now. Iss you know, how do yeh put it, not the best situation.'

'Still hustling?'

'Every night. On o right little earner. Anytime you fancy o rematch, we can put some real money down.'

'Al think abaht it. Yer still o cunt to some o my guys. Get what am saying? Gets me in shit. Those pussies get territorial.'

'An eye for an eye. Iss over isn't it?'

'Be careful is what an saying. Left here?'

'Yeah.'

'They like to put thuh muscle around, especially with o soldier. They got big beef with yow.'

'How abaht yer?'

'I don't go for all that shit.'

'Easier that way.'

'You were in Iraq?'

'Yeah.'

'Ever go Pakistan?'

'No.'

'Me neither.'

'Thell be in there next. Coalition forces.'

'Send em. Cunts been killing mah my lot on that border for fucking decades. Thass thing with West. They pick and choose who theh want to fight. One minute theh pals with Afghans, next minute theh bombing them.'

'Do yer remember those battles at school?'

'Nothings changed.'

'Don't pussy out solja.'

'Live lark yer mean it.'

'Makes me laugh. All the pakis and the whites, the same old bullshit arguments.' Malik carries himself well. An easiness tempered with danger that John likes - reminds him of how he likes to portray himself. These Asian fuckers love their bling, their belongings. Retro masculine. That phrase he heard on a TV show the other night suddenly comes bright and makes sense. Above the dashboard are two giant polka-dot dice.

FRANCESCA is on John's mind. He gets home at ten' o'clock and despite being promised a bed has to contend with the balding, arse-worn sofa. She's responded to a couple of his texts and has stopped signing them with her telltale 'X'.

Carl sleeps in his chair, resting on blubber of excess that buttresses his face when he puts his chin down. According to Popeye, Evelyn is in the bath and John takes a seat in the kitchen with the kid.

'Yow doht mind mah banter, do yer?'

'Nope.'

'Juss summit Evelyn said, doht matter. Juss got me thinking lark o silly bleeder. Starting tuh look big anyway, kidder.' After sixteen weeks of intensive training, hundreds of pounds worth of protein powder, mass weight gain and amino acids, Popeye is still pretty much the same size he was before. His biceps have maybe increased in tone. He asks John if he wants a beer and John can only stare at the invisible beard on the kids face: the old woman facial hair, a crop beneath his chin, some on his septum.

Popeye slams the beers down on the table, pretending not to be flexing his neck, his peanut deltoids.

'How's your dad?'

'Fine. Why?'

'With me living here, the bar. Things seem to get on his tits o bit. Stress him out.'

'Ant noticed if they yav.'

'I yav. Am wise that way. Iss summit yow get when yer get old: like nose hair or blood spots. Knowledge.'

'Yow having o laugh.'

'No kidding, yull juss have to see. Grow up. But yer wanna be taking amino acids for thah. I know o guy in town we can geh them on't cheap.'

'Dad says tuh lay off't supplements, ses theh no good for yow, yer heart.'

'Depends which ones. Iss all regulated Simon, everything in this country is. Yow can't scratch yer arse without some cunt filing o form abaht it. Putting it in some book or database. Most o stuff on't market is shit because it doht work; not because iss going to do owt to fuck you up.' He thinks of Francesca, how she would be impressed by his maturity. Evelyn sees through to a warmer side, but Francesca keeps to a restrained, distant understanding. Strict the way she doesn't give herself away. An idea flashes across Popeye's face, brimming through his eyes that are hooded in a furled brow, 'Have yow ever killed anyone?'

John pushes the brown-neck of the Budweiser bottle closer to his tongue, pressing against his teeth, 'Thass o funny thing to ask.'

'Yeah, but you have? I jus wanna know what'd beh like. Thess o guy at school, his allos going on abaht it. Does me head in. How he'd do it. What it'd feel lark.'

'Sounds like o cunt.'

'He yis, not saying his not. But iss o big deal.'

'Not for meh.'

'C'mon, yow kidding?'

'Yer really wanna noo?'

'Think so.'

'Lot o guys say o lot o bullshit. Thess not much to it. Iss

simple, comes more natural than yer noo. Than yow'd like. Lark iss something you meant to do. Yow think it'd affect yer more than it does. Maybe it does do, doht. Thess o lot o jocks and nobheads hull go boasting abaht woh thev done.'

'Did yeh ever cry?'

'Did a fuck. I liked it, theh first. Yer pull't trigger. Bang. Iss silent. Guy on't deck. Blood everywhere. And thass that. Lark been in o movie or summiit. Horrible, but dunt sim real.'

'Really?'

John leans his shoulders over the table, drawing tension through his silence, delays his answer whilst fixing a steady stare over Popeye to him who John is. What he's done. Shut up about Evelyn. Don't even think that thought. 'I'd love tuh do it again. Thess nothing like kick yow get, when iss legal. When yer killing for't Queen and country. To save yer own two bollocks.' John finishes his last inch of beer and nods slowly as he hears Carl's yawn; the big man unwinds from his sleep. Lethargically enough. Carl, animate and huge on his stumpy legs, strolls round the living room making grizzly noises.

The three blokes settle down to watch a double team of Clint Eastwood films: one about WWII from the Yanks perspective and the other from a Jap viewpoint. Carl talks throughout; missing things, not remembering who characters are and disrupt John's flow. He likes to get into a film as much as he can, escape himself. His time in Iraq will be made into films in years to come, overpaid actors bombing over fields in studios, putting on regional accents and doing interviews about how they got into character and how they sympathised with the impossible task. Then go back to their mansions and paparazzi gangs; the next film and the next Oscar. Carl opens the last of the beers. Cases brewery fresh. A perk. Evelyn hasn't appeared and John gets anxious: she's spending time with their baby.

Getting on side with it before he can – the idea of it cosmically bigger than the tadpole foetus beating the tiny throb of life in her belly. Popeye sends messages during the film. These kids text constantly in something like protocol but not even complex as Morse code.

Bedtime, with the second film over they're glad to get off the sofa. The TV screen was eye watering and their limbs needed movement. Blood. Oxygen. John peels off his yellow striped socks and jockeys upright on the sofa above the fault line where cushions dissolve into a backbreaking chasm.

This sofa is sanctuary. Other than the club, the only place he can keep his head down. During the day, whenever anybody else sits on there, they're on his patch. Can smell his scent; feel his heat. Doglike. He's made it his. Now it belongs to him earned through sleep and vivid dreams. He can hear Popeye open and close the fridge door; the sound of electricity hums and muffles a conversation upstairs and Evelyn's caring voice.

He dreams of Francesca. They're in a villa, where he imagines she's from in Portugal. Tiger-yellow sun. The hushing cadence of faraway waves. There's no sense of time, of day, or setting; he can't understand why they're there, but she's tussling off his trousers, appearing at his crotch with zeal and felicity. She pulls out his already uncreased penis, the lollipop brightness of his engorged head as her mouth, rough and rapid, allows her tongue to corkscrew and ripple over his glans. He pours his hand down the top of her dress and finds swells of breast, while she manoeuvres her head and bobs eagerly. He comes in a surge, in shots of plasma, white fluid that drenches her chest, catches the contour of her face. The image begins fade, to cease, to dissolve into a merge of colour and indeterminacy.

He shocks awake, delighted then disappointed in a room violet in the morning light before sunrise, wipes the sweat blemishes from his forehead and settles enough to wake up, resolves to make amends. Make things right with her and get out of this fucking house. Outside he can hear students battering bins, drumming them with sticks and grappling loudly in the street. He could kill them. The noise slows to chatter. Nobody is awake at this hour - not anybody decent. Guys like Malik stalk the streets, selling weed; ex-soldiers. There's a different society. Prostitutes. Coppers. Dealers. Drunks stagger pissed, vomit blood and bile into gutters. Something about this hour is honest, more in keeping with our inner nature than the daytime's bullshit. The full moon is chalky white, devilled by pesky clouds.

DRAGGED through another day, ducking to get in the car door and then driven smooth along the road for half an hour without speaking to Carl - John stares through his back-seat window and spots ghostly clouds chain link across the cold blue sky. There's a debate crackling on the radio about Toffs in politics and Carl flicks it over to another station playing a hair metal band. He has no time for Tory schoolboys who think they know about the state of things, the way things are. The house of Gaylords. His fat neck bulges through the head-rest, his wispy moustache twitching in what can be seen of his face through the wing-mirror; they slow for traffic, glowering at the business men in suits and portly middle-class families in minivans that look like deployment vehicles. Eventually the traffic unclogs, cars come free and they can move into the city, shrunk under the height of a broad new skyline and turn into a car-park in the centre of town where Carl parks up and pulls placards out from the boot that say things like say no to MUSLIM EXTREMISM and STAND UP FOR ENGLAND that Evelyn and Popeye have printed on in red-black ink. As they make it down to City Square to join the protestors who look more like football supporters - who are football supporters, horseshit and petrol fumes fill their noses and their footsteps are tense. There are hundreds of coppers on horse-back, on foot, kettling the meatheads into an enclosed plaza and the UAF clamber outside the pen – chanting well-rehearsed, better pitched slogans with middle-class inflections at the more brusque, bellicose Defence League, who simply and emphatically reply with England, England, England. Hard Yorkshire syllables. John's not sure who Carl knows here; there are a hundred blokes, some local, some with Nottingham and Luton written on make-shift, partisan hoodies.

Two helicopters swoon overhead, following their movement with a thermal-camera and then both hover at fixed points hundreds of feet in the sky. This is it. This is England, he wants to think but doesn't know why. There's solidarity between the men, standing, chanting at a common enemy and making them known and heard. Making noise for the jobs they fear losing, the home they see betrayed by the liberal elites – suddenly Carl's bullshit has purpose, and even though they're not sure what they're doing, what they mean what they say, they know that a deep anger is finding some sort of remedy – that this is a positive step. This madness is Basra. This scuffle of people and passion and anger; the twin helicopters overhead. He can feel desert dust in his face, a hand that aches for its weapon. There are men he recognises from the Snooker club, men he's never talked to before or even knew they were interested in anything beyond beer and the paper, wrestling with huge placards, joining the big chants.

'Carl, look.' John points at Paddy climbing onto a ornate balcony designed for flowers and hurls bullshit at the green-neon coated police, the UAF and passers-by trying to nosey up to see what's going on. England. England. England. He can see the Pakis from the club – the one's he's scuffled with joining alongside hippy lefties: the self same guys he knows hates everything they stand for, as he does, shouting down the guys who are kettled into enclosure, protesting between quaint water features and pompous statues; the cities heroes, men he has never heard of, men he doesn't know. Carl's fat heavy body and overbearing presence takes on a new demeanour; stately, empowered, he rallies his guys - a leader. A helicopter fixes over them: its beating blades loud above. They clap their hands twice then raise their arms in the air, and repeat. No Surrender. No Surrender. No Surrender to the UAF. Through the partition and hundreds of police forming a human barrier, arms-linked, like defenders in a wall, the two sides throw jeers and placards, coke bottles and burger packets. John gives them the two-fingered salute, and Carl is livid, bull heavy and riling against a gate, his anger finding something tangible to grip, his rants carrying the backing of a crowd, a riot, a march with a roar. Carl's eyes on his adversaries eyes. They'll be scores to settle, rivalries to be brought back to the Snooker club, money to be won on the table, fights to be fought on the street, a sense of England to be recovered, a future to shape, a thug culture ready to stand up. John forgets where he is, expects commands, cools into a calculated concentration, blood pounding and body ready to react against the pending violence. The city has been brought to a standstill, buses can't get down the streets, people are caught up in the blockade and can't get past, filling the space up with more people. The coppers have a video camera, they're on film. They'll be tagged and labelled extremists. John doesn't give a fuck and Carl is making new friends - offering his meaty fists to Leeds United fans, to blokes like him. England, England, England. The spirit of war. Camaraderie. The excitement of a football match, the purpose of war. England. England. England. John sees the guy who scolded his forehead - leaps dangerously over the square's wall, kicking off a copper's black hat to go after him and dives into the opposition crowd. He throws a right cross that misses. Follows up quickly with a left-hook, catches the prick under the jaw below the eyeline and sees his neck rock, expression contort and blood lasso from his bust lip. Neon-green arms seize his body, manacled by the law, a dull strike on his head dizzies and he's pulled into a police wagon, arms tied behind his back, happy. This is England. Day doing fuck all in a cell. Back to the wall. Arse on the water-resistant mattress. Around about six-thirty he's released without charge, his belongings in translucent bags after spending time to 'cool down'.

He kept his adrenaline high: alive by press-ups, sits ups and body weight exercise he's happy to teach Popeye. When they let him out the door, into the November sun, freedom. Free-dom. All that makes sense is a chant. The rhythm of words. Town will be filling up again for the night; he can't wait to get hold of Carl, the other guys, play pool, tell jokes and get on it.

EASY LIKE SUNDAY MORNING Evelyn lies on her bed, arms hugging round her rolled up legs. The pink starfish of his hand on her belly. Silently, John cradles behind her; back to chest. He puts his hand deadly cold on her gut. Holds his palm against her flesh. Scans on his mind, the foetus with features that are apparently the size of the Queen's face on a coin. Through her bellybutton's asterisk is a vividness for a child, a sleeping embryo floating in a cherry red womb. They are covered in silken hairs. They say Marilyn Monroe glowed because she was covered in fine downy blonde that glittered when camera bulbs flashed. John unbuckles the brass button on her jeans and curls his finger over meshes of sandy hair. Oiled sheets of skin; rosebud and petal. Her kisses collapse warm fades of breath. She obliges, wiggles free from her jeans and he feels round her back to unclip the hooks on her bra – her jugs shivering - regain their posture. Nipples stroke his bare chest. He rests his face on her belly, listening to the hollow. Sprung pubic hairs mingling with stubble.

'How woh today?' Evelyn asks quiet and horse. Over familiar Again.

'Won o few games, not too bad. Carl want around though, got suspicious. His usually on Saturday?'

'Eh took day off.'

'How come?'

'Thought you'd o heard? The march, yesterday, eh got himself in o scrap, beat up o guy.'

'Shit.'

'He ses it woh other fella's fault, but Paddy ses Carl juss went for him.'

'Any charges?'

'Police reckon iss race related.'

'Wunt surprise mah.'

'I know. Eh can't stand em.'

'Never known owt like it, his lark Alf Garnett. Even mah Granddad's noh that bad.'

'Am not sure he even means it, his politics. Thess summit unhinged about him.'

'It woh o good day, yesterday. Med me feel good, first time in ages. Lark been part of o regiment. Those EDL guys, iss not abaht politics. Iss abaht country. Abaht what matters tuh average man,'

'What abaht women?'

'Them too. Iss not for those clever twats who run't army but doht see service, or't politicians. Cunts.'

'Not like you tuh beh wound up lark this? Yow should settle down, I lark keeping mah nose out.'

'Got arrested.' She was about to comfort him, but he's given her the chance to maul him with a glance. She likes this - to scold him - pull him into line. He needs looking after, protecting and held together, even if he's a bastard.

'Why did yer do?'

'Not a lot, they let me out.'

'It's noh funny, I can see yer smiling.' Evelyn smiles too; she likes guys who break the rules, state their position. Francesca would go mad.

'Iss pigs, innit? Iss what they do, just round you up lark fucking cattle and take yow. They love it.'

'I feel lark o moll.'

'O woh?'

'Dunt matter.' Her hands link behind his neck, and her arms are again returned to his jawline. The quilt they're laying on has begun to warm with their heat.

'Wanna baff?'

'Can do.'

'Thought you'd be more bothered abaht Carl? If theh pressing charges, his in trouble.'

'Does it look lark I care?'

'Summit happened?'

'Noo.'

'His not hit you again?'

'Iss just that, I doht love him. I noo thah now. Am not sure I ever really did, it wer o mistake. Amma cold? Duh yow think am juss a fucked up, cold person?' He closes his eyes, the deep fragrance of her. He imagines the cells multiplying like he's seen on 3D demonstrations on TV films: spindled DNA churning into a person. Those sex education lessons at school he hasn't thought of for twenty years before now. Those 2D diagrams were too scientific: the way those biology teachers with bum fluff beards fucked. The Joy of Sex. Not the wank throb, the sex pest urges of the rest of us re-enacting pornos. The graphic slap to the hind: the red woven smack of arse. Ten years too late. He wants to know everything going on in there; the news on the baby, in the tendrils and circuitry of Evelyn's velveteen womb.

'Yer Klingon mark looks better.'

'Yer think?'

'Thell get some stick. Those raghead bastards.'

'Doht, it'll only cause more trouble.'

'Baff time?' She nods, assenting to the water. John goes to the bathroom and burnishes water with Radox. He adds cold and stirs with his thumb, preparing a bath like he would for a baby. Everything becomes so much more luminous, brighter, when you're living for somebody else. This is the next eighteen years. Evelyn and child. Why tell his family? Fuck those cunts. This is about Evelyn. He can get used to this fatherly feeling, proud across his chest. Wearing the added swagger and size like a tuxedo. The hot water comes out the tap too fast and spangles wild architectures of foam. Pockets of air in frigid little honeycombs. He crisps his blue and her yellow towels crinkly hot on the eggshell radiator. The bathroom is steamed moist.

A waving water level covers half their bodies up to the shimmering buttocks and rocky elbows cracking lilac foam. Legs redden: the waxen skin that's not been covered looks greasy and yellow, spotted with foam. Leaning back pushes Evelyn's buttocks between John's legs and he splashes water onto her midriff, cupping her breasts and fingering calming circles over her belly. When they rise, carefully, not to slip, the sequins of drip fall into chains of droplets. They pat one another dry in the warm bed knowing the time will come when he'll have to return to the living room and they'll have to pretend. An untruth lingers. He has this inkling something dodgy is going on between Ronnie and Francesca – the way they talk. You can tell when a guy like Ronnie falls for a girl. The cocky front disappears. The drinking and smoking stops. You know your distances.

He knows Carl suspect more than he lets on, but that's

forgotten now; Evelyn's apple-scented hair tickles. Her body ripples generously.

'Am gonna have tuh go soon.'

'Stay o bit.' She gently rolls a fist on his chest, fingers staggering open into a star as she falls asleep. Twitches of dream animate the Viking pale of her face. The TV's still talking. Always questions without answers. Always the strobe images. He liked the creepy girl with the ragdoll that used to come on when TV was terrestrial. You knew where you stood. The eerie face. You need a break. Awake in the ghost of hours beyond transmission. A guy called Billy Mason-Wood, a soldier he went on two tours with, believed he could hear the voices of dead friends on military radios. He's been sectioned now. Came from a good family and ended up in the rat house. Tonight the past looks bigger than the present. Everything that matters, the big events, have already happened. The country has no future. Two C-list celebrities are ballroom dancing, waltz-stepping through his blue mist of nearly sleep. The sand-bagged tiredness. John's on his back only seeing the flickering blur, colours on the ceiling. The long shadows of their closed positions. Evelyn sleeps deeply. Rigid, death. Hands balled together, knuckles-clasped, he prays. It is a poem spoken without words. The kilter of his remembrances and the things he is trying to say. The first since Iraq. The jailor on his knees. He remembers the fire of bullet and spray of blood, the metal fog of weaponry. These noises make you feel alive. They are the tugging call to adrenaline and an ecstasy of being – the fever of war. They were under siege. He thought he would die. He was imagining his ten-second obituary on the six 'clock news. The condolences before Prime Minister's questions. What would death taste like? Where would the darkness's go? He believes God and luck are the same magics. He's glad to have Evelyn in his life, really, though he doesn't deserve her. The annoying innocence of her love. She's too generous, too forgiving of his failure, his inhuman crimes.

When they fucked, John tasted Carl's dirt on her. The lips he was forced to kiss, licking rim flare of sluice flesh. The scent and bud of her cunt. It's another man's territory. Thinking about the things their bodies have done; what he tries to make her do. How far can he push her? Where does she draw the line? He has trained her to suck dick, built-up her confidence - under the sheets. And had to kiss the curdled warm saliva that thrilled his cock when she rose, sweating, from the duvet.

Now he's wasted enough time down the club smoking and drinking, kicking up a fuss with anybody who gives a fuck. He gets his clothes on his back and shambles downstairs to the colder living room where Dasha the dog stares at him dazed. When the door jacks open and Carl comes in. After midnight. John squeezes his eyes shut and fakes a snore. Soon as he's gone, he looks up through the curtains at the serene night and joins the stars up. Trying to pick out Scorpio amid the galaxies of pinheads. Stars are dead. Beamed from thousands of years ago. Slow time. He feels this about his own memories, his past. The heavy mass of remembering. Yes. They appear and their best days are gone. Their sparkles are white lies on the night sky.

PERCHED wobbling on the top of a high stool John raises a tulip pint glass of Stella watching as Francesca performs her finely tuned show of innocuous flirting. This is the new model specially sent from the brewery. Ruins the wife-beater image. Not a selling point. He can guess when Francesca will jolt her head, knows her ticks, flicks, quirks and wiggles. Her secret movements. He notices when she's bored. Halfway toward a daydream she tilts her head and licks her lip. She's on all fours, knees dirtied to wipe down the bottom of the fridge. This is one of those bars Carl hates. MTV on the flat-screens hived around the building. Loss leading offers on mixers and spirits. Free drinks for women on Tuesday nights. Students dossers Brill-Creamed and slim with hard bodies John can't compete with. No wonder Carl can't stand them. Even this place isn't as full as he'd expect. Glass in hand he gargling its swill as he walks to the door guarded by two black bouncers and lights up. Lines of unmarked cabs queue and solicit conversations from drunken teenagers. A train screams on a wet darkened bridge above the street. Rain. Heavy streaked lines stretch and splash into puddles. Four days of rain. His cigarette loses its flavour – his tongue's gone bum fluffy.

Francesca joins him, clinging to a tiny jacket. They slip down an alleyway. 'So how long yer been seeing Ronnie?' John asks taking smooth drags and spooling long, decorous smoke.

She takes a drag, 'Iss been o few months. On and off. Nowt too serious.'

'Yer weren't gonna to tell meh?'

'As if.'

'Don't be a bitch.'

'Fuck you. What abaht Evelyn?'

'We go back a long way, it wer o mistake.'

'Look after her. Lease yer can get that right.'

'No.'

'C'mon John, don't be a deadbeat dad too.'

'Yer know?'

'Do summit right in yer life.'

'We're not having it.'

'Bullshit.'

'Thes no way we haven't it.'

'Yer know how much she wants one.'

'Not with me.' Rain patters on his hair and styles a nineties fringe across his forehead. They dab their tabs out on the alley wall and embers spark down to the floor, bright and fiery.

'Is you a want, allos has been.'

'You've missed yer chance.' She turns to walk back into bar, John catches her hand.

'So I had a chance?'

'Don't beg me.' High on a stool the bar happens around him all evening. He orders a jug of lager and drinks his way through it, easily, taking no pause to piss or burp. Occasionally he goes out for a cigarette and gives a cocky nod to the bouncers.

He tries one last time, 'We could still meck this work, I'm getting me sen together. Take yer out for o nice meal.'

'John, go home.'

'Please.'

'Go be a daddy. I don't want to know yer.' She has levels of seriousness John can't match; parts to her that you can't go. Uncover. She silences him – his organs freeze and skin prickles. Realism sets hard into his body. Physical. You understand. A flopping, bruised heartbeat. The booze woozily grows into a headache. Alone he patrols his snug with a jug of lager.

When Ronnie eventually turns up, he kisses Francesca with his one eye scanning the bar. John sees them for the first time. Acting things out like a couple. Animated by seeing one another. John's hands are alert – violent, plastic with energy. He taps the table. Styles hands through his hair. Cracks his fingers. He can't see a pool table or anything to occupy.

'HOW YOU POPS?'

'Woh do yow care?'

'Juss been a nice guy – yer no?'

'Av seen yer.'

'Sin who?'

'You and Evelyn.'

'We both live here, so I guess yow would.' There's a tension to him; an aggression in his stance that John lets pass by. Guilt. Popeye thinks he can front John up. Got some big man ideas, let them go over the top of his spotty head. John can't take him seriously as a threat, nowhere near. Dickhead. It's a blow to his balls when jerk offs like Popeye think they can have a go. Popeye's downed his first beer. He fishes through the fridge for second. Then shuts it hard enough to shake the contents.

'Woss spooked yer?' John asks,

'Not a lot.' In his face, the way he forms his assault, there are the grains of the man he will become, like Carl, forceful and mouthy.

'How many of those have you had?'

'Not enough.'

'Put thah down. Run yourself a glass of watter and get your sen to bed. You look knackered.' Carl exhorts from the other room and reminds John he's still sleeping, doors away. Popeye leaves the room and runs up the stairs husking wanker under his breath, on the flicker of his tongue. John thinks about another beer; but waits for Evelyn as he stares at the square neon digits on the clock, yawns and taps his finger ponderously on the table. They have to be more careful. It's hours before the door opens and Evelyn stumbles in, wet from the worsening rain and she kisses John's forehead, looking over his head to the living room, two eyes on the staircase. John waits for her to get settled, put away the things she carries round. Her hair is blonder in the strobing light. 'Popeye knows.' Now a reflex: he reaches into his top pocket. Pulls out a solo cigarette.

She's pulling off her tights and steps into her slippers, 'How can he John? Where's Carl? What makes you think that? There's no way he can. No chance.'

'Eh said he's 'seen us'.'

'John, that's ridiculous. He's 'seen us'? Where's Carl? I need to speak to him.'

'He's asleep in't living room.' John eyes her the whilst tapping a cigarette on the table-top.

'You should stop thah.' He likes her teacherly way with him. Her cheeky eyes when she says these things: it gives John petty rules to break, a chance to laugh.

'So yoh not bothered?'

'Woh did he say?'

'He was, you noh, actin funny. And then he sed, I've seen yoh. Me and you.'

'What do yer think he meant?'

'Thass obvious.'

'Dunt sound like hard evidence to meh,' she rings her arms around his neck, leans onto his sitting thighs and gifts him with a soothing kiss, 'I woh looking at baby clothes today.' She giggles to herself. Delighted, she hunches her shoulders. Goes to the sink. Dippy. Giddy. Upbeat. Sickly. John dabs grey, black and white ash into his plate-sized John Smith's ashtray; the one remaining relic of his own place.

'Did yow no Ronnie and Fran are together?' He floats his question across the room, expecting a put down.

'Yer couldn't guess but she is o bit of o slapper. Who wunt sheh sleep with?' Me: John thinks. He goes on, smoking.

'Didn't see it myself.'

'Oh I did. It was plain as day. They deserve each other as far as I can see; both of them think the sun shines out of their behinds.'

'Is Carl going on that march?'

'He ses so.'

'Got fuck all to do, may as well. The last one woh lark o football match without football.'

'Load o yobs.'

'You got o problem with yobs?'

'No.' She laughs as John play-fights with her. Eventually the laughter fades and John's worn out. Eve gets her clothes together and kisses John goodbye; Carl wants her to go see look at some figures in the club, and when she leaves, John sits on the sofa and sighs. When Popeye comes down the stairs looking for food, suspicious of the recent laughter, John has fallen asleep watching today's Top 10 Music Videos. A well-choreographed troupe dressed as astronauts gyrate like lap-dancers.

FEELING HEAVY, HIS BELLY enlarged, arse bloated, John joined the gym about six months ago, made sure it was the first thing he did since he got back: but the thought of pulling himself away from the sofa, heavy with a moody hangover, and go walk a mile to the corrugated metal shed by the canal hadn't yet enticed him. But living on Evelyn's cooking and sitting opposite Carl every meal has put fear into him. He slumps his clothes in a locker and squeezes into his grey vest and black joggy bottoms, strutting out into the free-weights section where big men heave sets – grunting loudly and lacking body hair.

Somewhere reflected in the long mirrors that stretch across the open plan space is Malik, stabbing his legs on a cross trainer, iPod headphones in, and his stare, serious yet vacant, fixed at his sweaty reflection. John warms up and does wind-mills with his arms, warming his rotator-cuffs, gets the blood tingling and the muscles loose. His first set takes it out of them: staggered by rasping breathlessness, his lung capacity stubbed, his military strength weakened.

Gets to the bench press, three exercises in, he has to dab his forehead with his towel panting and wheezing, slightly afraid of the next bitching sets. Bench-press is a high power exercise, a compound movement, and he can't get away with lifting not a lot in here; the steroidal, squirm-faced men, the freaks will rib him, endlessly. He reclines on the bench and sees a brown hand grip the bar running parallel with his eyeline.

'Need o spotter?' He recognises Malik's voice.

'Cheers.'

'How many reps?'

'Am goin for eight.'

'Goo on then, I got it. Watch guards on't bar, theh fucked me up last week, loose.' John pushes the barbell off its rest and lowers it to his chest, breathes deeply as the weight comes lower and exhales with a big gush, pushing the downward pressing weight back up, skywards. He repeats the movement, three, four, five times and Malik starts speaking at length, 'Thass it, keep steady. Hold it teh bottom. There. Thass concentration point. Good.'

John booms another rep from deep inside his chest; feels his pec's flame and roar, the muscle breakdown, as he locks his elbows. You need to thrash our the movement, explode. The barbell and weights are crossways above him.

Malik goes on, 'This game you've been talking abaht – between me and you.' John's eyes bulge, 'There's still guys who want your ass. You know? And those white cunts, those skinheads, they'll be there?' John pushes out the eights, finally exhausted and Malik pushes his finger down on the bar; with John weakened, he can't raise it any higher, his grip wobbles. 'You bang one more rep o that, come on.' John squeezes, growling, asks everything of his body, his saggy chest and wilfully powers the last rep emphatically upward. Panting, John sits up for deep lung gasps of breath. He pours his fingers through his sweat-matted hair.

'Crazy bastard. Thall hurt like fuck.'

'No pain, no gain.'

'Those cunts still after meh?'

'You're not down – not a liked guy. Nothing's gonna change, those boys be plannin.'

'Part of meh likes tharr. Gives me summit to think abaht when am bored: on't shitter, sat on't sofa. I'm a wanted man round these parts.' They laugh and John sees a friendlier side to Malik that he keeps reserved by his natural coolness.

'Before yow go – this rematch. We'd have to mek it work on our terms though. Thell be heat from this, and if we can keep a bit of control, get it right, we could both make a more cash out of this than we thought.'

'Sweet.'

'Carl reckons he'll stake me as much as it takes.'

'Lotta trust there.'

'Woh?'

'Risky.'

'Theh guy thinks am the great white hope.'

'His a dizzy bastard, inne?'

'Weird bloke, but got a good heart, deep down.'

'Lark you?'

'More lark you mate.'

'Yer a bullshitter.'

'What's the situation though? With a rematch?'

'That lot are a bunch o pussies. You shit em up when yer attacked them. Most white boys pussy out. Thass why theh come after yer 'cos theh scared. Right?'

'Got enough on me plate without all that.'

'Theh think yer even, keep it that way. Play the game.'

'Hate the player.'

'I'll give yer a call.' Malik leaves John ready for another set with sweat drying on his clothes. Malik takes his fists to a heavy red punch bag and works the middle, throwing hook after hook, then mixes it up with jabs and five punch combinations, works the bag hot. Fist mark dented. Tough outside. The bag swings, acceleration and velocity, like a pendulum.

JOHN NIBBLES AT EVELYN'S hot red ear as she tries to take a shower and aims the nozzle. 'You're gonna get wet' she giggles and pushes him out. He pulls her, takes a firm loop of her middle and tugs her in a waist-lock, directing her to the bed that she's washed crisp and petal-scented. John slips of his jeans, prongs his cock out from his boxer shorts and they kiss straying back to the bouncy mattress and Evelyn twists the button at the top of her jeans and reveals a stark white, round belly. She rolls on her sloped front, bringing up her arse. He takes a hand of his cock and runs it up and down the wet smooth of her pussy, angling for the point of entry. He does and sinks deep into the middle of her. She lets out sharp sigh and John sinks deeper on his knees. Down the alley created between her cheeks, at the base of her spine by her arse is a bony whiteness, a few trim hairs and an X-rated organ. He closes his eyes with her pussy plucking at his prick. She makes throaty, orgasmic sounds. Faked. He shoots babbling shots. She pulls his lower back eyes focussed onto eyes.

They relax on top of the bedsheets, bodies warm. He rolls nearer her, into her back and hooks his arms under hers and holds her breasts, slumming his face between her shoulders, nose to bone. She's ticklish – responds to John's slight touches with giggles, laughter, squeezes her patchwork pillow tight. John can forget she's pregnant like this, when they're playing and he can't yet see any physical change in her, no big bump. To bring up the issue would start an argument. John wants to lay here and ease away his hangover and the excess alcohol oozing out after the run in Evelyn's warmth. He and Carl went to four bars last night across Leeds and won several games, though John thinks he spent much of the winnings, there's change spilling from his jean pockets as he steps out of bed and gets ready for another day. Evelyn sits on the bed, cross-legged, naked, speaking:

'Thought any more about what we're to do?'

'Get a job, get out o here.'

'Iss that easy?'

'Truss me.'

'Yer an idiot.'

'Lotta people tell meh that.' She's playing John's t-shirt in her hands, his tough body underneath and doesn't press further. When Carl goes out and with Popeye in college – John and Evelyn spend their mornings bickering, joking, play fighting in bed. She worries about evidence, signs and smells. The stains on the bedsheets or socks, underwear, anything that can give them away. John likes how women are detectives, conspiratorial. Keen to protect their betrayal. She cleans twice as hard. The price of eternal vigilance is fatigue. A stray hair or minor detail could ruin her. Downstairs, John's smoking the yellow off a butt on the sofa, finding out about his world with his dog-eared copy of The Sun that spent all day rolled up under his armpit. Benefit cheats. Asylum fraudsters. Bent politicians. Dodgy coppers. Overpaid footballers. Why do people believe the myth of the world? That the state and the law rules? When it's the thugs on the backstreets and the gangsters on the black market and the bent arms firms and illegal wars that hold the sway? Evelyn arranged flowers in a bowl. Blue. Pink. Orange. Yellow. Long-necked, bulky stalks proud stiff with life and obviously unaware of their impermanence. One day Evelyn will be older and thicker round the girthy middle. She'll get the middle-aged mum short haircut and her skin will parch and thin. John will grow grey and heavy like an elephant remembering a livelier past. Those flowers will see out their days in the window opposite mucky walls mosaic-like with graffiti, spray paint figures and abstract colours. He has to get out. The stillness weighs heavily. He wants to be back in the club playing the Paul Newman hustle. He wants the crack with life-worn characters drinking slow death at the bar. Wrapped up between these walls: there's desperation in a lover's kindness.

'Do yer have to smoke?' Annoyed, her lips tut. She wants the air clean for her unborn child.

'Sorry.' He stubs it out, his cigarette, 'Am juss fidgety, trying not to drink. Makes me go barmy. Need to have summat to do.'

'Why doh yow go for a run?'

'I yate runnin.'

'But dint you run in't army?'

'Yeah, even more reason not teh.' On the TV there's an unlikely family who rant and rave, only to be told off by some middle-class twat about the ways of the world, what's right and wrong. The new clergy. A mother shambles from the green room, bigger than Big Fat Carl, as the bickering intensifies, becomes cuttingly personal.

'Popeye ask any more questions?' Evelyn tries to shush her cup of tea cold and takes a seat beside John.

'Not since the other night.'

'Ormones.'

'Doht underestimate him. Hiss a clever kid. We're not as clever as weh think we are, either.'

'Doht work your sen up – hiss been like this for years, up and down. Moody. Suspicious. He's a teenager.'

'You say that.'

'Doht go working yourself up, thess not a problem.' The TV slips into commercials about car insurance presented by rodents, a gang of multi-ethnic bankers perform a dance routine and an earnest grey-haired man talks about funeral expenses and the burden on your family.

Out in the garden, fag hanging from his lip, he has a new mobile. Evelyn made him buy it to keep tabs on him. He has an app where he can see the football scores. There's GPS tracking like he used in the forces. Everything is touch screen now and he wands his finger through the phone book, finding Francesca. His gut tightens as the dial tone rings:

'Fran, iss me.' There's silence on the line: he knows somebody has picked up.

'John?'

'I need to see yer.'

'No small talk with you is there?'

He laughs, 'Am all business.'

'Yer don't take no for an answer?'

'Don't act like you don't lark a bloke to be persistent.'

'I do. Just not you.'

'Meet me. Outside work. Properly.'

'I'll think about it.'

'How's Ronnie?'

'As if you care.'

'He is me mate.'

'I haven't seen him in o while. Not sure if we're on.'

'I'll leave Eve.'

'It rhymes, so it must be true.'

'Not kidding. Serious.'

'We'll see. I've got to go. Let me think abaht it. A don't know if I can trust yer.'

'Trust me.' The lines goes. He's been give a number of duties around the house; and, upbeat, he gets two wheelie bins in his grip and runs them jerkily down the gravel pathway.

SUNDAY AFTERNOON. The Snooker Club. Carl turns up the volume on the TV: Leeds United are playing Kettering Town in the FA Cup and the pitch is a clod, the same white jerseys that were playing in the Champions League a few years ago were struggling to put on past a pub team. A fat bastard goalkeeper having the game of his life - tips a belter round the corner. Clips a toe poke over the bar and barks at his raggy defence - doesn't let up on the game and let his attention stray. John drums the table top. Thumps in time to the Leeds chants. There's no other atmosphere – the place half-dead. These places used to be full. What are people doing? Not everybody drinks Tesco lager. Not everybody drinks out in the metal and leather bars in town decked out like bordellos or boudoirs. Carl slams down the phone. John ignored his bawling, desperate for no good reason to hear the commentary. He shuffles out from the back, the staircase where the phone rings every five minutes and pulls a pint for the sake of pulling it, 'Here, have that,' he pushes it over the counter to John who downs the last of his sloppy, backwash froth.

'Cheers.'

'Doht know woh they expect o me. Fucking idiots, the lot o them. Now thee want karaoke back on.'

'Woh good will that do?'

'Who knows. Dohnt tell our Evelyn. Have to get my head round thiss me sen first. Theh say they're sending one of their guys down on Thursday. Some sort of product assessment, lay-out, that sort of thing.'

'Iss all bollocks to me. Dint have this in't forces. Thass why I liked it.'

'Not lark old days – remember meh old man's pub down on't Kirkstall Road? Thass before it started going silly in't nineties with themed pubs and too many game nights. Mr Qs and all that shite. Breaking down snugs, open planning everything and scrapping lounges.' Bemusement rolls through his cheeks and John sighs in agreement; there's the ghost of Francesca, somewhere, beyond this conversation, mocking Carl and his bawling and then laying into John for doing something stupid that he'll have missed. The bar in daytime without being boozed; the stale light, the glasses and bottles waiting like props.

'Where did all't local trade goo? Muss be boozin somewhere?'

'Four pubs close o week mate. A week. Britain I knew when I woh a boy – iss all fucked. Thes no other way to say it. Fucked. No Labour movement. One party state. Bending over backwards for't Pakis who want to kill us: hate the way we live. Pubs closing. Fucking benefits. Drugs. Shit.'

'Iss all gone to dogs?' John shaped to laugh, but Carl goes back to his argument, gets serious.

'Am thinking of getting rid of Car lot too.'

'Really?'

'Even if weh got more trade, overheads are enough to finish yow. Government's tax crazy and breweries thall do owt for a quick buck – doht think ahead. Shud put meh in charge. Ad show em thing or two.' Craning their faces toward the TV, John and Carl watch, humbled, as Richie Partridge floats in a free kick and Ian Roper heads the ball clean into the back of the net, onion-sack billowing. Carl pulls himself another pint. They don't speak: both light calming cigarettes.

'What a load of shite,' John says, 'Makes you feel like a rite twat following em sometime. I woh there when Valencia did us in't Champs League. It woh between tours.'

'Not so long since we had Cantona and won bloody league before it woh Premier. Iss all money now. Everything's about bloody money.'

'Yer not wrong.' John's pint pulls him toward a deeper tiredness; he can see snow through the window and the passing traffic, red car, blue car, red car, green car, he counts them by wondering where they're going. He always wanted a grey Ford Capri and to belt about Leeds like he was in the Sweeney. He's licensed to drive, has a BFG military license but can't afford the insurance let alone a car and the price of petrol. One thing he thought the war in Iraq would do was bring that down. Maybe it has. Maybe things would be worse had they not gone in there. Some bighead in a University might know. Then again, they probably don't. Carl is the wisest man he has access too; standing there, slowly raising his pint to his mouth, he can see he's struggling to find a way beyond life working behind the bar. John can see him being heavily involved in the EDL – taking things forward or helping get them organised if they ever got their act together; he won't do BNP, says there's too many Front members in and Combat 18 who he can't stomach. The fan noise from the TV echoes through the piled up seats of the other room.

When Evelyn and Popeye turn up in their puffy winter coats they're carrying bags of shopping. Evelyn's excited about the presents she's bought for Carl's birthday next week and Popeye seems cool with everything; not in one of his mardy strops or giving John a stern eye.

'Owt for me?' John asks, his smile warning Evelyn. Remember who you love. They go in the back, as a family, leaving John to fill his own drink and stare at the boring football. When your teams losing like Leeds are losing – outplaying the opposition, stripping them back and missing every chance that comes, you know you're fucked and the game drags. You're incapable of changing anything, so you drink. He gets a text from Fran which breaks up the monotony; she seems to have relaxed these past few days, forgiven John for his mistake when she was stupid enough to go along with him.

There's banter and noise and it's not coming from the TV screen. John cranes his neck and some of the Asians have arrived wearing baggy joggy bottoms and boots and black sideburns shaved into geometric shapes. Leeds are working the ball up the pitch. The Asians take a table and one winks at John, pointing at his own forehead where they got him with the cigarette butt and they laugh. He expects them to come and have a go. Robert Snodgrass shoots and Jermaine Beckford gets a touch on it, finally sending something past their goalkeeper who's having the game of his life. John shakes his fist with enjoyment, remembering bigger games and his younger self. He gives the Asians a camp wave and they laugh, tickled and tell him to fuck off.

It was when they protested against the soldiers coming home from their tours, that's when it tipped John over the edge who's usually keen to keep clear from politics. There was no need for that. Folk should leave each other alone, leave them be, that's the best way. Seeing the Asians squaring up to one another over the pool table makes him itch for a game himself and he can't wait to get Malik on the table and show him a lesson. Do a match as tense as Dennis Taylor and Steve Davis.

Carl comes back to boss the bar and sees the Asians playing their games on the tables, turns on his heel, shakes his head sighing and ambles into the back. Urdu becomes the dominant language in the room as the football comes to the final whistle: the rapid intonation, takes him back to Basra and the hot sun, guns and sacred houses.

FRANCESCA SEEMS NERVY AND then alert and then suddenly interested, propping her chin upward and waiting for John to speak, to tease out his gossip with her flirtation. Cycles of interest and disinterest. He wants to unravel her, work her out with his index finger, his hands. They're in a Chicken Bar where they had to pay before they came in, before they even ate, and John lashes his whole spatchcocked bird with spicy sauce, dipping his chips in it too and Francesca watches, reviewing his table etiquette. Her mother Elda – a thick-hipped, hard-working immigrant kept her old world values. Francesca has been hard-wired manners, ways of being.

She had promised herself she wouldn't end up like Elda, arthritic with three children, working day and night, cleaning relentlessly and always on guard. She would be a model – she would have a better life. But she was pregnant at nineteen; in love with an older man, and her modelling only took her so far as a topless photoshoot that embarrassed her, and she had to go to court to get them withdrawn. So now she was here with John who was tearing chicken-muscle. She notices his hard-worked skin and crooked lines, day old stubble. Green eyes. She watches the hands that have held her, coarse and workman-like.

'Yow a right caveman you are.'

'Starvin.'

'We've not talked for weeks.'

'Yer right.' A teenage waiter in a black shirt comes to see if their meal's alright, and if they want anything else. John orders a second bottled beer and Francesca waves him off. Her earrings are huge gold hoops.

'Ows work?' He asks.

'Shit. How's the Adam's Family?'

'Thee do meh head in.'

'Got yourself into a right little set-up theh, ant yer? Evelyn fancies you too, thass obvious.'

'Really?'

'Way she looks at yow. Surprised Carl's not caught on; iss not as thick as eh looks.'

'We've got history.'

'No! Really? Any other dirty secrets?'

'Like woh?' He stares back at her, dense, goes back to his food and hungry as he is, tries to mute the noise of chewing gristle and tissue, white breast and elastic skin. Without thinking, he flips the conversation round.

'Sin Ronnie lately?'

Francesca raises an eyebrow and curls her lip, there's cuteness to her disdain. 'Wass he got to do with owt?'

'Just aksing.'

'We broke up.'

'Didn't tell me yer were together. Looks like am not only one keeping secrets.'

'We weren't talking, remember? An it wohnt serious. Like I should tell yow anyway.' There's a nervous energy between them. Different face-to-face. Not buttressed by a bar, a situation. It clears the air – them getting their jealousies, their gripes out of the way; they talk freely about the small nothings that animate their days, with the words feeling light and swift. He imagines them old. Their bodies rankled, heaving the resins of a well-lived life. The thought is secure like a Kevlar vest. When John finishes his meal only bones and grease are left. Francesca had stopped eating halfway through hers, stirring chilli through rice, watching John. Stirring chilli through rice, to keep her hands busy. Younger couples, first dates, teenagers with gullible, grease-pored faces are eating alongside them. There are some business types in Reservoir Dogs suits and twenty-something postgraduates in block colours. They take a walk to the bar next door and she takes her arm in his; John gives the bouncer a nod as they pass through the door. He's never been drunk with Francesca. She likes Bailey's and a few drinks have made her loud and unguarded. Sober, she's alert and watchful, John enjoys her blathering, seeing her loosen up. They work their way through several cocktails, then sours. Jelly-legged, arm-in-arm, they make their way out as the barman bellows last orders. John doesn't drink this quick: the pace has wobbled him; he likes a slower sozzle, drowning himself gradually through a binge. Silently, with the intensity of enemy fire, they stare at one another. Francesca's husky-blue eyes. They walk out the exit and into the shopping plaza; on the escalator they hold the rubber grip that loops long and elliptically through the length of the rolling staircase. They make it to a backstreet, where Francesca's backs onto the coarse red brick wall. John's cups her face in his hand warmly on her cheek.

'No,' she says, 'Iss notta good idea.' John takes a breath,

fills his lungs and exhales, letting go. He sidesteps her and stands with his back against the wall. They're side-to-side.

'What the fuck are we doin?'

'Iss complicated.'

'I noo that, it allos is. Evelyn's pregnant.' It takes a second for Francesca's eyebrows to go crimp and then ease jagged. The new reality sets in across her face – a sense of epiphany. John groans and Francesca's angry. 'Get away John, juss fuck off.'

'Eh want meant to be.'

'How canna trust yer? How? Am not o fool.' He reaches out to her and she throws her arms away, crying. She starts a high-heeled clack down the street and John chases after, struggling to catch up. They're under the halcyon light of streetlamps. 'Francesca' John shouts, 'Francesca, I'm in with love yer.'

She stops, turns. 'You doht mean it.' Her palm holds her other palm and she looks up at him, eyes begging.

'Fran, I do.'

'Evelyn?'

'What about her? Iss complicated. Lark you say. But it alloss is. Things get more and more complicated, every day, it never stops. It never will. I juss don't give o fuck. About anything. Honestly. Other than you.' She understands, letting him pull her nearer. The movement brings her body round and their hips meet groove on bone. They kiss, the same electricity as the last, John cups her head. Hard skull. Soft hair. She rubs her palm with her fingers outstretched, searching, her nails preciously across the papule shafts of his cock. They back into an alleyway where it looks like deliveries come in during the day, round the corner, into an alcove. He feeds two fingers facing outward down her pants, feeling the tight restriction of her jeans work against his wrist. He dabs the squint of flesh, the oyster of clitoris and its slick hood slowly circling. She lets him have his way reluctantly – tastes his pleasure then pulls him away – his hand glides past her ear through her hair. They kiss trailing lip from tongue, and tongue from lip. He steadies his pace, hearing a jet sound by overhead, carries on. He nibbles her ear, kisses the cool violet flesh behind her lobe and slows his fingers to a delicate pressure. They clinch, warmly held, neither lets go. A hot tingle soft as butterflies wing-beats upward through his gut. She pats his arse and cradles her slender arm round his broad, muscular backed waistline and they walk quickly through loud scrums of clubbers holding onto one another in drunken packs and students becoming two figures in a dizzying crowd rushing on their way home.

A TEXT from Ronnie. The Snooker Club has gone into the first stages of receivership. He's at the kitchen table in his underpants and his white vest gone grey over its lifetime, cornflakes dropped down the y-neck. There's a posh sounding DJ who keeps playing wank music, darkie shite off the chart. John thinks it's an odd vocation for that sort of guy. Dinner party type. Evelyn sleepily makes tea and toast in one of his white t-shirts. Pantless. Oversized, the cotton just about covers her arse and hugs at her sexy oval outline. Undersides of cheeks.

She wanders around the house without her pants on – modelling her whiskered strip of fanny hair with childish glee. An impulsive, addictive song comes on by a new girl band that has John's fingers rapping rhythmically on the kitchen table. There's a dirty grit to their voices you can't teach: comes from deep velveteen throats. Rasping and sordid. Evelyn turns a blunt knife over her toast: one piece in her mouth. She pulls up her seat next to John. Crumbs on her breasts. Her belly has swollen. A handful of weeks and it's already bigger than John's oversized beer gut. They had a warm-hearted lecture from a doctor last week about cycles and biology and what was going on in her belly. Morning sickness. Embryology. Evelyn took it in and relays back to him every day – too much information for John to take enough in and properly remember.

'You got a text?' Evelyn asks.

'Yeah, nothing to worry about,'

'Someone special?'

'Just Ronnie.'

'You still speak?'

'Why wouldn't we?'

'No reason.' Daytimes seem longer here, in the suburbs. There are noisy birds and posh kids in the morning. Mums ferrying three kids into hummers. Weapons of consumption. Ready to grow into another load of jumped up tossers.

'Yer get in a mood when I mention him.'

'Am not in a fucking mood, OK?' John unrolls today's edition of The Sun and he reads an article about a paedophile preying on kids on Facebook, fucking paedos, shoot them all, chop their cocks off – that'll teach them. Evelyn's doing what John finds women do when they're angry, pretending not to be, despite the odd articulations of her face. Her sideward glance. The fidgety, stiff pouts are petulantly, angry. He retaliates and turns back to page three where a nineteen year old model has luxurious Double D tits not dicked about with by cruel gravity. Evelyn crosses her legs. She seems hidden, closed off from John.

'You've got anger management issues.' She starts her assault, a war of attrition, asymmetric.

'No I doht.'

'You can't take criticism, either.'

'Would yow lemme read meh paper?'

'Those tits must take some reading, lot of mental effort. Good to noo father of my baby is a reader.'

'You're fucking crazy.'

'Not me who wakes up shouting in the night.'

'What the fuck is that meant to mean? Not a sober moment wi women, is theh? Allos some fucking pantomime.'

'You're o dick.'

'Eh?'

'Don't act lark yer don't know.' She acts tough, head swaying, but it's a punch thrown too far. She's off balance. The tone has gone in her voice and she's shrieks, verging on tears. He's never seen her so worked up. But his tempers turned on; he thumps his fist on the table after his every point.

'I know.'

'Yer know what?' John holds his newspaper still: hot guilt rushes up through his arms. She knows.

'Am pregnant with yer baby.'

'Am not sure what the fuck yer on abaht.' Carl. The fallout. A burning, rushing shock of blood rinses through him.

'Don't fucking lie to me!' The phone starts ringing. A shrill burbling tone and Evelyn rips the handset off the wall, smashing it into the square-tiled floor.

'Yer wanna calm down.'

'Juss stop lying. Please.'

'Am not.'

'I don't want this baby.'

'Evelyn, c'mon.'

'Am not messing about.' He opens his arms out: first in protest and then catch her in a hug, console. She doesn't this – running upstairs and slamming the door. A filthy pop song comes on the radio and he picks up her toast, still warm and strokes marmalade across the stubbled bread. Carrying on as normal, letting her know he isn't bothered is relaxingly satisfying. He waits to bluff her but she doesn't come downstairs. It's been twenty-minutes. Carl will be home in an hour. Popeye in two. He's got good at working out where they'll be, and why. He fishes out yesterday's clothes from the laundry basket and runs some water through his greasy hair. The roads here are long and with the houses all the same: chunky terraces, he feels like he's been walking down this street for days, heels sore, calves tightening. To walk is to labour. Eventually he takes a right turn. Inside the windows of houses - some covered with curtains, others with choppy blinds - he can see the bright invitation of people's living rooms. Where some goofy Dad-type is home after work, shirt unbuttoned, talking to the wife about the day's trials and the kids are play fighting in front of the TV. His old man used to launch him up into the air bellowing Peepo! In a second-hand cane chair wearing a brown-white triangle cardigan. His face was a big, oval laughing Buddha. He'd have been about twenty stone then; thickset with muscle. The pounding chest. Every boy wants to be their father; then spends their adult life trying not to be. Since he joined the army he hasn't seen his mam or his old man. They've talked on the phone and swapped Christmas cards. But he doesn't want to take sides since the divorce, get involved in their bullshit. He can't deal with them. Not with Evelyn. His head. One side of the street is red brick Council Houses: the other has cosy semis painted sour-cream white. Squirrels bound around the traffic over a cone-dimpled roundabout. A football pitch two hundred yards away. Clod and dirt. White chalk. Where he played in goal as a boy because he was already too stocky, too meathead girdered to play outfield. He once saved a penalty in a semi final like Gordon Banks clipping the ball over the bar with a crooked elbow flick. Your father chain-smoking on the side-lines. He'll bring his own kid here one day. Girls can play football now. The world changes. Anybody can do anything except be happy. What progress is this? Grey snow crisped across the pathway crunches underfoot. Rows of low-dangling willow tree branches wave a shore white-edged with snow; he hasn't strolled round here since he was a teenager. Evelyn had given up herself for him. Her belly round about to grow into Zeppelin-shaped pregnancy. Spaces for life, ever creeping, moving in secret like cells of bacteria. It's always the invisible things that fuck you, that hurt you. The everywhere dangers. The everyday threat. Evelyn knows about his night-sweats. She thinks she knows about Francesca, how? Gossip travels fast through Burley. The twisting and turning in the night. How he hates the white eyes of the brown faces and the photo flash. The porn star flare. You photographed them giving blowjobs. Crazy shit. You whip their arses and sit your balls on their faces. Tea-bagging. You can't remember if it was them or you The squad you were with. This is the war you fought. Soldier. You watched them do this. All guilt is white. Naked: you kick them in the balls and in handcuffs: the rest are made to wank their mates off. Guzzle. Belly laugh at their weasel dicks. The force of total will over another human: the thrill of evil enjoyment. You're not the worst. You've not fucked them. Bummed their hairy arses. Naked. Cock. You've done nothing to stop this. That's true. Guilty by association. You will be out the door. Dishonourable. Gun sweat rings your fingers; that aching trigger pulling. There's no litter round here. He will be another deadbeat Dad. His child will be another one like him; without the motion in their life's to move forward or toward anything. All John knows is how to survive; how to do it by sapping the life from others. Inside is always the gnawing hole, that God-shaped space. The prayer that echoes hollow like a coin down a well or voice to far away to hear. It's not good to be back – away he had the memory at least of what it was like; the fiction of home, of growing up round in his backyard. Now Burley has a palooka on a moped, riding the warbling cobbles. The ice-cream man sniffs coke. Selling twenty-bags to kids. You have been trained to kill and have fucked death. The dead are living in the wounds and the memory and the gunshots. The gravel in the rain. Shit and death and sleet and cunt. Soldier. Soldier. You are not worthy. You are a crime of war. Soldier. The bodies of the naked; the naked and the dead. The gunshot tremor. He hasn't told them he's back: his Mum, Dad, Brother. The happy family. They're like Reality TV. He can't be bothered with their fanfare, the accusations; the backlashes against one another and the way everybody has to take a side or pretend to have warm memories about times you remember weren't very good. And if you don't – somebody will turn against you and make out you don't care. Everybody believes he's too laidback. Nobody thinks he cares about anything. He knows his Dad was made redundant from the railway without much compensation, and that his Mum was trying to get enough capital to put down on a good house now the market has slumped. Some poor bastards are in negative equity. Living on promises in cardboard boxes. These Squirrels' have a nest and hoards of nuts. It is natural to save. Human nature to be impulsive. To want more than we can ever have. Tonight's breeze curls upward in his face as he finds the end of the street: a junction. Some punched up boozer on a corner. He gets his head down, and goes inside. Cranky old cunts guard their sports pages with laboured pints of Guinness. A panda-eyed, ancient landlady caked in make-up. This'll do. He turns his phone off and orders his first pint, leaning on the bar. One becomes two, becomes three. Four. Five. Three hours later and he's slurring to one of the old guys about tonight's match, accumulators.

'There's good odds on Owen.' The old man suggests in a nasal, tightly strung, middle-class voice.

'How'd yer know I liked a flutter?'

'Looked liked sort.'

'How's that?'

'You're in here, first. Second, you're drinking your self silly. You look reckless. A gambling man.'

'Only had o couple. Juss warming up.'

'Trouble and strife?'

'Summit like that.' They exchange knowing looks, two men propping up the bar. After the first match has been on (an exhaustively dull 1-1) there's the talking heads in the studio, well-tanned ex-footballers doing well for themselves; then there's the adverts aimed at guys like Ronnie and Carl. Razors advertised with F16 Falcons, online gambling and steak-flavoured crisps. Following the break, another game comes on. He raises his pint and looks around for a pool table that isn't there. The landlady gives him the eye and he avoids it, disgusted. The game gets into the second half and the old guy enjoying their silence is confident enough to retry the conversation.

They talk politics, crack a few gags then get onto women. The old guy's a windbag. 'Tell them what they want to hear; keep 'em happy, that's best thing you can do.'

'Then yer lose every fight tho?'

'Who's winning? I'll tell you now, if my Elsie were still alive lad, as God is my witness, I'd let her do what she liked.'

'Really?'

'You got kiddies?'

'One on't way.'

'Them's another reason. Keep it quiet.'

'How long were yow married?'

'Thirty eight years.'

'Good innings.'

'She drove me potty, she did.'

'Think they all do.'

'God put them on earth to make us better, son. Now that's the honest truth.'

'You think? Am not religious myself.' The other stiffs at the bar swap glances. They know he's getting into this old guys favourite territory, sermonising.

'World didn't make itself, stupid.'

'Dunt mean God did.'

'Who else: weren't you?'

'What did?'

'Like toh think of it as a sort o magic.'

'Who's magic?'

'Am not saying I noo.'

'You've a lot to learn. We all have. But though, I Daniel, shut up the words, and seal the book, even to the time of the end: many shall run to and fro, and knowledge shall be increased.'

'Not o clue woh that means.'

'Think on, think on.'

'I'll give it a goo.' They talk alcohol sodden words, dreary. The old guy starts to fall asleep into his drink. Divine knowledge. John likes being told off, corrected by an older head, even if he is a crank. They've been in life longer than he has. Done their time. Decades, cholesterol, pain.

The landlady has been watching and is keen to but in, 'Don't listen to this old timer. Talks nonsense.'

'Shut up Caroline.'

'Allos in here, talking about bloody God.' John notices the sparkle of a cross necklace under the cut of her blouse.

'He seems lark a knowledgeable bloke.'

She is holding off serving a punter, 'My advice to yer is yer look depressed. Yer wanna get yourself out with some lads yer own age.'

'Alcohol won't solve nothing.' The old man chimes.

'Cheers, the pair of yer. For yer help and that.'

The old man grabs the scruff of his collar, drawling into his ear. 'She's wanted me for years that tart.' By the time

John stands upright to go – juggling himself between his two shaking feet, he feels sick and guilty. He retraces his steps through leafy sludge, following the willow trees along the path. He pisses up a bush. Burps and farts. This street is endless. Dreamily staggering and plodding through the urban streets and looting foxes. Greenery. A pen barracked with oak trees and uniform gardens. He sees the trellised outline of his house. Orange bright. Closed curtains red like a matinee. The braggadocio night.

JOHN FEEDS HIS ARM through his marine-green jacket. About to leave, Evelyn catches him by the doorway's cloudy glass. Shapeless silhouettes if Carl and Popeye were to turn around from their Rugby match – speaking loudly.

'Where you going?' She whispers and puts her hand on the front-door and plants her feet down to form a barrier charged with John can't squeeze past.

'Am noh under house arrest.'

'No need to be such a grump.'

'Juss want some air.'

'Iss that it?'

'Yeah.'

'You ant asked me abaht scan.'

'I woh gonna.'

'I don't think you realise how big this is John? What this is going to mean for me? For us?'

'Trust me.' Her eyes are crushed diamonds, the corridor's twilight. Her hand slumps onto her belly and she nuzzles her head on her own chest, swan-like. John feels remorse burn through him, stinging hot at fingertips that reach out for her body and hug her, secure, tight. Strength compensates for brevity. He imagines Francesca watches and remembers her musk. Their silhouettes disfigured through glass.

'It'll be OK,' he says, 'We'll get out of here, away from all this and somewhere new. Where we can be us.'

'Please, promise meh.'

'On meh life.'

'Love yow.' Rough as sandpaper, his cheek grazes her lips as she gives him a kiss. Goodbye. He's on the move. Wades out into oceanic night; a lazy breeze blows creases into clothes hanging on washing lines. Long strides down the centre of the road. White lines between his steps. Tiny bats shriek through the early evening sky. Blues and yellows slowly swirl a deeper darkness. Already the paths are frozen smooth with black ice and he ignores the rows of parallel redbrick terraces that form a maze for miles around, the same street multiplied and repeated. Gardens spotted with the colours of Coca Cola cans and Carlsberg six-packs. Single-mum's appear at doorsteps like meerkats calling their feral children in for an overcooked dinner. This is England. He has fought to fuck. Fought for human rights, Fought to walk the streets without being terrorised. Disorder through the force of the state. But those days in the Iraqi sun are memories now, dreams you've lived distant as echoes. Night sweats. The thrilling ecstasy of battle. Warfare a calculated chaos. Sex is the nearest thing to violence. The powerful intimacy. Sacrifice of selves. He climbs the stairs to the Elbow Rooms up four heart rate elevating floors. There are posters of bands he's never heard of and gigs he'll never go to. Long-haired, angry little fuckers playing with rage and guitars. Tonight the bar is busy with students. Not the giddy workers who pile in on the weekends. Easier prey. Cocky. Overconfident. You can exploit their bucktoothed stupidity. Leaning her weight awkwardly to one side, spilling her curves into a contortion, Francesca's being chatted up by rah rah teenager in love with himself. She deflects his flirtations with a toothy smile and shirty sarcasm – though it's not working. She's a tough girl. Can usually handle herself. But this guy won't let up and has started to get pushy. John carefully puts down his pint and strolls over to the bar, inspired to protect.

'You alright Francesca love?'

'John. Leave it.' She announces with drama, her forehead creases and her eyes spell no. The rah makes a quiet exit as Francesca offloads her spite onto John.

'Thought he was hassling you.'

'I can handle myself, and anyway, he wasn't.'

'Thought you'd be more pleased to see me.'

'Yeah, well.' She dwells on the 'well' and watches John's confidence crack. Facial muscles slacken. With a white cloth she polishes herself into the surface – her morphed reflection denies the hard curves of her beauty.

'Who's that perv you're hanging with?'

'Some guy I went to school with.'

'Looks wrong.'

'He is. That's why I like him. He's o dirty bugger, bumped into him t'other week in One Stop.' John has ignored the texts Phil has been sending him, let's him sit alone in the corner of the bar and wait.

'What you here foh?'

'Drink.'

'Nowt else I yope.'

'Well.'

'The olly thing you good for is fucking things up.'

'Thass not o nice thing to say.'

'Evelyn.'

'Iss still not too late.'

'Do the right thing.'

'Am not sure what that is.'

'Yer should be.'

'Yeah, I know, but am not.'

'Iss not just you you've to think o.'

'My old man walked out on me. But meh step woh good, probably better.'

'Yow not lark him.'

'And I doh wanna be.'

'Good.'

'I mean what o say about yer.' John takes his pint and finds Phil in a semi-circular leather booth. Neon blurs on the menu in front of them as Phil excitedly tells him about the kind of porn he's into – web cam girls, late night adult chat rooms and then lists what everybody they knew at school are doing now. Students play boorishly on a nearby table. Boisterous in trash talk. Cunts faces: at least the Pakis can banter.

'What yer been up to then?' Phil asks, smiling, open and reclining into his seat.

'Bit o this, bit o that.'

'Where yer living?'

'Do yer remember Carl Brown?'

'See him every other week at petrol station.'

'Am there, with him, his kid and his missus.'

'Shit.'

'Gotta get out o there.'

'Bet thass weird. There's o lad I work with, his been living with some Poles in o house share.'

'Rather that, to be honest.'

'Right noisy buggers thee are.'

'I'd soon shut em up.'

'Got o bird? Bloke lark you must do alright. Got that soldier thing goin on – man in't uniform.'

'Not so easy any more.'

'No uniform?'

'Summit lark that.' He's left his mouth on autopilot and he can't take his eyes away from Francesca, hypnotically the way she works the bar, her presence. He sucks his thumb, licks a cut, remembering the other night.

'There's o couple I lark.' John answers.

'Fitties?'

'Fitties, fatties, I'll take any. Black. Brown. Green. So long as theh easy.'

'Easy as Snooker?'

'Pool now.'

'I've heard abaht that game o yours with the Pakis. Loads of us putting cash down on that.' John remembers why he hasn't spoken to Phil for years; he was a little pervert at school and would look up girls skirts (which John found funny) but he'd go on and on about things, got cheep thrills from everybody else. Francesca slowly fills a branded glass with lifeless lager. This shouldn't be attractive – her hand on the pump, modulating the gas flow – but he finds everything she does fit as fuck. A cue ball shoots off a table like an Oreo and knocks down a glass. The students to John's right – including the one who tried to chat up Francesca are arguing with some pissed off mosher cunt whose beer they've spilled. Bolts through his ear holes. They should back down. But the mouthy twat has balls and stands up the rocker, twice his age with a greasy, blonde beard. A fight breaks and there's no security early evening. Francesca freaks out and drops the pint she's pulling. The student and the mosher are tearing into each other and John runs over to break it up, getting one in a half-nelson, ripping him from his grip on the mosher and then gives him a slap, let's him know who's boss. The mosher stands John up and has a rant. Tells John he's a pussy. John pulls him tight, wraps his arm round his back in a hammerlock frogmarching him out of the bar and tells him to fuck right off.

Francesca sobs; arms hugging her knees as she crouches on the floor behind the bar. The other barmaid frantically tends to a growing queue, between pulling pints, she yells at Francesca who can only lip-read her anger, too panicked. John takes her wrist, strong in his hands, kisses her suddenly. Crying eyes to his chest to absorb her shock.

'I hate fighting.' She rocks, crying, 'Makes me sick.' When

the bar's closed and the night's over, John's waiting outside in a taxi. Talking about the fate of Leeds United and the glory days in Europe a few years before. They are wordless riding in the silence of the twilight streets; the taxi driver, a bull-necked darkie starts trying to get a handle on their situation, it makes John burn, his rubber lips in the wing-mirror. The white inches of Francesca's bare cleavage. The taxi stops short of the house and they get out, unwilling to argue for a few extra steps and walk hand-in-hand toward the white-crusted door; green mould toys, dogshit and packets of crisps. The air is crisp with night. That turmeric of humid leaves. Necklaces of weed underfoot touch texture with the slush gravel drive that their slow waltz is scrunching Twisting toe-steps. Tonight he sees everything – the walk to the door happens in slow-motion. His senses alert to new configurations. Key scratches on the lock: eternally slow. Their hop and skip up the staircase is clumsily non-intimate. Another door: a second lock. The slow key. Her flat is a room in an old Edwardian house: it would once have belonged to some rich dick and busy with the graft of servants and cleaners. The likes of us. Francesca says a weird, muscled bald man (who does odd jobs for the landlord) lives downstairs and smokes weed every day with his shirt off. He has his five year old lad over on weekends. Broken families. Those of us carrying scars. The other flats are taken up by young couples and professionals she barely sees. They keep their own time, their own hours. John takes out a carton of cigarettes, top open, and sticks his tattooed arm toward Francesca. There's sadness and shock seeing how poorly she lives: the communal landing that smells of retro damp and the tiny bedsit with the strip of kitchen she's done her best to make her own. Candles and pictures and clothes all over the floor. The place is rich with the musk of her. He feels like he's smoked two or three packets of cigarettes.

Sitting on the edge of the bed, their hands close to touching, wrinkled in touches of smoke; they smoke their cigarettes. Halfway to sleep, ashtray white ashen, Francesca docks the side of her face into his shoulder: her hair is straggly, deeply auburn up close and roseate-scented.

'Thes dirty socks everywhere love.'

'Shurrup.'

'Yer o dirty one.'

'Not now, eh?'

'Am not avin o go. Juss. Yer know.'

'Dick.' They laugh, falling over the duvet, Francesca turning into his kisses. Her mouth full, face sensitive to his nuzzling, the three-day beard. She cups his face in her hands. They kiss like the RomComs they've been watching. They didn't feel like a thing they could do that they hadn't already seen. John loves to spend his days thinking he's in a low-budget action movie. Discarded layers of underwear. Bags of make-up tossed across the floor; bandy leggings, the lobster pincers of a hair-straightener. Their breaths are fire. Slipping from their clothes, pulling t-shirts over their heads and down to their underwear, hands pressed to arse, swimming under fabric. The squid rubber of skin. She teases up his shirt with a brave hand, curved nails trailing and kisses his manly gut, the hairy paunch above the burping crater of his belly button. They are smiling. Dumbly. Thick with love. He is jealous of the night's darkness: anything that steals away his precious sight of her, supple flesh, coming free that he had lusted over so many nights, so many days. The fullness of her lips. The richness of her breath. He sees wisps pubes and her warm wet gash. Overcome, he thumbs down his own briefs, tangling around his ankles and guides her hand, unresisting, over his stabbing penis. He is surprised by her shyness, her reticent slow stroking that quicken and milk as she gains confidence. There's not been time for his usual trick of washing his foreskin in the bathroom. His gesture of respect. They bump heads. John's rhythm doesn't seem to be coming as easily as it usually does and her mouth is warm and damp, the mists of breath and ecstasy thrills his cock. Pounding. The throb and tremor of higher heart rates. This pleasure is unbearable as headfirst, in a tickling outpour, the Medusa's head of flickering hair and her mouth, twisting tongue that takes him deep into the suck and gag of her slaying rhythms. Their body's are land and ocean, elements. She fingers stroking his bollocks. Gently, John finger frigs her wet cunt and rib-eye of clitoris. She's careful with the toothless sucking her lips. His cock in her mouth. Physical warmth strobes across their skin. She's electric. John gasps and groin punches with spasms and that urge to thrust, to fuck her dark-tongued mouth. Feeling close to coming, the tempting itch in the fraenum; he returns the gesture, the split of her legs and curling his hands around her the her tan lined thighs, licking hungrily between the precarious descent of gash. Eating cunt: he recoils nuzzling his face in rough curls of pubic hair. A teenager, recalling the vibrant instinct of his thirteen year-old self, the fooling around in the park, he slides the inches of finger and feels beckoning for the spot that has taken him a lifetime to find. Toward deeper, twisting spasms. He can't believe he's gonna deep-dick her; sweating, his heart throbs. She sucks salts from his fingers, licking between joints. Put it in me. Now. John Usher. The condom is inside his jacket pocket in a compartment of his wallet. Fuck. Streamed wet with lubricated arousal and gorged supple, he slows his pulsing length into her. Foreskin raging backward, head stabbing. Breaths stagger sharp. You dirty bitch. He had been afraid of not being able to satisfy her. Idiot. Nothing has ever felt as natural. Love. He could fuck anybody. The World. These thrusts dimpling his buttocks: she absorbs him deep inside the muscles of her.

Screaming orgasm, she rips tiger-stripes in his back. Thrusting, sinking: he groans, sinking, with pleasure. She has hunks of his hair in her hands, whispering. This is real. His face beams hot sweats. Remembering they're bareback, not wanting another bastard child, he pulls out. Sudden bolts cumshot her belly. She rubs the semen hot into her peachy flesh, licking the vanilla from her fingers. This way she tastes the sea-salts of a man.

Weak and silent, he lay his face on her breasts, defeated. Her hand brushes the side of his head. They lay breathing slowly, becoming cold, careless, on the semen-drizzled duvet. John goes for a piss and has to wait for the pipes to flow, the light swaying under the crazy strobing light bulb. He is suddenly embarrassed by his nudity and remembers he's in a communal bathroom, dick stinking of sex and pubes rusted with the dribble of her cunt. Shrivelled into a wrinkled wattle, seeking warmth, his penis returns to his body. Back in the bedroom after a nervous shuffle across the landing, he finds her under the sheets pretending to be asleep. He sees her prostrate shoulders and the brightness of her hair, the way he feels his life has been leading to this moment. There is nothing else in the stars or the sky. She is his little everything. He climbs back into bed pressing his cold slab of muscled chest onto her smoother, slimmer slab of back.

'Night love'.

She rolls onto her side, clutching the sheets, 'Am not sure this woh o good idea.'

John's jaw hardens, 'Why?'

'This is not o good idea.' She makes a cheerleader squeal, thrusting her face into the pillow, 'Can you go?'

'Can weh talk abaht it?' She feels his hand on her shoulder, the tremolo in his voice.

'Don't touch meh.'

'OK.' His dick feels ridiculous, exposed. Rapey.

'I can go if yer want.'

'No, no. Am been stupid.'

They gather in a cuddle, 'Am not easy, me yer know? Yer won't want me. Not when yer know me. Am not with all this. It dunt come natural to meh. Av got Jake too. Iss not fair on him to confuse him.'

'Relax, yeah? Take it easy.'

'Am trying.'

'We juss had sex. Thass it. Nothing more. We both grown ups. Wiv done this sorta thing before. Don't get carried away – it wer just sex.'

'Alright.'

'Seriously, don't get funny.'

THE MORNING is bright. A breezy cool. Daylight scours John's unseeing eyes that are gummy as he wakes. The scents and sex fluids of last night are dried like bruises, pressed into the paper of his flesh. Francesca's already alive, wrapped in a dressing gown and playing Domestic Goddess in the kitchenette. An old-style kettle chugs puffs of steam.

'Thes not much for breakfast. Do yer want scrambled egg?'

'Yeah.'

'Put telly on if yer want.'

'Can yer come here?'

'Got these cups o tea on go.' Her system is all wrong, the eggs in the pot are being frazzled, growing the chewy crust that John hates. The kettle still needs taking off the hob.

Eventually, he turns off the hob. Her breasts swaying scandalously under the cleavage of her dressing gown. Stops.

'Am not going till we sort our sen out.'

'John, you're a lovely guy. But.'

'Yeah. Go on. Say that.'

'I can't get involved with somebody – not now. Not you.'

She has come to sit beside him on the bed, he has to resist sliding his hand between her thighs. He has been inside her. Whatever happens. Whatever is said, that can't be taken away.

'Am not gonna mess yer about.'

'Yer said it woh just a fuck.'

'Iss never just o fuck.'

'Yer expect meh to believe that?'

'Fucking too right.'

'I need to be single, for me. To get myself together. You don't even have a proper job. Yer o pool monkey.'

'Shark.'

'As if that meks it any better.'

Last night has made him confident, assertive. His performance a money-shot in his mind, like elegance. Thinks of rhyming bodies, screaming feelings, the sex was enough for her to come back to him; he doesn't need to beg. Shush.

'I've got this rematch with Malik. Am not doing that badly for myself. I earn more than you – with me dole and what I pick up playing the tables. I hate it. But on the dole, yer get everything paid for yer. Am better off than if I yad some dead-end job.'

'So that's alright, is it? Mugs lark me go out to work and then thes John Usher ripping us lot off. Yer not in some silly film. I can't believe I even fell for yer. Yer ridiculous.' When she's angry, a rippling creases the middle of her forehead. Growly eyes. Traces of other accents: foreign.

'Iss not me ripping yer off. What decent bloke would work one of those jobs? Theh not for me. Am not one for gossiping round the fucking water shed or whatever they yav. I yate admin. I can barely read or write. Them's not a man's job. Am a big useless cunt I yam. Women don't even need yer no more. They've got benefits and IVF. Blokes lark me: well, weh juss fucking dildos. Six-foot dildos.'

She can't help but laugh. He has a silliness about him, a boyishness when he tries to say sound meaningful. 'Yer not a dildo ... Yer just a nobhead. Don't take this personally. I know everybody says it, but iss not you. Any other time. It'd be different.'

'I'd love to work. I'd love to work down o mine. Or building ships or whatever. Am not working in a fucking coffee shop. And security works is o slap in the face.'

'Won't work or can't work?'

'I don't know where yer get yer morals you.'

'Some of us were brought up right.'

'OK. Whatever. Can weh juss shag?'

'Yer juss said o fuck is never jut o fuck.'

'I want you, love.'

'Yer can't have everything yer want. Thass your problem, John. You want it all. Your way. All the time. Life's not lark that.'

'It can be. Life's what yer make it.'

'I want a quiet life. A man with o job for a start. And I'll have Jake staying with meh again soon. Thass partly why am so stressed and trying get things straight. You know thah.'

'A proper bloke. Not just a six-foot dildo?'

'Would yer stop going on about that? Jeez. Yer not o dildo, yer are a big nobhead though.' She smiles, shark-like.

'Av only been out of army for two minutes. Listen. You just wait. Wait, yeah? I'll get me sen sorted. Turn myself around.'

'Yer bad news you.'

'Aren't we all, aren't we all love.' The walls are a Victorian green in the stodgy daylight: the condensation trickled window left open last night with a breeze chiming the blinds. A framed photo of her young lad Jake on the mantelpiece with a bull-necked darkie who must be her abusive, ex-boyfriend.

EVELYN AND FRANCESCA. Francesca and Evelyn. John aligns his fingers expertly on the table to form a bridge: shoots. Soon this will be for real – the club will be full of punters who have put their bets on. The atmosphere will change. Evelyn had been the bookmaker, doing the dirty work while Carl had come up with the maths, the odds, the money, the stake horse. Whatever happens John will make money and come out better than he was going into the game; the only thing he can lose is his pride, his ego by taking a dive for Malik. But if he wins – he wins. There isn't another option. Abortion. His body feels good today. Without the musical pops and creaks in his joints, the stucco flex in his fingers. Works his body into the shot, fires a spot with pinpoint accuracy.

There's been discussion on who referees the game. How they'll keep things fair and the crowd from laying into one another? Have the police heard? The dried crisp walls are crumbling; the game machines turned have been turned off to save money giving the place a new silence, without the incessant, overactive background noise. Last night they left Stella Artois off. Criminal, to John's mind. A vast conspiracy is working against him. Things are rough and bare. Memories bigger than dreams. Reason to get out. He wouldn't be able to hang around in Francesca's trendy metro pool circuit for long: he'd be an outsider, a weirdo with nothing to do. Exposed. The place smells of disinfectant – Evelyn has a mop and a bucket and goes to work on the stale floors. Somewhere Carl's trying to balance the books for a visit from Head Office.

They begin to argue, loudly. Evelyn's shouting voice is polished and high-pitched, humblingly Yorkshire. Cutting to the rougher edges of her upbringing. Those layers of smoke and sex and years of false sophistication. John is open to argument. Sensitive his people and their quirks. Now they're not the salt of the earth. The scum on the streets. Death has given him eyes. Carl barks expletives, doggedly; when he's at the Headingley for the rugby; at EDL rallies.

These voices are shawn. A smack. Carl stands soothing the back of his hand and Evelyn buckles to her knees, crying. A violet bruise swells quickly on her cheek. John squeezes his cue, tight, then tighter; hearing knuckles crack to grip the wooden base. The fight dies down, Carl tending to Evelyn, apologizing for his fists. John has to ignore it, block it out, avoid the distraction - and eyes the table, sees only the bright baize and the coloured baize, around him, around the table is fluid darkness. He walks the length of the outer edges, counting his steps, heel to foot, working the angles. Practice makes perfect. Time passes and the table is cleared, then cleared again: as night catches up on the place, crowds of thugs and hard-nosed locals, gamblers and gang members gather around the four sides of the full-size American table, squaring followers of John and Malik. Strangers caught up in the excitement come over from other tables, give up their solo games to see why this gathering has divided brown and white faces?

'Money's sorted, John.' John pulls the long zip of his black plastic cue jacket, a gift from Carl. A fat cylinder of cash in his hand. They've collected the bets. Crinkled notes and rancid coins in a charity box. Evelyn beside on a makeshift table. She's good with numbers. Understands the odds and has a log of everybody's stake. Carl has given John a down payment of one thousand. Keep him sweet. Make sure they know whose boss. John feels the nerves not of potential loss, but performance anxiety; knowing he's going to have to put on a show, work out escape routes.

'Good luck.' Evelyn says with her pencil in hand, hair locked in blonde curls: she's lost vigour since she's fallen pregnant. No lump visible. But John can see. Throbbing like a pulse on a radar screen - glowing red. Carl hasn't seemed to pick up on anything yet. Hard to see in the dark - her bruised cheekbone struck salmon bright.

'What's that?'

'Nothin. Just banged my head on the door. Anyway, not long now. Good luck.'

'As if I need it.'

'I mean for us.' She smiles and John thinks of himself as some kind of cunt. Francesca has a position the other side from them, nearer the Asians, and smokes a cigarette with a cool calmness, a moll chick from those gangster movies. Malik's getting directions from a man with a matt black beard, the proud darkness invites sparkles of light and seems devout, more religious than Malik could ever claim to be. There's a crackling of chatter and not much action. John doesn't know who's meant to be adjudicating, who's in control? The two competitors circle the table, away from the other, waiting for direction. A method. John gasps and takes his pint in his hand. Watering his dry mouth, babbling beer through his molars feeling its slow kerosene sink downward into his burning gut.

Francesca taps him on the shoulder, with Evelyn watching from the other end of the table. She greets him with a smile that he's not seen before, something accepting and vulnerable about it; so he squeezes her hand white and says, 'I'll leave her.'

'Yer don't have to.'

'I want to.' Carl has since taken charge of what's going on and has directed a flunky to arrange the balls, and keeps handing off Malik's posse who keep getting in his face. 'Fuck you.' Says Carl and pushes his heft through a thicket of people to find John.

'Money's no object, mate. Remember that.'

'Cheers mate.'

'I'll stake yer all night long.'

'What the fuck are all these pakis doing here? Thell kill me.'

'Who gives a shit?' Carl sweeps John's face in the palm of his hands, like a boxing coach and the uplift of stench repulses John, beefy armpit and cigar smoke.

MALIK TOSSES A COIN that flashes a streak of light and decides who'll take the break. He huddles low, scrum-like, to uncoil the contracted anger, the hidden power of his thick muscles, steering the cue ball deep into the triangular pack, spilling them like coins, a hard firm contact, the spank of a sweet strike. He pokes a four stripe. Comes back strong with a nick of the seven and into the round hole, billowing in revolutions, as if warm, into the loose netting. He misses an easy three - pulled it? But that would make the game too easy, too put up, even if he is meant to win. Does Malik think John's that bad? Shivering resins of sweat shine on the heads of the crowd. John tees up for his first shot with rising excitement from the crowd, the odd whistle and clear shout of encouragement. He assesses the fallout, the wreckage. He refines a plan in his minds eye, carrying the dimension of the balls like CGI, the special effect of his head - to poke a ball through two spheres. With enough force he'll be round the back and able to tidy up from behind.

John's plan works before he comes unstuck when he scuffs with his dry nib, forgotten to chalk-up. Malik takes the table, rejoined by a different accent of noise, the latent Arabic in the cheers of his support. John only has two to pot and Malik's making a mess of it. He can't pick up a steady rhythm. Instead his play is slow, stilted, with fractured shots that snap rather than play smooth and long, free from jangling nerves. Malik's final miss collides into the cushion, rocketing back with increasing force separating his clear sight of two balls paired around the black. At a glance, Francesca and Evelyn share facial expressions – a pouted gasp, a sense of dread, and fear. Carl's mood barely wrinkling his stare. Steely-faced, woody-headed, demanding victory. As if victory could reverse a decline. There is a new kind of zeal in his face; like when he's ranting, expect more controlled. Measured. John disposes his last three tidily and weighs the black's heavy stillness, untouched, the duration of the game. Simple shots are the hardest. John plays it safe, striking as he was taught by his pervy step dad, That's right John. That's right. The shot follows the easy mathematics, rolling the black into a crowded pocket.

The crowd roars like Elland Road. Yorkshire. Yorkshire. Yorkshire. He takes a sip of his pint; the game has made him thirsty. He can feel a ping in his heartbeat, a stiffness in his walk, how he can stand in front of that crowd and lay his game when two months ago he couldn't play a soul. He doesn't fear Malik, or Carl, not any more. He sees his opponent talking tactics with the bearded man. What the fuck does that guy know about pool? John's played pool for twenty years. He knows the laws of the game, the way to bend them to your will, to get the luck. The light dab and the power push there. How a good player always plays several shots ahead, whatever the outcome of the next.

There's a crick in his thumb that catches the flow of his break; stunts the shuffle of the balls that no longer belong to him. It's a capricious turn when luck deserts you and you're a piece of shit again, a no good piece of shit, who can't muster any explanation as to where it's gone or how you ever did it.

'Thass right John. Keep to the plan. Don't you be riding me.' Malik works on the crest of badly separated balls: clockwise with a sharp peck of the cue, rifling downward on the angle, he two-steps, sideways, following the curve of opportunity, gaining confidence that slips from John.

'Fuck me.' John drives the black rubber back of his cue into the floor staring round at the angsty faces, the huddle round the table. Eighteen feet. A cell of baize. They're on the centre table: slap bang in the middle of the upstairs floor. Malik feverishly drives the black. John knows this is a stage game: the money is already his, already won. But there's pride at stake between Malik and John. They can't deny their rivalry, their want to appear better, to save face in front of a partisan crowd. John goes three games down, then four, five. When you're in full flow you cannot help but win, and then the inverse is true. His facial muscles feel manipulated, under pressure by the judgemental glares.

Alone, at the corner of the game, he balks his cue. Carl's hand appears, as it has a habit of doing, on his back. Then the gruff voice and the gestures. 'You keep going mate. Yer can turn this round. Money's no object. You focus on yer name.'

'Am better than him, I know it.'

'Well bloody well a go.' He wins the next: gets a feeling of rhythm in his hands, the inner percussion of his bones. The way the game emerges from you, instinctively, edgy and alert. Then the fear of Malik's power play puts him on the back foot. He slips four more in a row. The crowd are edgy. A break in play.

Carl is in his corner again. 'Thass twelve grand, I make it.'

'Sorry, Carl. I've got it in me. I know.'

'Thass desperate talk.'

'Seriously, one more chance.'

'Yer don't think am paying?'

'What?'

'Thass how much it costs to fuck my wife. The whore.'

'Carl?'

'Am not a monster. Don't flinch. Just remember what a cunt you are mate. What a fucking cunt.'

'I've not lost yet.'

'No, I have. Hope yer happy.' Turning toward the EXIT he elbows through the crowds of thick shouldered Asians and whites, shouting you're all fucking dirt paki bastards, rapists, whores and reprobates round here. You nasty little cunts. Dirty paki bastards. The fat cylinder of cash in his hands.

JOHN KNEW THE GAME would become too tempting, too seductive for him to simply throw away. He watches the table, catching a thought that will be his next shot. There is no reason to lose. With Carl gone his arms come free, he has the freedom of the table. He can take free aim. A strike at whichever one impresses, chooses for difficulty, the toughest shot. Dashes the cue with ticklish chalk and lets the shots work through his body: from ankle to shin, shoulder to back. Keeled, his eye sternly upon the table, the purple lamp lit baize and he pots the game's hardest shot - styling a seven that had got tucked behind a pair of heavy spots in front of the far pocket. The shot courses through him and already he's thinking about the next, the one after, the one after. The shot-paths align in the brain-shaped labyrinth of his mind.

He wins two more games. Malik is shivering. Malik doesn't follow what John's doing and only watches as he screws and pots, slams and swerves every ball in sequence, as good as he has. Whether it was the barracks after a hard days work; when he was a kid, after school playing in his Granddad's summer house; when he'd come in this place to play by himself and drool over and dream of Francesca - just to get away from the chaff daze, the noise and pictures of war that stay in his head and the montage of violence; how his day feels bruised, open, empty without the necessity for war, for structure, the MoD's guidelines on how to live your life, every day. But that's gone. No more bombs. But the rattle stays in your head, still combs through your thoughts. You can't escape it, you can't let go of yourself, the way you were and the things you did. Every explosion. Every clenched fist and brutal persuasion. The light of searchlights on midnight patrol and the cool of the Iraqi streets after sunlight, after the skirmishes that last long into the night and the constant background noise of bangs and explosions. You've given that up. And that pain: that wobble you felt in your belly and the nail-bomb in your head the first morning you woke up as a civilian; turning on the TV to the morning news - to stories about Kabul and Afghanistan, other troops, other boys, guys doing your old work. That is not you any more. The big piss-up of freedom. Wondering how you'd fit yourself back into an old life that doesn't fit any more? The pressure of hours, the tedious days, the daytime streets, the boring air. The silence of it. Stillness. A calm day, like a civilian sky. You don't want mercy and you don't want to work. You shagged the birds you wanted. You tricked and hustled the games and the pricks you had to. There is always war. Constant war. The two selves. Now you're winning. Luck is with him. Now he top spins the black hovering over the pocket before it drops and the crowd rises to cheer. A riot breaks out. The first to ten. Francesca claps knowingly and John thrusts his cue fiercely into the air.

III

THE MONEY from the game is enough to tide John over for a couple of months: he artfully joins Francesca's name in black ink on an envelope with a sum twice that she lost in the original game. He writes his name bold in unjoined letters. Over his shoulder he hears Evelyn coming down the staircase. Pregnant steps. Heavy as a baby's life. Two weeks since they moved in and Evelyn has a theory for everything. What goes in the kitchen. The colour the walls should be painted. How to spend his cash. He nature has changed from playful and girlish, to hectoring and subordinate; needing John's affection and assistance. She gains self-confidence and big ambitions from property shows. DIY SOS. How to get on The Housing Ladder? These unchanging, middle-class, one-size fits all blueprints for how we should live.

John and Evelyn sit in front of the commanding TV: both feel pregnant. Her cooking was adapted to suit Carl's requirements, greasy and carb heavy. Oven lumber. Her huge portions are man-sized. Sat deep in his chair John thinks sympathises with Carl. How he saddled himself here chain-eating peanuts, weightless corn puffs and round-tipped chocolate biscuits. Riled about the world. Hungry for anything he could to graze. Off-duty in front of the TV like John is today. Ronnie rang him up last night and Carl's in denial. Reckons Evelyn will come back to him. Thinks he's being punished for his affairs early in their marriage. Bullshit. On the glass oval coffee table by his feet – there's a copy of Glamour and it's the same old stories; movie premières and dresses, gossip about affairs, unloved lovers, sordid romances, who's got cellulite and who's got skinny. Silence overwhelms him as he walks out into the leaf heavy garden. A cigarette his firebrand in the night. The dusky moon botched by darker clouds. Starless. The sky bigger than any thought is larger than any mind. There are no words. That aren't shale and matter. He exhales a fug of smoke through his mouth and nose. These houses are semi-detached terraces with bay windows and carefully tended, miniature gardens. The streets are the same for the next square mile. Verged with green bushes, occasional streets: jams of unmoving cars. His aunt lived here for a good twenty years with her girlfriend. They never came out. Easier to pretend they were sisters. They've gone to live in the Bahamas and Paula lets them rent the place for cheap. John's something of a surrogate son. Aunt Paula was short, dark featured and Christine's nose was like a beak, her hair grey blonde. They never wore make-up, or dresses. It annoyed his Gran. In The Lion King their spirits would be cast against the sky, another phase in the circle of life. But that was bollocks. There is life. You walk about, do things, feel things, have a laugh, get pulled along by your gut and then die. Death. He used to think about it under the sunsets, wrapped up in his gear in Baghdad. You didn't talk about it. But when you missed a target. It was always the women who made the most noise. In their black shawls, brown faces, in groups of threes, and fours bawling wildly. The hedge needs trimming. She'll have him on that tomorrow. The gut. The house. The wife. Baby in the oven. He's growing middle-aged. Because Evelyn screws when he slings a tab in the garden, he walks out into the road and tosses it through a grate into the fast, furious sewer.

Evelyn becomes easier to deal with at night, pliant, relaxed loving in a clinch on the sofa; her hand calm on crotch, warningly along his thigh. He resumes position, grooved in the sofa and tonight's property show's about a couple who want more space in their house: a pair of blacks, richer and more eloquent than John, he feels the torrent of words preached to him by Carl feel good, then spiteful. The presenter is a Geordie architect twat who's better looking than John, everybody on the box has something that you don't, they are who you can't be. John can see the images and information filter through Evelyn's eyes, waits for her tiredness to kick in, so he can have some time to himself, Match of the Day. Somewhere in her gut is the next John Usher, some tadpole-like creature. He's not old to be having his first kid. Half the guys in his class at school have; half the guys in the army. His watch ticks ten-thirty. Francesca will be pulling pints and giving banter that knocks those pervs back down to size.

The lamplight and central heating create a sleepy, hazy atmosphere. They hug: Evelyn hugging tighter. Then the grip comes slack as she falls asleep, gently snoring. They don't talk about Carl or Francesca. Sometimes she talks about Popeye, wondering how he's getting on. The pool games. The long nights round the baize. The cramped weirdness of living under Fat Carl's roof. That's all forgotten, or not talked about. Evelyn's weight numbs his leg. He kisses her hair. Tonight's matches are Man United against Aston Villa. Portsmouth have to go to Upton Park. Leeds United had played at Carrow Road: these days you only get a thirty-second snapshot on the local news just before the Weather. A hard-on warms his thigh, begins its pointless swell. The highlights are getting started. He cracks open a can of Budweiser and Evelyn murmurs in her sleep. When Match of the Day finishes, an acidic sting burns through his stomach. He should eat. His belly lining's running on low. 'C'mon pup.' He lugs Evelyn onto his shoulder and spanks her rump arse. Lights out. Climbing stairs to the Egyptian Mystique scented bedroom. Window opens. Thrilling with serious cold. Door closed and light on the landing. John's silhouette is a dark cowl projected onto the ceiling. Evelyn whispers her sweet nothings snuggling deeper under the covers and John reclaims her, down to his white vest and baggy boxer shorts. She's stripped to a t-shirt and no underwear; under her top he feels her fluid breasts – filling the open cup of his palm. Something's not right. Twenty minutes pass and he's awake. The darkness alerts him. He's on guard. Has to move. His muscles doesn't fit his bones – tightly cramped, the twisting sinews and loose conditioning. A tense muscular armour. But this isn't Iraq. This is different. He senses that. This is the set-up. Screams are muffled inside him. Scar his heart's tremulous fabric. This life is spooky. Poor Evelyn. Any other girl and he would've already bolted. Even though he's hot he rolls Evelyn in his arms. She's deep in oblivious in sleep. Nightmares.

Two or three in the morning, she catches him asleep, screaming. His body shocking. Night sweats. 'John, love.'

Exasperated, sucking breaths, 'Yeah.'

'You were screaming again.'

'Sorry.'

'I read online that if yer talk about it, yer might get some resolution.'

He is facing away from her, 'Resolution? Jesus.'

'No need to play hardman now.'

He breaks into tears, still facing away, 'I've done some bad things, yer know? Some terrible things.'

'I've seen reports, it wasn't you.'

'I was there. I didn't do nowt.'

Shivering, 'Then there's you, and Carl, and all the rest.'

'It'll be alright, everything will be alright.'

EVELYN'S sitting the kitchen table reading a book of baby names. 'Come on now, is this o good idea?' She turns her head, expressionless, grey and vacant.

'Me Uncle woh called George, we could call him that. '

'Too posh.'

He takes a seat beside her, 'Am not being presumptuous. Have I said that right? Yeah, presumptuous.'

'Sally said she liked Graydon.'

'What the fuck? That's a Gaylord name. He'd get the shit kicked out of him.' He picks up a newspaper, 'Who's Sally?'

'Just an old friend. Been nice not working, or having Carl breathe down me neck.'

'What about Bruce?'

'No. No.'

'Jack. Thass a solid name.'

'Don't sound too enthusiastic.'

'Iss early days yet.'

'Maybe if I was called Francesca?'

'Don't start this up.'

'Yer don't deny it, d'yer?'

'Yes, I had feelings for her. Thass over now. We're together now and yer having me baby.'

'And if I weren't?'

'Maybe am not ready to be a Dad?'

'Yer better start getting ready ... Because iss happening.' She knows this has been coming. She had done nothing wrong: she had loved him, angrily. She seems more of a women now, wounded; he can see the stern apprehension in her eyes, the wasted, abortive look in her face.

'Look. Am off for a pint with some of the Burley Liberal lads later. Can we talk when am back?'

'Anything for a quiet life.'

His face is still in the newspaper, 'This is the thing with women, right. When yer not with them, theh normal people, theh con you into it. Then they turn. Go ape shit.'

'Big man has his masculinity threatened?'

'And what the fuck is all this feminist bullshit yer keep throwing at me. Are yer nuts?'

'Am starting to think all sex is rape.'

'Jesus Christ.'

'Don't fob me off.'

'Wish someone would rape me. Good God.'

'Don't say the Lords name.'

'Would you fuck off telling me what to do?'

'Tell me how you feel.'

'You can fuck right off missus. Right off.'

'Let me in, please.' She offers her hand, the knotted bridges of her fingers and the moon-cuticle nails with particulars of life, grooved underneath. Later, in the hallway, he comes back from the pub. Evelyn has a mug of soup in her hand. 'Am so sorry.' He has broken into tears, salty cheeks; they are standing with feet a yard, a universe away.

'For what?'

'I've tried, Eve.'

'Don't do this.'

'You've got Carl, yow married.' Her body crumples, and she starts coughing as she's choking.

His hand on her shoulder, 'Yer a lovely woman.'

'Get out!' She has him by the collar, pushing, 'Get out! I gave everything. You nasty cunt.' In the evening, Evelyn sits in the spare room that could be their baby's, hugging an oversized Winnie the Pooh teddy bear and twirling a spaceship on the cot's mobile. There are no curtains up, and late in the night, she thought she could hear the sound of pool balls coming into contact, rhythmically over and over again. But John, redeemed, was laying arrogantly in their bed, sleeping.

BY MID-MAY the weeds have taken over: the crowns of green root and dagger between paving stones. Several weeks since the big game; the fallout. John makes it home his eyes are drunk and bleary. He opens the door carefully.

Expecting shrieks and weak fists, cutlery to be coming his way, he shields his body with the door and pokes his head round. Nothing. No noise or sound. He makes his way toward the living room and then upstairs, trying his best to find his pregnant girlfriend. Lost her, he grumbles to himself. Lost me girlfriend. On the landing outside the toilet, she is unconscious. Wrapped in his England shirt and naked underneath, she shivers on the floor. WAR CRIMINAL is written on the oval mirror in wild red lipstick.

'Eve? Fucking hell. C'mon.' he kneels, his hand on her shoulder. Her look is blank, doesn't say what's wrong, 'Fucks sake? Evelyn. Can you here me?'

He dials 999 on his phone: and is redirected to the regional call centre operator. He goes through all the usual commands. Is she breathing? Yes. How long has she been in this state?

'Eve, love.'

'Don't patronise me, you misogynist.'

'I've called an ambulance.'

She is baby small, in his hands, confusedly drawling, 'Yer don't want me. Yer never have.'

There's the glossy cover of a Abortion – Your Questions Answered on the toilet seat.

'It'll all be over for yer soon, John.' Her stare is hollow; contains vertigo like distances. A recrimination. Fall.

Closer, collar to cheekbone. Cheek-to-cheek. Her limp body. The hospital smells like microwave food and has the buzzing background electricity of his old TV set. He female whispers through knots of sweat-fingered hair.

'What's happened? The air is heavy. Pressure comes from the four corners of the room – Evelyn's silence. Cold and rigid, she shivers and sobs onto floral pillows. His body is warping through shapeless space; twisting through oblivion. In a few decades he'll be a child again, under somebody else's care, dribbling into a bib and too past it to know. Then death. The Raven on the horizon waits for you. Ashes. On the killing fields. Stiff corpses jagged-limbed in their death poses. Evelyn holds her tummy. Won't let go.

In the white bed, lined up to several drips and scanners, her voice croaks: 'Yer got what yer want.'

'Eh?

'Don't touch me.'

'Am sorry.'

'No, please. Don't. Am sorry. All me life I've been messed around, let me self be second-best. Not no more.'

'What about baby?'

'What baby?'

'No.'

'I never want to see yer again.'

'But the baby?' He does as she says. At home, in the basement, there's only the black to pot. Sitting by the far right pocket, in acres of green baize. John's plays himself again. His toughest own opponent, like Ronnie the Rocket. He's nervous. He's not done this for months. Not since he got back. Or the games with Malik and living with Carl; before Francesca and Evelyn. Eyes move across his body, self-conscious. He missed three or four sitters on the run up to the black, he's out of practice. He pushes on the four pads of his fingers, eye on the trajectory, the cue wiggling over the crook in his fingers. Eyes the ball, noses the cue. Eyes the ball and the light shifts, sways. A scythe. Light and darkness swaying. The cellar is old and dank, strewn with cobwebs and chalky walls that powder his back and elbows, as he moves through the tight spaces a couple of feet too short for a table. He bought the thing yesterday at a dodgy auction a guy in the bookies told him about. When pubs and snooker bars close down, like any other shop, the liquidators step in and sell the assets and strip the place down. Probably what'll happen to Carl's place in Leeds. They'll find new jobs. The world moves on. Life never escapes you: Death. Where the suffering began. Would its dark balm bring him peace? He wonders about the stories, the characters that have been round this table; its baize frayed, the outside wooden rim is burnt scarred. Evelyn asked him how he could buy a pool table at a time like this; when they had no money and things are getting strained, they are falling out of love and she doesn't understand, this is why he needs it. The only thing that calms him these days. The black still sits at the far end, he's afraid to miss. She says she doesn't blame him. He wants to feel more grief and do what's right for once – when he gets near, a current electrifies him, stands the stiff hairs on his neck. His belly tightens. His hands feel clumsy and rape-fingered. Everything he says is bullshit. The kind of crap you read in greeting cards. Words that aren't worth saying. Useless. She told him yesterday and she was afraid of seeing the blood, the dark richness filling the bowl; this shouldn't be the resting place of a baby. Dead Babies. The sewers must be full of misery. Waste. Last night, hugging on the flat-backed sofa he believed he loved her. Whoever you get with they'll always be other girls, things you can't have. Sweeter arses and tighter pussies. Every day we lose something. Energy. He takes his shot with the broad light in his eyes. The glove-white cue strokes the black and the eight-ball saunters slow and portly stopping before its drops. The resistance of these worn-out tables makes him think he may as well be playing on AstroTurf, the bobbled surface. Some days you pot what you like. You really are Ronnie O'Sullivan. Some days you're not. He hears Evelyn's voice in his head – motherly and guiding – showing she's tried to enjoy his interests – some days Ronnie O'Sullivan doesn't turn up. Some days we are our own shadows. Whatever people say he is, that's what he is. A deadbeat piece of shit. Playing this stupid game is a conversation. Every shot a question begging his belief for answer. He'd feel a cunt explaining it to anybody. He stalks around the table and draws his cue, ready to strike-though this eight ball. Firm and high. The cue screws-back. Then with table bare, balls potted, the cellars dusty walls surround him in the cold basement. He needs to come up for air. He doesn't know whether Carl will be back from the rumoured questioning about his involvement in the threat of an attack on the Muslims. A gloit at the sub-branch of the English Defence League unit he was running has bragged he'd bomb the Super Mosque. When she cried, he withered. Burned. Vertigo swings through him: staticy nerves jangling in his body. He has a scrapbook and a chest where he keeps his chocolate-chip camouflage helmet clipped with the chaff of quick-fire bullet debris and circlets of dust.

TOGETHER, both their wages can just about afford this place. A two-bedroom semi with a gravel drive and a tiny garden. They've moved to the other side of Burley, near Horsforth, where the flowing River Aire and the white suburbs break up intermittently for by-lines of football pitches and the conspicuous remains of Kirkstall Abbey. Francesca is on the phone: she spends all day talking to people who John has never heard of – who she never sees. He has a running total in his head. The many zeros of rising costs. What happened with Evelyn, living with Francesca and her kid has urged him back into work. Security. Four nights a week he patrols one of a chain of Health and Beauty pharmacists. Sometimes Francesca comes in to get discounts on eyeliner and all the other mad shit she buys. Their bedroom smells like work. The aisles of cosmetics and shelves stacked with potions. She has the phone high pressed against her ear, through waves of hair. She has so much to talk about. So many issues.

John decamps to the kitchen where Jake is doing his

homework. Black children are more beautiful than white ones, like baby elephants. Concentrating so hard he doesn't at first hear John standing over him; the black curls of his short afro, the mud honey of his half-white, half-black skin.

'Need o hand?'

Jake smiles, eyes only briefly making contact, 'It's OK. Mummy can help. Shis better at maths.'

'Yer not wrong theh.'

'Thanks for yer offer.' John laughs: shocked by the kids politeness. Where do they learn the things they say?

'Yer gonna be o good boy for your mammy?'

'I allos am.'

'Good lad.'

'John? Can I ask you a question?'

'Yer juss did.'

'No, no! I mean another question!'

'If yer lucky.'

The boy is giggling, and feeling brave, 'Why aren't yer o black man?'

'Because am white?'

'Yeah, but why?'

'Yer mummy not told yer?'

'Yeah, Daddy's black. And so am I. But why are some people black and not others?'

'Don't know.'

'Yer don't?' The boy is over eager, and stamps hissing out his frustration in a little jig. Already his mind is chasing new things. Thinking about the world as he bounces a ball on the treated living room floorboards. It's eleven thirty on a Saturday and John is scared to put the TV on and watch Football Focus in case Francesca moans at him again; she loathes the game and the argument isn't worth fighting. He saves his vetoes for when things get serious. Not to watch the BBC shitty arses bang on about Fergie and the glorious state of the Premier League. A shimmy of cold flesh on his knuckle, and the kids has his fingers in his hand examining the lucky scars and rawhide skin.

After breakfast, Jake has been washed and patted dry. His curly hair carries the dewy shimmer of dawn. John has his jacket on and has been waiting for Francesca to get ready for thirty-five minutes. That's one thing about getting old – you get used to waiting. The unmoving stillness of the day. The past growing bigger in your head. A lifetime of jokes and shags, naughty games of pool. The freedom of being pissed off your face. Half a lifetime, hopefully. Living here has sometimes relaxed him.

Francesca bundles down the stairs clacking in heels.

'Right, am ready.'

'A thought we were olly going shopping?'

'We are.'

'Alright.'

'What?'

'Juss dressed up.'

'And? A woman can look as good as she wants these days, whenever she wants. Jake? Where are yer?' The child comes running through the door and John is planning his days treats: where can he squeeze in a cigarette? How many girls can he double-check without Francesca seeing? Will he be allowed one of those hotdogs the shopping centre does? It's still early enough to have the morning's cool rising, remnants of moisture and the hard glittering night that shrunk into grey shadow. In the car they listen to R & B intercut with the ravings of an overactive DJ. Francesca has told him her plan for the day.

'Did yer hear abaht club?' John speaks through his teeth: concentrating too hard on the road.

'No.'

'Iss gonna be made into student flats.'

'Yeah?'

'Part student, part luxury accommodation. Them hotels yer can live in.'

'Who's gonna do that?'

'No idea. I can't work out who these fuckers are with money. What do theh do?'

'Not o lot, probably.'

'Yeah, not o lot.'

'What do you wanna be when yer older Jake?' Francesca shouts into the back, over the cuboid headrests.

'An astronaut or a soldier.'

'Stick with astronaut. Trust me. Be o spaceman.'

'Thass what you wanted to be, innit.'

'Iss what everybody wants, surely?'

Then he thinks about it, deeply. His face going sullen and bloodless, cheeks liquidly responding to his own question.

'John?' Jake's inflection is falsetto.

'Go on tiger.'

'D'you have any kids?'

Eyes slide toward Francesca. 'Not that a know of. '

'I wish I was a kid forever.'

'Why's that?'

'I wouldn't want to be without me toys.'

'Yer mum's still got some.'

A harsh kick in the shin stops John going further, Francesca takes control: 'Yer won't want them when yer grown up. You'll be a big man. And not lark fatty John.' Fucking bitch. Looking after your kid and putting up with your shit. Foot down. Though emerald leaves are crisped dry and flow around the tyre treads they move toward the outer belt of the city and the ring road; Francesca is still upset that he thinks she's underdressed. John is angry that Francesca won't stop calling him fat, and poking her middle finger into his belly. Jake laughs: clapping his hands in the backseat. 'Why are you two alloss arguing?'

Francesca, laughing, hisses. 'We're not. This is called being in a relationship, Jakey. You will be one day.'

'Because yer mother's allos right, Jake. Thass the real reason. Aren't yer love?' John says half-turning his head and rolling the steering wheel into the newer, longer streets of grey and the static Saturday traffic. With Francesca working nights on the weekend and John having them off: they've been going to the out of town shopping centres more often. Drive-thru eaten in the car. The cat and mouse with the saloons and the land rovers into the slim gaps for parking spaces. John puts his hand on Francesca's bird-like thigh.

He is impervious to her moods, the swings of jubilation and love, giddy sex and defensiveness. His anxieties and shell-shock have been replaced by chores and nagging. These few happy weeks with Francesca and the kid. It's like the way some people get annoyed by the cries of babies. He lets it all wash over him, barely touch his ears. There are other things to worry about. Ronnie hasn't been in touch lately; he's not surprised, the sort of guy who carries injured pride. But how would it have been the other way? John would've had to have sucked his lip in and carried on as if nothing was wrong. Shooting pool. The inactivity is changing him; the way he doesn't need to get a day started, there's no rhythm to anything. His shifts are long and lonely, standing over the aisles in his street clothes, undercover. Occasionally he has to catch a teenage shoplifter or some shit-faced smackhead. But filing the reports and calling in the police becomes more work than it's worth. Sometimes: he gets a bit of banter with the check-out girls before being moved on by an imperious twenty-something manager in a short-sleeved shirt. Occasionally, he talks to the bitchy gays who work the men's department. So why does he wake up and wish he wasn't alive? Why does he cry himself to sleep? Sterile air, of light, the electric blur on the packages and the barcodes:

the white shelves and slippery floors. The reckless abundance of things makes him penitent. John. Her voice is soft and pliant hung like a question: walking hand in hand to the blue corrugated hanger where the sofas and the beds, the desks and the tables are sold and you have to walk around following their yellow lines through the set of their retarded adverts. Waiting.

'A can't work out if we need new lampshades.'

'I yav no idea, love.'

'C'mon, yer must do.'

'I like the one's we've got.'

'In't eh boring Jake? Am big John Usher. Too manly for interior design.'

'Thass me.'

'Yer wanna wake up yer feminine side.'

'Thass what yow for.'

Her voice is soft and crumbly, 'Lovely.'

'Stuff theh say abaht single mum's. I wanna prove em wrong. Thass all.'

'Fuck em. Yer don't need to have good furniture to show yer o good mum. And yer not single.'

'Love yer.' Her lips press against his with a new familiarity. The tastes and rhythms of her spit. Love you too. He answers: and at this moment feels interplanetary, his body, form flowing through the rich darkness of somewhere like space, the guilty depths of Evelyn's womb and the spawn of an unborn baby. The child he pleasured her to kill. Home. The sudden strength of Winter. Outside, through the door he can hear male voices on the wind. The scent and musk of male bodies. A Sunday League team playing football reminds of Iraq. Reasons for men to be men together; all the larking and the banter. Fast towels whipping bare naked arses. The sincere screams of pain as the contact reddens into something like a welt. This is a blessing, to be trapped, here. Touching his shoulders on his way onto the patio and the hyacinth-purpled garden, the sun is Baghdad orange. He hears Paki kids playing cricket in the street, fielding with Yorkshire accents. The second innings. A boy caught out. He was happy, contented and that's why he has to play pool. Get out. Shark. Hustle. Move. Francesca's napping in black lace underwear; her tits shapelier in the curved cups sprouting out over the see-through lace and satin underwire. A final kiss and her whispery breath on his lips. He has his belongings in a khaki bag: a few photos, a couple of books, his three outfits and an electric razor. He has left her enough money to pay the rent for three-months and knows that her single-parent benefits will kick in. With the door pulled against his shoulder to muffle the noise, he steps out into the bright morning, squinting in the daylight stretches of open road. Coming back into town and revelling at the prospect – he's not forgotten the enemies he loves, sweat beads along the greasy top of his sun-glowed forehead. He's already spent a wage on loose-fitting jeans, bomber jacket and lumberjack shirt. He heard a joke that Carl got two years for GBH on a paki at an EDL rally. Though that'll be halved after an appeal. No doubt Carl will be go on about his Human Rights. There's a rumour that he's going to convert to Islam to get special treatment. Guilty men don't deserve their freedom; they pay their penance. That's why John can't live in that idyllic house. What used to be edgelands where dirt streamed with water, fields along the road, is another multiplex. Places where families can waste their boredom. He hears Evelyn got a first class degree form the Open University and is in a relationship with a teacher she met at a reading group. Unlike Francesca, who knows nothing more than she needs; Francesca who has Page Three quality tits always secretly fancying being famous, Evelyn wants to get on and to know things. You can't speak the things John knows. When he was beating professionals at Pro-Am tournaments, it only meant pressure to succeed. He approaches the sandstone viaduct where the Queens Rugby Club is tucked under one of its arches; and he goes on remembering how he'd call for an echo when he was a kid under the hollow arches. The sides have been graffitied: he once wrote YEAH I LOVE ESME YEAH. The many living. The many dead. Towards the complex, the field renamed to something more marketable and public relations friendly: the Harley Davidson store has closed down and smiles seeing the Snooker Centre's goofy signs with it's giant American balls. The low-rent muckiness: Las Vegas style neon signage and the odd angles and brown shit-brick of Seventies buildings. Yorkshire dirt. The entrance is boarded with plywood and windows are cracked into crooked peepholes. Days before this place is gone. The traffic picks up, a crawling line going four ways of shunted gloss. Sheet-metal pounded into cars.

At the shadowy bar, John's eyes adjust to the light. Like the last drill on a sinking ship, the place is spotless: smelling of fructose and air freshener. As if that'll keep it open.

'Anybody serving?' He yells rapping his tattooed hand on the blue steel bar tap. A twenty-something blonde moves deliberately, viciously slow – white vest and rolling breasts.

'Yer alright?'

'Now av seen you.'

'What do yer want?'

'Bourbon and a table, please love.' She laughs, small round sparkling eyes with a bead of sex, being on top, slamming her minge over his cock and she jerks her shoulder up to pour a bourbon, showing her curved sideboob. A few weeks and the liquidators and asset-strippers will have done their work. Across the room into the shadows he takes the double-bourbon and absorbs the taste on his fat tongue: mash on his lips. There's Motown playing with fragments of the same video at different sizes and angles on the several screens throughout the bar. Shards of Diana Ross and The Supremes ghosting from a screen. The brassy Northern laughs of the snug. England. Francesca. The shadow of days. Now the lights come on. The table backlit with serious glow and the Air Con chills. He sets up: triangle over the balls. Arches his shoulder, turns to lever and strikes up. Twitches two strokes of Silver Cue tip and stands with his back this barmaid who sees his elbow jerk and the white cue spank with a cracked break and a pace and an aggression to see each ball chase distances out from the centre.

'Iss been awhile.'

'Alloss is with you.' Heads turn. John has his arms open wide, for Ronnie. The two men, friends, pick up cue sticks and start the game again. Triangle over the balls.

'What's all that shit in yer bag?'

'Going to me mam and dad's for the weekend.'

'How's the missus?'

They exchange a knowing glare. 'Hard work.'

'Thass why I left her to you.'

'Fuck you.'

'Yer ready for a pasting?'

'As long as you're getting drinks in.' Chest to table, nose to baize. The shocked balls scatter. Don't be afraid. Shark.